Book I

The Realm

Dakota McElhinny

Table of Contents

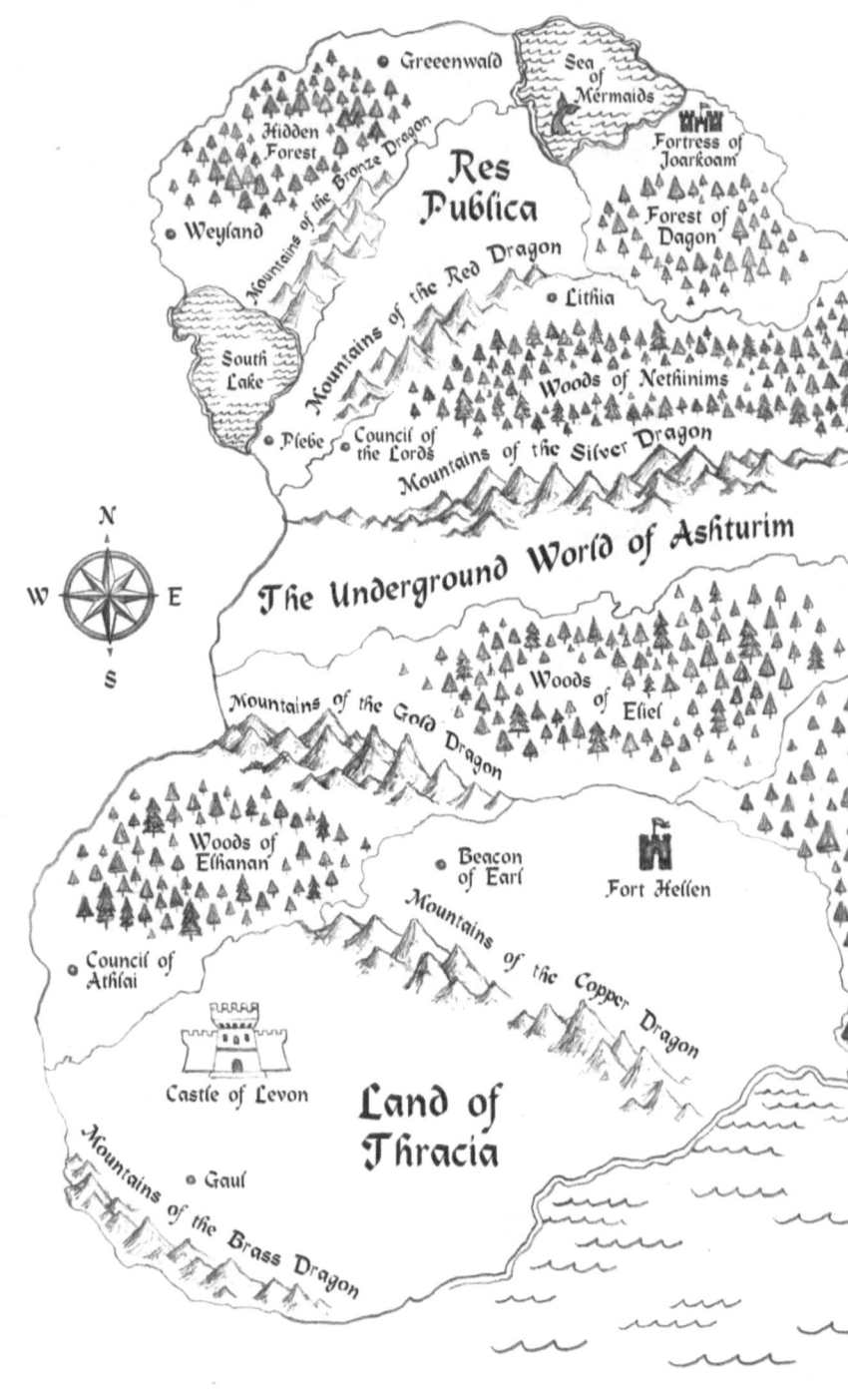

The Map of
Padavona

Pilate

Mountains of the White Dragon

Saint Benedict's
Temple

Castle of Dalian

Mountains of the Green Dragon

Land of Gilon

Belfast

Mountains of the Black Dragon

Ben-Hadad

Forest
of
Shiloh

Mountains of the Blue Dragon

Knossos

**Land of
Ashdod**

Marshes of Cameroon

Lake
of
Abdullum

Mountains of the Great Sea

Tower of
Heathens

**Great
Sea**

Mount Abyss

Part I

Telezzar's Doings

CHAPTER 1

The Unexpected Gathering

"Keep up, Basil!" the wizard barked. "We don't want to be late!"

"I'm coming, Telezzar," the fox replied. "I can't help that my legs were made shorter."

"Your legs shorter and your mind smaller, I know," he said, grinning to his companion and familiar, Basil.

"Why is it important that we reach the Blue Dragon Tavern?"

"I've already told you; I have business with the tavern's keeper."

"Can't you just write him?"

Telezzar paused and turned to the fox. "Do you think that thought never dawned on me?"

"Perhaps, but then again..." Basil's words trailed off as Telezzar departed, and the fox resumed chasing after him.

As northern winds blew southward, a beautiful day rested on the City of Ben-Hadad, the city where the Blue Dragon Tavern resided. Telezzar, the Blue, and Basil were making their way to the tavern.

"Basil, when we arrive, I need you to fulfill an errand for me," Telezzar said, as the tavern came into sight.

"You never let me go anywhere. Are you ashamed of me, Telezzar?" Basil asked, snickering.

"No," Telezzar replied, "only afraid you might drink too much and reveal all my good stories."

"Ah, too bad there aren't many good stories to tell, except when I save you."

"All right, Basil, here's a list." Telezzar handed the fox a small piece of parchment paper that had several lines scribbled down on it. "Run along and see to this, then meet me back here."

"Such a harsh task master," Basil replied, as a sly grin escaped, "but then again, I guess I must make do."

"You better, and don't be late," Telezzar said, turning and entering the Blue Dragon Tavern.

Telezzar stepped into the familiar hall, full of unfamiliar people. Warriors, travelers, and merchants made conversation with one another, but the wizard simply made his way to the tavern-keeper. The tavern-keeper seemed hesitant at the sight of the Telezzar, but as the wizrd approached the bar, the keeper grabbed a jug of red wine and poured them both a glass.

"Any news?" the tavern-keeper asked. He turned away, to place the jug of red wine back, and as his back was to Telezzar, the wizard slipped a powder into the keeper's glass.

"None, save Ashdod."

"Shhh!" the tavern-keeper whispered loudly. "I can't have you referencing such dark places in the tavern." He reached under the counter, grabbing a bag and sliding it to the wizard.

"My dear, Salvatore, I cannot help that such dark places exist," Telezzar replied, looking down at the plain, brown bag. It felt like old cloth, something a peasant might wear, but the wizard placed it in his pocket.

"I'm worried," the tavern-keeper said, changing the subject. "Is this the only way?"

The wizard gave a calm smile. "Have I ever let you down, my friend?"

"That remains to be seen," Salvatore replied sarcastically but honestly, and he watched the wizard walk away from the bar counter.

Telezzar knew the tavern well. He frequented it often, and his deep, sea-blue eyes gazed over the crowd, looking this way and that way. Then, a smirk found his lips, and he made his way to a table where four bystanders sat.

"Good afternoon, might I join you?" Telezzar asked, looking at the members.

The closest to Telezzar—a dwarf—glanced him over and nodded her head. "Have a seat, we shouldn't be much longer. We are waiting on our kin while they tell tales outside."

"Oh, why don't you join them?"

"They know one another from a battle, or something of that nature," a malobathron giant replied, fixing his eyes on Telezzar. "We decided to come in and pass the time with drinks." He extended his burly hand toward the wizard for a handshake. "I am Dar Caine Condorian, son of Njord McAdoo."

"Interesting, and what business would two malobathron giants have in Ben-Hadad?" the wizard asked, as they shook hands.

"My father's business is his own," Dar Caine replied with a grunt, for he did not enjoy strangers putting their noses into his business.

"Forgive me, Dar Caine, I was merely making conversation," Telezzar said. "Who are the rest of you?"

"I am Troy Red-Dragon, and I traveled here with my brother, Achren Red-Dragon," the elf at the table replied.

"Red-Dragon?" Telezzar whispered, musingly. "Between your last name and your garments, I must presume that you are a paladin, yes?"

"Indeed," Troy replied proudly.

Before Telezzar could reply, the dwarf interrupted: "I am Leda, daughter of Uther. We are here searching for a bounty."

"Bounty hunter? You strike me differently than the bounty hunters I know," Telezzar said, looking at her oddly.

She smiled shamelessly. "Nothing seems to get pass your intuition. You are right, my father and I are rangers under the command of King Dalidon. We are hunting a bounty for him, though."

"Yes, a ranger," Telezzar replied, softly, "now that, I can see." He smirked with delight and looked at the last member. "And what of you?"

"I am Lars, here with my brother, William, and we are from the Hidden Forest," the leprechaun said.

"Hidden Forest?" Telezzar whispered, again to himself—the four members thought perhaps it was only a bad habit. "You are from the other side of the world."

"Yes, but my brother and I are fishermen. We are traveling to the Great Sea to test our skills," Lars said, with dazzling excitement in his voice.

"Well, it was a pleasure to meet each of you, but I must be going. I'm sure we will all meet again," Telezzar said, rising from his seat.

Dar Caine shook his head. "I hope not," he whispered to the other three, and they chuckled at his words.

"Until—" Telezzar was unable to complete the sentence, for outside, shrieks filled the air.

Those inside the tavern fled under the tables, or for their rooms. Quickly, Telezzar ushered Lars under a table, and he handed the leprechaun the bag, which the tavern-keeper had given the wizard. Lars glanced at the bag. He thought it was peculiar, but his thoughts turned elsewhere.

Dar Caine took hold of two handcrafted axes, of the type that only malobathron giants wield. One side of the axe head was a blade, but the other resembled a hammer.

Leda unsheathed her sword, and the blade glistened with a silver tint. It had been fashioned for her forefathers, in the Days of King Ashturim II, and she preferred to wield it over any other weapon.

Troy owned several weapons: a spear, a short sword, and a bow with a quiver of arrows, but the elf readied his short sword for this battle.

Whatever lurked outside, it began hammering on the two-front door of the tavern. *Thud! Thud!* Thunderous, earsplitting strokes pounded one after the other, until finally, the doors fell inward.

Through the broken doorway, emerged several skeletons with ivory-colored bones, and three gargoyles, with grayish-black hides and long, gruesome fangs.

The lead gargoyle jerked its head about, sniffing the air, and its sickly yellow eyes pierced through the crowd, as if searching for something. Leda waved back her reddish-orange hair from her freckled face. She did not fear this enemy. The gargoyle approached her, its gangly hands in an attack state, and it gave a low growl, attempting to insert fear into the dwarf. Leda raised her sword, the blade twinkled in her emerald eyes, and she swung.

The gargoyle jumped back, avoiding the dwarf's blow, and it reached out to grab her, but she swung again. As the blade whistled back through the air, it cut off the gargoyle's hand. The creature howled, grappling at its wound. Leda huffed aloud, and drove her blade forward, straight through the gargoyle's chest. The creature gnashed and fell backwards, dead.

Dar Caine met the skeletons head-on. Each skeleton held a sword and shield but being undead had consequences. When the skeletons attacked, their arms fell off due to the swords' heavy weight. The giant grinned at the sight. So, the skeletons threw down their shields and picked their swords back up, but the same thing happened again.

Dar Caine turned his axes over to the hammer side, bashing the nearest skeleton's bones to pieces. The others tried to run from him, but having no arms, they fell over. He crushed each of them, too, and when finished, the giant shuffled the animal furs on his back, and combed back his charcoally black hair.

Lars—still hiding under the table—peered out several times, watching the others battle on. He fantasized about joining them, and battling the gargoyles, but he quickly shook these thoughts from his mind. A cautious fear lingered in his eyes, while a numbing sense seemed to paralyze his body.

The last of the enemies—two gargoyles—went straight for the tavern-keeper, who was still behind the bar counter. The creatures avoided Leda, after seeing her strike down their leader, but they could not avoid all the companions. Troy Red-Dragon jumped over the bar counter, acting as a barrier between the gargoyles and the tavern-keeper.

The gargoyles began foaming at the mouth with pleasure, for they could smell the tavern-keeper's fear. Troy's hazel eyes met both of theirs: one had bloody red and the second—the new leader—had dull yellow. The elf pointed the tip of his short sword at both, but this only angered them. They readied themselves, preparing to pounce, but Troy took no chances and attacked first.

Lunging forward, Troy's short sword missed both gargoyles, and the closest one retaliated by throwing the elf backwards. The yellow-eyed gargoyle stood over Troy, ready to end the scuffle, while the red-eyed gargoyle leaped onto the counter and crept toward the tavern-keeper. Troy swung his sword upward, but the gargoyle leader stepped back, avoiding the blade. Quickly, Troy tossed the short sword upward, but his hands reached back, grabbing his bow and an arrow. After strapping the arrow into the bow's shaft, the elf released it, and the arrow lodged itself in the gargoyle's throat. The gargoyle gagged, choking on the arrow. Wasting no time, Troy picked up his fallen short sword, rose up, and finished the creature off.

The smell of the gargoyle's blood was sickening to Troy. He buried his nose in his sleeve, and as he turned around, he caught sight of the red-eyed gargoyle grabbing the tavern-keeper. The feeble fellow's eyes filled with terror, but the gargoyle showed no mercy, sinking its fangs into his throat.

Troy's heart sank. He had failed the tavern-keeper. Coming to his senses, though, he leaped forward and swung his short sword, letting the blade sink into the creature's back. The gargoyle howled in pain. It did not bother to fight back, instead fleeing the tavern, wounded.

Each of them was relieved. It was all over, or at least they thought so. Their eyes turned to the doorway of the tavern, fixated on a peaceful sight. There, a figure stood clad in golden armor, and everyone was mezmerised by his beautiful appearance and apparent power.

With a friendly smile, he walked into the hall and gazed down at Lars. "I know what you have, little one. Hand it here," he whispered in the Black Dragon tongue.

Absentmindedly, Lars reached down to his pocket, fingering for the wizard's bag. Telezzar, not easily enchanted, extended his staff with one hand, and pulled Lars back with the other. "May the Staff of the Scythians avail you, you slithering, serpent-tongued Demon!"

The portayed beauty faded, as the figure seethed with anger over his failed charm spell. He glared at the wizard. "We will meet again, my friend. In the name of Dunbar, we will." With that, the figure disappeared.

The remaining evil creatures also vanished, along with Troy's brother, Lars's brother, Leda's father, and Dar Caine's father.

"They will return, so we must move swiftly," Telezzar said. He shut the front doors. "Mr. Lars, if you would be so kind, please unlock the trapdoor beneath the carpet over there." Then, with a hushed whisper, the wizard placed a lock spell on the front doors.

"We cannot run," Dar Caine said to the wizard. "They took my father, and I must save him."

"No, it's too dangerous," Telezzar replied, hoping Lars would be quick with the trapdoor. "Trust me, more enemies will soon arrive, and we must be far from here, when they do. I am taking you to safety, in the mountains, and once away from here, you may pursue your father's captors if you wish."

"My brother was taken, too," Troy said. "What if they kill them? How can you guarantee their safety?"

Telezzar gave an understanding, yet saddened, look. "I cannot make such promises, but I can provide you safe passage from here. Once we are away, I will help you find your family members."

A grieving silence stole the room, but Lars popped up from the floor. "I have unlocked it."

"Good," Telezzar said, happily. He looked at his new acquaintances. "If you wish to make a pursuit, then you should leave now, but I am taking a different route, and any who wish to join me may."

The four exchanged glances. They were unsure of what would be the right choice, but the wizard grabbed hold of the ladder, ready to descend into the mountains. "Oh, Mr. Lars, whether you stay or come with me, please lock the trapdoor back."

The four watched, as Telezzar climbed down and disappeared into the darkness below. Without any hesitation, Troy followed the wizard, and after weighing her options, Leda followed, too.

"What do you plan on doing?" Dar Caine asked the leprechaun.

"I'm not quite sure," Lars replied, peaking down the trapdoor, and then glancing to the front window. "I won't be able to save my brother alone, so I'll join the wizard, and he'll help me."

Dar Caine grunted. "I will join, then."

"Very well, but you need to go first, so I can lock the trapdoor behind us."

The giant grabbed hold of the ladder, and with a heavy sigh, he descended into the mountain. Lars looked about. The great hall and bar of the tavern sat empty and quiet. The leprechaun waited a moment longer; then, he climbed onto the ladder, locking the trapdoor back, and following the others down.

CHAPTER II

Creatures of the Darkness

Lars did not know how far the ladder went down. He climbed and climbed, until he felt sure there was no bottom. Of course, this was not true, but after a very long climb, he finally reached the ground, joining the others.

"I am glad to see each of you decided to join me," Telezzar said.

"Where are you leading us?" Dar Caine asked, as his grasp tightened on his weapons. He did not trust the wizard since he—and most giants—viewed magic in an ill light.

"Into the Mountains of the Blue Dragon," Telezzar replied, looking over the pathway ahead. "I am a wizard."

"We each assumed as much, since you were waving that staff around," Dar Caine said.

"Yes, and who was that, that you scared off?" Leda asked.

Telezzar raised his hand, gesturing for silence. "In due time, all questions will be answered, but for now, you must follow and trust me."

"I will follow you," Troy said, supporting the wizard.

Telezzar gave a thankful nod, and then, he turned around and led the group onward, down a dim tunnel. Water dripped from the ceiling, making the ground wet and slippery. The tunnel was cool, too, and it bore an unfavorable stench.

Set within the wizard's staff was an orb made of stardust, which gave the staff its power. Telezzar dismounted the orb and threw it into the air. Immediately, the orb provided a source of light while floating in midair, and it was a pleasant surprise to each of the companions.

From the orb's white light, the group could see the rough cavern walls, but there were drawings and carvings, too, and these made the companions feel uneasy. The chiseled works depicted a mighty behemoth, a lesser demon—still taller than any giant—that served the greater demons and devils of Hell. Of course, not all the behemoths were in Hell, some had escaped their masters, and they were loose to roam the Seven Plains.

"These drawings of the behemoth bother me," Telezzar said, making conversation with the others.

"I agree with you," Lars replied, jittery.

"We will not meet a behemoth here. The wizard has not taken us low enough into the mountains, and he will not take us any lower," Dar Caine said.

Telezzar stopped and looked to the giant. "Dark times have arrived, Dar Caine, and I cannot make such promises."

Dar Caine grunted. "My words were meant to comfort those with a faint heart."

"But wouldn't the truth be best?"

"Perhaps, but if you are unsure of such things, then perhaps another should lead."

Telezzar gave a reluctant smile, knowing the giant only wished to make his authority known. "Dar Caine, why don't you tell us about yourself, while I try to lead us from this place."

"There is not much to tell," Dar Caine replied, as the group started moving on again. "My grandfather is Draul McAdoo, the renowned High-King of Prixem before his passing. I live in the Fortress of Joarkoam, which lies in the of Dagon. Before that, my people lived in the Void, just as all giants did."

Being curious, Lars cut in: "You lived in the Void?"

"No," Dar Caine replied, shaking his head, "all of the giants from the Void have passed, with my grandfather being the last."

"Oh," Lars said, not certain of what to say.

"It's all right, though. When my people were sent here, we learned to berserk in battle."

"What is a berserk?" Lars asked, having never heard of the word.

"A berserker—such as I—is a giant who wears the skins of wild animals, and in battle, we have the ability to take the wild beast's form, depending on which fur we choose."

The giant's answer surprised the leprechaun. "I have a mask that allows me to do that; I call it the Mask of Disguises."

"Mask of what?" Leda asked, bewildered, just as Dar Caine and Troy.

"I will show you," Lars said, giddily, as he pulled a simple, clear mask from his jacket pocket. Carefully placing it over his face, he began to morph. "See!"

"I can't believe it," Troy whispered, staring at Lars, who now appeared as a malobathron giant.

Dar Caine was in awe, too. "The mask did that?"

"Yes," Lars replied, taking off the mask, and reverting to his leprechaun self. "I found it long ago, but do not remember where."

"That's nothing. I'm a paladin, just as my father and forefathers, though I enjoy studying and training animals," Troy said, gaining everyone's attention. "Someday, I hope to train a gryffin as my war-beast."

"Oh dear, we have a fantasy dreamer," Leda said aloud, as she elbowed Dar Caine, and the two sniggered.

"Not all dreams come true," Troy replied, seeming to fall short of speaking his thoughts. "My father passed in battle, long ago, forcing my grandfather to raise me. Though I love and respect him, he is quite controlling of my life, and that is why I am a paladin."

Leda felt sorry for her quip. "Forgive me, Troy, I meant nothing by my words."

Lars watched as Troy returned a friendly nod, but the leprechaun felt sad for the elf. "Troy, what is a paladin, exactly?"

Troy smiled, enjoying the attention. "I am new to the Paladin Order, but Archbishop Malcom Ballimore rules over it, though my grandfather oversees the paladins of Lithia. Paladins protect the free lands from goblin hoards, eldred—evil elves—and the Bdellium Knights of Death."

"Do not speak of them!" Telezzar snapped, stopping the group. "They hold dealings with foul kings and align their allegiance with Dunbar's descendants. I will hear no more about them."

Lars was too intrigued. "Telezzar, what are these knights?"

Telezzar closed his eyes. "I will not utter any words about them. Troy, explain."

"The Bdellium Knights are seven warlords, created by Segomo for Dunbar. When Balor sentenced Dunbar to Hell though, the Bdellium Knights fled here, to Prixem, and they now roam freely. As Telezzar said, foul kings deal with them, but forever, the Bdellium Knights are cursed to serve Dunbar's descendants."

Lars gave a confused look. "But why are they feared?"

Troy smiled back, hesitantly. "They cannot be killed. If a Bdellium Knight is in battle, then there is great reason to be frightened by it."

"Enough," Telezzar's voice said, booming from the front. "Leda, tell us of yourself."

"Well, my father was once a bargeman and I have many kin that still are, so I know the trade quite well. When my father married my mother, though, King Dalidon anointed my father as a ranger, and I followed in his footsteps becoming one, too."

Leda was silent, thinking of her father. "He says, I am stronger and wiser than most dwarfs, but my temper will be my downfall."

Dar Caine grunted. "I can see it."

"Watch it, Giant, or I will cut you down to my level," she replied, winking at him. "Tell us more about yourself, Dar Caine."

Playfully, the giant cleared his throat. "Well, I have a natural gift of farming and tending gardens."

The others erupted with laughter at the way Dar Caine had told them this. "Now I've heard it all!" Leda exclaimed.

Dar Caine laughed with them but became serious. "I do enjoy farming and tending my garden. I can also tell you, my eyes change colors between blue and green, depending on the couplet."

"Aren't you special," Leda replied, with another good laugh.

"She is right, you are quite the character, Dar Caine," Telezzar added in. "Lars, anything else?"

"Well, I am from Hidden Forest, specifically the northern region of Greenwald—most leprechauns live in Greenwald, while most short elves live in Weyland." Lars paused, scratching his curly, light-brown hair. "Um, I always wear this dark-green jacket because it gives me luck." He showed it off to the others. "My brother, William, and I are fisherman and trappers, and that is why we were going to the Great Sea."

"Interesting," Dar Caine replied. "Lars, is it true that leprechauns are shorter than short elves?"

"Nonsense!" Lars exclaimed, somewhat insulted. "Short elves are shorter than leprechauns."

Troy grinned, realizing the giant's jest. "I don't know. I have heard otherwise."

Lars huffed and did not reply. Both Troy and Dar Caine laughed, though.

"Telezzar, tell us about yourself," Leda said, wanting to learn about the wizard.

The wizard was somewhat surprised. "There is not much to tell." He paused a moment, thinking. "Each wizard has a special power. I possess two: controlling water and creating illusions."

"Illusions?" Dar Caine asked, wanting the wizard to elaborate.

"Yes, illusions, but they drain my power quickly," the wizard replied, holding up his staff. "This is the Staff of the Scythians, which was crafted by Segomo of the Void. Once, it belonged to DeAth, before he fell from grace and became Death."

The companions were impressed, and Lars was eager to learn more. "Telezzar, what is that floating in front of us?"

"Ah, my wizard orb," Telezzar replied, "the orb gives my staff its power and each of us—the ten wizards—own one, and the orbs are made of stardust."

The group continued treading down the hollow tunnel, but their bodies were weary, wishing to rest on the cold, damp flooring. The wizard urged them to stay strong, as he guided them on. They did not get far, though, before meeting trouble.

From the darkness, twenty-four hairy legs emerged, for the group had wandered upon panda ants. The creatures were monstrous in size and covered in white-and-black fur, which gave them their name. They were not dangerous, unless frightened, and in this instance, they were terrified of the orb's white light.

Leda unsheathed her sword. The orb's light made the blade glisten in the dark tunnel. The closest panda ant hissed at the dwarf, since it did not fancy the glistening blade. Leda crouched, slowly sidestepping around the creature, but it was not easily fooled. It lunged at her, and she swung her sword. Both missed each other. The panda ant stood on its hind legs, attempting to kick Leda, but she jumped back, avoiding any blows. As the panda ant re-planted its front legs, Leda drove her sword forward into the creature's leg. With a painful squeal, the panda ant fled back into the darkness of the mountain.

"Watch out, their stingers are poisonous!" Telezzar shouted, alerting the companions.

Lars, standing near the front, slipped on the wet cave floor, and landed at the feet of a panda ant. As the creature opened its pinchers to grab Lars, Dar Caine rushed forward, swinging one axe upward into the panda ant's chest, and the other downward into the pinchers. The creature shrieked from the painful cuts. Then, sounding like thunderous claps, the two axe heads hit the panda ant in the head; it swayed back and forth before falling, dead.

Dar Caine helped Lars up, but a third panda ant grabbed the giant's waist. As it hoisted Dar Caine into the air, he dropped both of his axes. The creature jutted its tail end forward, toward Dar Caine, but the giant grabbed and pointed the stinger upward, and the panda ant stabbed itself. It squealed with pain, but fell over, releasing Dar Caine.

Now, while Leda and Dar Caine battled the panda ants at the front, Troy took on the last one. It had climbed onto the ceiling, attempting to crawl over the group. Troy jabbed at the creature with his spear, but it was useless.

The panda ant had, had enough, and it jumped down onto Troy. Terrified of the outcome, the elf ducked his head and closed his eyes, preparing for the worst, but nothing happened. He opened his eyes, finding Telezzar had saved him by freezing the panda ant in midair.

"Kill it, Troy!" Telezzar urged, as his magic drained, and he tired.

Troy thrust his spear upward, ramming the spearhead into the creature's head. After several jabs, he moved from underneath the panda ant, and Telezzar released his spell. The last of the panda ants fell.

Everyone was silent, save their heavy breaths. Telezzar looked at the companions, and he realized they were surprised, since they had expected safe passage.

"I cannot control everything," Telezzar said to them.

Dar Caine grunted. "The leprechaun fell, and you did nothing. Where I am from—"

"We are not where you are from," the wizard replied, sternly. "You are in the Mountains of the Blue Dragon. I warned you that this could happen."

Feeling sympathetic, Troy chimed in: "He was busy saving me."

"Yes, and I am well. Perhaps, we should carry on and trust our guide," Lars added.

"At least some of you have their senses about," Telezzar said, with a kind smile.

Dar Caine said nothing more about the matter. The group moved on, continuing their path. They all grew more famished and more tired, especially the wizard who felt drained of all power. They pushed on, though.

The Realm

The cold, wet stone pathway became dry and sandy. Though the air became heavier and hotter, the group became joyful, as they found a vast, open room. Telezzar could travel no more, and he decided it would be best to have them rest.

"We will rest here and regain our strength. Each of you must rotate standing guard, while I restore my magic."

Dar Caine offered to take the first watch.

"Telezzar, may I ask you a question?" Lars asked the wizard, privately.

"Does the one you have asked count?" Telezzar replied with a smile. "Yes, my friend, you may ask."

"Well, the bag you gave me at the tavern," Lars said, hesitantly, as he scratched his elongated nose. "What is in it?"

Telezzar mused for a moment, understanding the question, but he seemed at a loss for an answer. "The bag holds something valuable. You must not lose it, and you must never let the figure, who appeared at the tavern, gain it."

"What is in it?" Lars asked again, wanting to push for an answer, but keeping mindful of his boundaries. He handed the bag to the wizard.

Telezzar's face seemed to grow reluctant. "As I said, you carry something valuable, but it is best you do not know yet." He studied the bag, running his fingers over the worn-out cloth. Then, he looked to Lars and handed it back.

"I understand," Lars replied, lying to the wizard, and he walked away.

Telezzar sighed. He wished to tell Lars, but he knew it was better not to. The wizard rose to his feet and walked over to Troy.

"Are you well, Telezzar?"

"I will be fine, nothing some rest cannot cure," the wizard replied, as he sat next to the elf. He began unwrapping some cloth that held a mysterious object. "You are a paladin, so I am entrusting you with this. It is the horn to the gargoyle you slew."

Troy took the horn, studying it with fascination. "Why are you giving me this?"

"You do not know?" Telezzar asked, and Troy shook his head. "Any horn taken off the head of a gargoyle will turn pure white after three days, and when those three days have passed, one may blow upon it as a trumpet, summoning a unicorn."

Troy stared at the horn. "Were you able to retrieve any others?"

"Sadly, no," Telezzar replied, "but keep the horn safe, and only use it when you need it most."

Troy smiled, thrilled about the gargoyle horn. "Thank you, Telezzar, I will wrap it in my rope, and keep it safe in my pack."

"You are most welcome, Troy," Telezzar replied, and he walked back to his place of rest.

The wizard settled in, as sleep began to take him. His thoughts bustled about, remembering his home—the Void—and his father, Balor. Balor was Lord of the Void, and the Void was home to other immortals too, who helped Balor rule the Seven Plains. Telezzar missed the Void and his father.

The Realm

The wizard's eyes glanced about, one last time. Lars lay fast asleep, Troy ate pizzelles—a special elf bread—and Leda was replacing Dar Caine at the watch. The wizard combed back his long, black hair and closed his eyes, drifting off to sleep.

As Leda stood watch, she glanced about the room, noticing the drawings and carvings on the walls. She wondered if the space had once been a throne room, perhaps for some lost civilization.

She studied the drawings and carvings more closely, realizing they showed the behemoth again. This time though, the behemoth fell to a naga. Leda speculated the story was one about creation. Some believed there was a Divine Naga, who carried the sun and moon upon its back, slithering around the plains, bringing day and night.

While Leda stared at the walls, pondering her thoughts, a creature made its way into the lair. It took out a small crossbow and paralyzing dart, which resembled a beetle. It carefully placed the black dart into its handmade crossbow and shot Leda. At once, the dwarf was stunned and fell still, but she could see her attacker, which was a lizard man.

The creature proceeded forward, not realizing there were others in the lair. Telezzar—feeling a disturbance—awoke and saw the lizard man. He shouted and alerted the others, who immediately woke.

The creature's greenish-yellow scales faintly glistened in the orb's white light. The lizard man charged towards Telezzar, but Dar Caine cut off the creature's path.

The lizard man stopped running, when it saw the giant, and it quickly took hold of another dart. As it fumbled around, attempting to strap the dart into the crossbow, Dar Caine reared his axes back and unleashed several powerful blows. The lizard man let out several painful hisses, but the axe hammered the creature's scaly body flat and gooey.

Then, the lizard man attempted to crawl away, but Dar Caine stepped over it, raising his axes and bringing them down. The lizard man lay dead, like a flat lizard pancake.

"Will she be all right?" Troy asked, seeing that a dart had hit Leda.

Telezzar removed the dart and looked at the wound. "Yes, she will be fine. She has only been hit by a paralyzing dart."

"We have tarried too long, Telezzar," Dar Caine said, impatiently. "You must lead us on, and we must leave now."

"Leda cannot be moved," Troy replied.

"He is right, Dar Caine. We cannot leave until she has recovered from this state."

Dar Caine grunted. "I will carry her."

"Don't be a fool, you cannot carry her for almost half-a-day."

"We have not journeyed far into the mountains, and we have already met creatures of the darkness. Please, let us go before something fiercer finds us and attacks. I will carry her."

The wizard saw the giant's determination, and he understood his concern. "If you will carry her, then we will move on."

Carefully, Dar Caine picked Leda up, while Troy and Lars gathered her belongings and carried them. Telezzar led the group away from the vast room, back into the winding tunnels of the mountains. Little did they know that fate would soon intervene with their quest.

CHAPTER III

Riddles, Trolls, and Secret

Passages

Time slowly passed, but the dart's toxin soon wore off and Leda was fine. The group continued down the rough path, traveling deeper and deeper into the mountains.

Then, within the darkness, a vague figure appeared in their path. "Halt, friend or foe?" a deep, bellowing voice asked.

The group stopped, watching the figure's outline come closer and closer. "We are friends," Troy replied, looking at his companions.

"You better hope," Leda whispered back, as her hand clenched the handle of her sword.

"Friend or foe?" the voice asked again, but this time with greater authority.

"Let's ambush it," Dar Caine said, thinking the figure was possibly evil.

"No, let's use a different tongue," Troy replied. He cried out in the goblin tongue, "Who are you?"

No reply came. "Should I use a different one?" Lars asked, with a tremble in his voice.

"No, let me use the dwarf tongue," Leda urged, before anyone else could answer the leprechaun.

The figure was almost upon them. "It is coming," Telezzar whispered.

Panic flooded their minds, as silence stole their tongues, and their ears beat hard with fear. "We are friends of Telezzar!" Troy shouted, not knowing what else to say.

The others seemed relieved by Troy's choice, but the wizard gave a hard glare. "Telezzar?" the voice questioned. "Telezzar, are you there?"

"Carlton?" the wizard asked, vaguely recognizing the voice.

"Yes," the voice replied eagerly, and from the darkness, the figure quickened its pace to the group.

Telezzar turned to the companions. "All is well, I believe. Carlton is a minotaur, so why he is here, I do not know. Do not speak to him."

"A minotaur?" Lars squeaked.

"Yes, a minotaur. More specifically, Carlton is a prince and the heir to the throne in Ovid, so he is far from his home."

Carlton could hear their conversation. "Yes, I am the son of King Claudius, and Prince of Ovid." He gave a friendly smile, and a respectful nod to the wizard. "Telezzar the Blue, what brings you to these parts of the mountains?"

"I cannot reveal our business," he replied, noticing Carlton's three brothers approaching.

"Surely, your business has no relation with centaurs," Carlton mused aloud, as he picked and combed at his matted brown-and-gray fur. "That filthy King Pindar still hates my father, since they do not see eye to eye on matters."

"I assure you, no centaurs are involved, but I cannot reveal our business," Telezzar replied firmly, for he had not seen Carlton in some time, and he was unsure if the minotaur could be trusted. "We head onward, though."

Carlton stared at the small group. What he thought of them, no one could guess, but surely, he found them to be a rag-tag lot. "Ahead, you will find a fork in the road. I have never ventured down the left path, but the right path ends at a wall of runes."

"What language are the runes in?"

Carlton gave a hearty snort. "I do not know, but my brothers—Crokus, Caelan, and Caneal—and I have been here for many couplets."

Telezzar did not understand Carlton's cryptic meaning, and he was going to ask for clarification, but something approached from behind the group. Troy pulled an arrow from his quiver and took aim.

"You fool—stop!" Telezzar shouted. "That creature is my familiar, Basil."

Humiliated, Troy lowered his weapon. "Forgive me, I did not know."

Shaking his head irratibly, Telezzar knelt before Basil, and using telepathy, the two spoke.

"Basil, what happened?"

"I fulfilled the errand before the madness broke out, but we are in trouble. Two eldred are hunting the elf, they know he is a

paladin, and they are accompanioned by six gargoyles, who know about the missing gargoyle horn in the tavern."

"This is terrible news," Telezzar replied, quickly pondering over options. *"Go now and hide in the shadows, for Carlton and his brothers are here, but I do not trust them. We must learn of their purpose for being here."*

"Telezzar?" Dar Caine asked. He and the others found it odd that the wizard knelt before the fox, without uttering a word.

"Basil tells me, there are two eldred and six gargoyles following us. The eldred want Troy, and the gargoyles have learned of the missing horn."

Troy smirked. "So, the enemy only wants the great warrior," he said, with a playful jab to Leda's shoulder.

"Then perhaps, we should leave the great warrior behind. Surely, he can fend for himself," she replied, with a smug grin.

"No, I fear something else is with them. We must move on," Telezzar said. At these words, Basil slipped back into the shadows.

"What evil have you brought?" Crokus asked, worriedly.

Carlton snorted at his brother. "Back down, Crokus, for Telezzar is a friend."

"What friend brings enemies upon us?" Caneal chimed in.

"Caelan, control your twin," Carlton ordered. He turned to Telezzar and continued: "We will hold off any enemies that pursue your company, Telezzar."

The wizard thanked Carlton, and the group journeyed on. They went down the tunnel, and shortly, they reached the fork in the road, just as Carlton had said. The air smelled cleaner, and when compared to the old ones, the walls appeared newly carved.

Telezzar led the group down the right path, since Carlton had traveled it. The path was short, and at the end of it, they found themselves before a mighty, smooth wall. The only blemishes on it were the runes, but disturbingly, the characters were in the language of the eldred.

"The runes read: 'What goes up, but never comes down?'" Telezzar said, for none of the companions knew the eldred tongue.

"That is too easy," Leda replied, with confidence in her voice. "The answer should be mountains."

The door did not open, and Troy chuckled. "Leda, with time, the mountains will erode, but surely, the answer is trees."

Once again, the door did not open, and this time Leda laughed. "Give us another joke, court jester."

"Stop, this is not humorous," Telezzar replied, as his patience grew thin. "We must open this door."

"Telezzar, I doubt we will open the door," Dar Caine said, staring at the runes.

Telezzar sighed, as a grimace swept over his face. "We must go back and take the left path, then."

"We do not know what lies down it," Leda said.

"No, but we do know what follows us," Telezzar replied, "if no one can fathom an answer, then let us go back."

The companions agreed with Telezzar's reasoning, and they traveled back to the fork in the road. Once they reached it, they started down the left tunnel. The walls did not seem newly carved, like the ones down the right tunnel, but dark sand hid the original stone flooring of their path.

As the group turned around a bend, the floor gave way, and they fell helplessly into a trap full of spikes. The spikes were jagged and dull, and thankfully, their injuries were mere flesh wounds, nothing severe.

"Curse that minotaur!" Dar Caine shouted, angrily. "He knew of this devilry and did not speak of it!"

Telezzar tended to his own cuts and scrapes, not defending the minotaur, for he did not know whether Dar Caine's assumption was correct or not.

"You believe the minotaur made this?" Lars asked the giant.

"Of course, who else would?"

"Quiet," Telezzar whispered aloud, peering out into the pit. "We are not alone."

A low grumble came from the far side of the pit. Then, shining like two dim lanterns, the dull, yellow eyes of a troll appeared. By the troll's side, there emerged two hivittes—evil dwarfs—and they both had white, crystal eyes and orange, scruffy beards.

"Beware of the hivittes' weapons," Telezzar said in a low voice. "They are armed with special spears. One end of the spear holds a pole to trip you, while the other holds the spearhead."

"Can we speak with them?" Lars asked, terrified of all three.

"Due to their temper, hivittes rarely speak with outsiders, for they are a mad race."

"That's reassuring," Troy replied, with a wry smile.

The Realm

Dar Caine grunted, taking hold of his axes. "The troll is mine."

"What are we waiting for?" Leda asked, as she unsheathed her sword and charged the closest hivitte.

The hivitte thrust its spear forward, but Leda swung her sword, deflecting the spear. She dropped her sword, and grabbed hold of the spear, and two began to grapple over it. Leda—being stronger—overpowered the hivitte and took the spear. The hivitte attempted to slip past her, but she ran the spear through the hivitte's throat, lodging the spearhead into the rock wall. Pinned, the hivitted gasped and gurgled, extending its hands, and ferociously trying to grab Leda. The dwarf reached down, grabbing her sword, and she cut off the hivitte's hands, so it could not free itself.

Troy met the second hivitte in the middle of the pit. He lunged forward, swinging his short sword, but the hivitte ducked. Troy slid back, trying to avoid the hivitte's oncoming blow, but the hivitte was quicker. The spear whipped around, pulling Troy's legs out, and the elf fell. The hivitte raised its spear, ready to finish Troy.

Telezzar knew he had to save Troy. Using magic, the wizard produced a fiery, flaming whip, and it knocked the hivitte down. The evil dwarf lay burnt and crispy. Troy rose to his feet, pitying the hivitte, but he could not bring himself to finish it, so the elf left the hivitte to die from the wounds.

The troll roared, as it flung its flails around. Dar Caine received several blows that would have killed most men, but he was no man. Tightening his grip on his axes, the giant rushed forward and swung, recklessly, and the blades hit their marks. The troll was not used to pain. The creature's flails flew forward again, pounding Dar Caine, but the giant had enough.

Dar Caine reached for his bear skin and changed into a bear. The troll was confused, even taken aback. The giant wasted no time, though, and he attacked.

"That fool, he is more vulnerable," Telezzar whispered, realizing what Dar Caine had done. "Troy, shoot down the troll!"

Troy hesitated, fearing he would possibly hit Dar Caine, but he had to take the chance. He grabbed three arrows and simultaneously fired them at the troll. The arrows stunned the troll.

Between the shots and Dar Caine's transformation, the troll had not noticed Leda, who snuck up behind it. Raising her sword up, she thrust it forward, piercing the troll's back. The troll roared in pain. It turned to face Leda, but Dar Caine turned back into his giant self, and taking hold of the troll's flails, he swung them downward, crushing the troll.

All fell silent, save their heavy breathes. Telezzar began rummaging about the hivittes' and troll's possessions, seeing what they carried.

"Dar Caine, you should keep the troll's flails," Telezzar said.

The giant knelt, tired and lethargic from the scuffle, with the troll. "I have my own weapons."

"You will not find better weapons," Telezzar urged.

Dar Caine looked down at the flails and nodded his head. "Very well, I will keep them."

Telezzar continued searching through the troll's pack, finding emeralds, diamonds, gold, and a black marble with white swirls.

"I slew the troll, so I deserve to choose my share first," Dar Caine said, commandingly.

Leda smirked. "It was my blade that allowed you to finish the troll."

"Dar Caine, take the diamonds, and, Leda, take the emeralds and gold," Telezzar said. Both exchanged glances but agreed.

"May I have the marble?" Troy asked. He found it intriguing.

"Yes, it appears harmless, and I detect no magic," the wizard replied, handing the marble to him.

"It could be a magical tracking device that belongs to an evil sorcerer," Leda replied, somewhat playful, but somewhat serious.

"Nonsense, if Telezzar detects no magic, then I will keep it."

Leda huffed at the reply. "I don't mean to interrupt, but how are we getting out of here?" Lars asked, inspecting the pit walls.

"Troy and I will climb out first, then Dar Caine will hand you and Leda to us and, after Dar Caine gets out, we will put the fake floor back," Telezzar said.

After removing themselves from the pit, the five laid the fake floor back over it. Then, they swiftly made their way back to the fork in the road, and headed down the right path, again. Just as before, they found the path blocked by the beautifully engraved door.

The riddle still stumped them. "What goes up, but never comes down..." Telezzar mumbled to himself, rummaging his deep thoughts for an answer.

"Perhaps, the answer is the gold of an aged dwarf king," Troy said, with a wide grin.

Furious, Leda snapped back: "No matter how old a dwarf king is, he will always have more gold than you."

"Dwarf king?" Telezzar whispered. "Old? Of course, the answer is simple. It is age."

The ground shook beneath their feet, unsteadily, and the door with the runes opened, revealing another passage. Happy to be moving along, the group gathered their belongings and prepared to leave, but a familiar voice stopped them.

"Wait!" Carlton shouted. He came running, with a thunderous *thud!* in his steps. "You have something I need."

"What is going on?" Telezzar asked, knowing that Carlton held a secret.

The minotaur gave a depressed look. "For five years, my brothers and I have been searching for the king of these caverns. He holds my father in his dungeon," he said with a heavy sigh. "The elf has found the key, the marble with the swirls. There is only one other like it, and it belongs to the king."

Telezzar eyed the minotaur closely, but he felt that Carlton spoke truthfully. "Let us discuss the situation."

Casting a Spell of Silence around himself, Telezzar motioned his companions to gather around, so they might discuss the matter.

"Who is the king here, Telezzar?" Dar Caine asked.

"Carlton is speaking of the spidermite, Kaulthar. He and his minions live in the lower caverns."

"We have no business fighting spidermites," Leda said. "I have heard legends of the half-man, half-spider creatures, and I have no wish to meet them."

"There may be other prisoners, though," Lars said, chiming in. He had never heard of spidermites, but Leda's description made him shiver.

Telezzar looked to Troy, who was the key-bearer. "What do you think?"

Troy was silent for a moment, pondering the decision carefully. "Since I have the marble key, I think we should free King Claudius."

"Very well, we will go to Kaulthar's kingdom," Telezzar replied, "but we must move quickly, for our enemies are almost near."

The group followed Carlton back down the tunnel. It was strange. A sensation hung in the air, one that seemed to lighten the mountains' spirit. Everyone could feel it.

Something still bothered Troy, though. He felt the mountains' happiness, but lurking in the shadows, something foul was afoot and performing dark deeds. The darkness still stirred.

"Telezzar, we are not alone," Troy whispered, as the group moved quickly to the fork in the road.

"You feel it?" Telezzar asked, hesitantly. "It has been following us since we arrived here, in the tunnels."

"A servant of Kaulthar?"

Telezzar's pace slowed, as he looked to Troy. "No, it is a brounie servant, which has been manipulated into a familiar."

"A brounie," Troy said, amazed. He remembered reading about brounies, when studying different animals back home. He could picture the knee high, brown-skinned creature, and he thought of its gangly limbs with long slender fingers, round button nose, and rabbit-like ears, which protruded out to the side. "Kaulthar has a familiar, like you?"

"No," Telezzar replied, with a chuckle. "Kaulthar is not wise enough to enchant an animal, or creature, to become his familiar. No, the familiar belongs to Dentar."

He did not know why, but Troy shuddered at the name. "Who...who is Dentar?"

Telezzar opened his mouth to reply, but Dar Caine called for the wizard. "Telezzar, we have stumbled upon spiders!"

"We have no time for a battle," Carlton said.

Raising the Staff of the Scythians, Telezzar made his way to the front of the group. "May daylight frighten you to darker places!"

The staff's orb let out a white light, which shone brightly. The spiders fled in terror, for the light scared them, and it pierced their bodies, inflicting wounds.

Dar Caine grunted, quite impressed. "Forgive me if I ever questioned your guidance or power."

Telezzar smiled back. "We all make mistakes, my friend, but some of us make fewer than others."

The group laughed at Telezzar's quip, but Carlton urged them on. They shortly reached the trap floor. Under the wizard's instructions, Dar Caine tossed his flails onto the trap floor, and the floor collapsed inward. The group and Carlton then entered the pit.

"Ah, we were fools. Our enemies were guarding something. Surely, there is a hidden doorway, which will take us to the lower parts of the mountains," Telezzar said.

Carlton looked over the troll and hivittes. "If Kaulthar had servants here, then why didn't they attack me and my brothers?"

"They were not placed here to battle, only to guard, and you never stumbled on them," Telezzar replied, as he glanced about the walls, looking for the hidden doorway.

"Here, I found runes," Lars said excitedly, finding more eldred runes.

"Not this again," Leda moaned.

"The runes read: 'What goes down, but never goes up?'" Telezzar said, interpreting them for the companions and Carlton.

"You spoke too soon, Leda," Dar Caine replied, with a smirk. He had no answer, and he doubted anyone else would, too.

Before anyone else could make a remark, Troy replied, "Rain."

Just as before, the ground shook beneath their feet, unsteadily, and slowly, the wall split apart, revealing a hidden door. The door remained shut, though. Examining it, Troy found a small, round opening that appeared to be a keyhole. He took out the marble and dropped it into the wall. Nothing happened.

"Wonderful, you lost the key," Leda blurted out, after several moments of awkward silence.

"No, it must be the keyhole!" Carlton shouted, full of rage. He swung his axe against the door, but the axe blade shattered.

"Carlton, don't be a fool," Telezzar barked, as Dar Caine grabbed and restrained the minotaur.

Carlton fell to his knees, defeated. "Then it is all in vain, my father will rot in the dungeons of Kaulthar."

Before anyone could console the minotaur, a low rumble echoed through the pit, and the hidden door opened. Filled with relief, Carlton grinned at the sight, but the companions huddled around the new tunnel, gazing into the darkness.

"This is where our journey becomes more interesting," Dar Caine said, with a wary smirk.

"Come, we must be on our way," Telezzar said to the companions, ushering them into the tunnel. "Carlton, you must place the trap floor back."

"I will, and I will remain in this pit and keep guard, until you return."

The wizard nodded at the minotaur and entered the tunnel. As he crossed over, Telezzar found the marble key, which had only fallen on the other side of the wall, and he returned it to Troy. Then, the group ventured off.

CHAPTER IV

One Wrong Makes a Right

Telezzar's orb led the way, shining brightly and guiding the group along safely. Not all of them were pleased though, for the tunnel was very narrow and constricting.

"This is eerie, even by a dwarf's standard."

Dar Caine grunted. "Eerie? It is ridiculous." He had to bend and squeeze his way through the tunnel.

"It's not that bad, though the smell could be better," Lars replied, holding his shirt over his nose.

"Of course, the tunnel is spacious for you, you are a leprechaun."

Lars stopped, abruptly, which forced Dar Caine and Troy to stop, too. "I am tall for a leprechaun, thank you."

"He did not mean anything by it," Troy said.

"Your present state in this tunnel represents the state of your ego in your head," Lars continued, heatedly.

"Are you talking to me or Dar Caine?" Troy asked, confused by Lars's slight.

Dar Caine laughed. "Does it matter? We're still taller than him."

Telezzar could hear their bickering. "An answer for your complaint lies ahead, Dar Caine."

The Realm

The group stepped out of the narrow tunnel, finding themselves in a gigantic room. Widely vast, the ceiling of the room stretched high above their heads, and they could not see it. They stepped further into the room, though, but met a ghastly surprise. Bones.

Bones lay all about, some even in piles, rotting and reeking of decay. Blood splattering stained all the walls, too. Terror grasped their hearts.

"We should not have come here," Dar Caine whispered, as his grip tightened on the handles of his flails.

"Dar Caine is right," Troy replied, peering about, "we must make our way back to Carlton."

Lars shuddered and pointed up. "Is that what did this?"

Everyone looked to a gap in the wall, where a creature lurked and stared at them. "A purslain," Telezzar whispered to them.

Leda huffed. "As if hivittes and trolls were not enough, now we must deal with purslains."

"What is a purslain?" Lars asked.

"Ask Troy, he is an animal expert," Telezzar replied, pondering on how to deal with the purslain.

Lars turned to Troy, but before he could ask, Troy began to explain. "Purslains are huge armadillo-like creatures with long snouts, crab-like claws—which they use to cut off limbs—and a tongue that creates a poisonous toxin." Troy paused, remembering what else he had learned. "Most importantly, never touch the tongue, or you will enter a drunken stupor. As you can see, they create lairs by digging holes into cavern walls. They're also supposed to be rare."

"Really, Troy? Rare? There's one right there," Dar Caine replied.

"Dar Caine, I hate to correct you, but there are three," Leda said, eyeing a pair near the opposite wall.

"Enough chatter! Shoot them down," Telezzar instructed, as the purslains began to descend upon the foreign flesh.

Troy and Leda took hold of their bows, and they began firing arrows. The purslains moved slowly, but their shells protected them. Though the arrows did not harm the purslains, the arrows did cause the purslains to lose their balance, and one by one, the creatures fell to the ground below, landing on their backs.

"Dar Caine, take your flails and crush their bellies," Telezzar said, pointing to the pair.

The creatures screeched and snapped. Dar Caine took his flails and crushed them, and a greenish-orange substance gushed and oozed out of their wounds.

Telezzar approached the third purslain and, placing a Spell of Friendship on the creature, he began extracting information. Having not slept to charge his powers, though, the spell wore off quickly, and the purslain began to snap at the wizard, feeling violated and wanting revenge. Dar Caine stepped next to the wizard's side, and at his command, the giant swung his flails, ending the last purslain.

"Our friend was most helpful," Telezzar said, feeling fatigued. "We must continue this path for a day, and near the end, we must keep our eyes open for a secret passage."

"Telezzar, we should turn back," Troy said, remembering their conversation before the purslains appeared.

"No, we have made a commitment, and we must try to fulfill it," the wizard replied, trying to keep their spirits high.

Dar Caine sighed. "Telezzar, we let our small victories make us believe we could do this, but we will face worse foes, as we journey deeper."

The wizard heard the giant's words, but his eyes stared off, to another purslain lair. "I sense a powerful treasure in there."

The companions looked to where he pointed, and Troy was eager. "I will go get it."

"No, there could be more purslains!" Telezzar shouted, but the elf had already dashed off and started ascending the wall.

Swiftly, Troy climbed up the wall with ease. Once he reached the lair, he peered inward, but he could see nothing. To remedy this problem, he decided to light a torch and throw it into the lair. Immediately, he regretted this.

The torch aroused and alerted four purslains of the elf's presence. Quickly, Troy bent down, grabbed hold of the wall, and descended back to his companions. As he climbed down, he noticed the torch had caught the attention of six other purslains, who all exited their lairs too.

"We can defeat them, just as we did the others," Telezzar said, reassuring the group. "Shoot them down!"

After strapping arrows into her bow, Leda shot at the six purslains. One by one, they lost their balance and fell to the ground. Then swinging his flails wildly, Dar Caine crushed the bellies of the purslains, splattering greenish-orange ooze all over himself.

"This filthy slime is sticky," he complained, trying to shake and scrape it off.

Leda—wiping some from her face—looked at Dar Caine. "You couldn't have been more careful?"

"Yeah," Lars chimed in, wiping it off his lucky jacket. "What if this stuff was acidic or poisonous?"

Dar Caine grunted. "Then you'd be dead, and I would be spared from hearing your complaints."

Troy leaped from the lower part of the wall, rushing to the wizard's side. "Telezzar, I'm sorry."

"You fool; you left your torch lit in the lair! Go retrieve it!"

Troy sighed but did as the wizard instructed. The elf began to scale back up the wall, but from the lair, the four purslains appeared, and they began to descend toward Troy.

Seeing the predicament, Telezzar raised his staff, casting a Spell of Sluggishness. The four purslains seemed to freeze, though they moved slowly. As Troy passed them, he kicked the four off the wall to the ground below.

Entering the lair, Troy stopped, as the overwhelming stench of decay filled his lungs. He stumbled and looked around. Blood and bones were everywhere, even more than what filled the gigantic room.

Troy picked up the torch and turned to leave, but one last purslain blocked his path. Without hesitation, Troy charged the creature, shoving the lit torch up the purslain's snout. At the same time, the purslain extended its limb, attempting to snap off Troy's arm, but the elf escaped, barely.

The creature reared up on its hind legs, letting out a hideous screech. Leaping towards the purslain, Troy kicked it down to the ground below. It was over.

Troy stumbled back and sat down at the edge of the small graveyard, breathing heavily. He glanced around and noticed—a little ways inside the lair—a ring on the finger of a dwarf. He crawled over to it and took the ring, and as he examined it closely, he realized it was made of starlight. Pleased with what he found, Troy pocketed the ring.

After several more deep breathes, he rose to his feet, preparing to leave. As he took one last glance over the small graveyard, something caught his eye. He stepped to the back of the small lair, discovering a surprise. He had found a secret passage.

CHAPTER V

Gneiss

Kneeling and examining the secret passage, Telezzar finally gave a grin. "Your foolishness may have helped us."

"It is safe to travel?" Leda asked. She was trying to peer around the wizard and giant, who stood between her and the secret passage.

"It appears safe, though I do not know what we will find at the end."

Dar Caine grunted. "Any place is better than here."

With that, the giant stepped onto the first stair, leading the way, and everyone else followed. The stairs were bulky stone slabs, and the stairwell seemed old, surely carved out by dwarfs, since it was narrow. None of the companions complained about this, though, not even Dar Caine. They were each glad to be rid of the purslain lairs.

Climbing and climbing, the group descended the stairwell, deeper into the mountains. They mused and guessed the time of day or night. As their venture seemed to be going well, an unpredictable predicament arose.

Dar Caine stopped in his tracks, and everyone else ran into one another. "Telezzar, several of the steps are missing," he said, staring down the dark abyss, where the steps should have been.

"Can we jump across?" the wizard asked. He squeezed around the others, making his way to the front.

"I doubt even Troy could make the jump," Dar Caine replied, knowing elves were renowned for being light on their feet at times.

Telezzar arrived at the giant's side and looked. Sure enough, several steps were missing, and in their place, a gap of darkness sat, plunging down. "We have wasted time coming this way, so we must hurry back to the purslain lairs."

Being at the back of the group, Leda turned to lead the way back up the stairs, but a part of the wall stuck itself out, tripping her.

All at once, a gigantic boulder detached itself from the wall. The creature rubbed its eyes, as if groggy, and then looked down at Leda with giddiness. "I-I haven't seen your kind in a long time!"

Everyone stood in amazement, but none more than Telezzar. "A gneiss," the wizard whispered aloud. "We come in peace, my friend."

The gneiss were ancient rock folk, built sturdy and strong. But with great stony dimples, and an innocent smile, this gneiss was merely a child.

"I love dwarfs," the gneiss said, while reaching down and helping Leda to her feet. "I'm here guarding, I'm guarding for my master, my master saved me from hivittes. M-my brother, he, uh, he is at the Mountains of the Green Dragon. I always, um, I always obey my master."

Taken aback by his quick speaking, Leda could only smile at first. "Well, I am Leda, daughter of Uther, from the Underground World of Ashturim."

"I'm Odie!" the gneiss shouted, throwing his head forward in excitement. Giddy with excitement, he sat down next to her. "M-my master, he dieded long ago. I love dwarfs. Do you have the elevator key?"

They all stared at Odie, confused, but Telezzar realized the gneiss was trying to help them. "Elevator key? No, where might we find it?"

"Oh, um, the nasty purslain leader, he, um, he has it," Odie replied, hurriedly. He made a dirty face, thinking about the purslains, who he had only met once or twice.

Telezzar cursed under his breath. Then, with a sigh, he looked at Dar Caine. "Take my familiar, Basil, and go retrieve the key."

Dar Caine looked around, and then he noticed the fox sitting behind the group. Basil had followed them. The giant nodded in agreement and left with the fox.

Telezzar stroked his black beard, musing to himself over all that had happened. "I must rest and charge my power," he said to the others, and he stepped aside.

Odie stretched his stiff rock body and looked at Leda. "To-today is my Birth Day! Would you, um, would you like to play a game?"

"What kind of game?" Leda asked, curiously. She was interested in the gneiss's proposal, especially since it was his Birth Day.

"Um, a game of chance. Th-they are my favorite."

"All right, let's play."

Lars and Troy joined them, sitting in a circle. Odie stuck his hand into his mouth and, after making a vomit-like gesture, he pulled his hand out and held a wooden box. Troy stared in awe, while Leda gave a pleasant smile, but Lars felt he would faint from such a sight. After fumbling with the lock, Odie opened the wooden box, revealing a deck of cards.

"Um, do any of you know how to p-play Rabbit Hole?" The companions each shook their heads. "Well, um, this is how you play. W-we each place something val-valuable in the middle, then we each will t-take turns placing a card down, but you m-must play a number that comes be-before or after the number played."

"So, if Leda plays a three, then I must play a two or four?" Troy asked.

"Yes, and say Leda pl-plays a three, but you, uh, you have no two or fo-fours, then you, um, you lose," Odie said. "And who-whoever wins gets the tre-treasure."

"Why is it called Rabbit Hole?" Lars asked, thinking the name was peculiar.

"Because we, uh, we place our cards around the tre-treasure, making the hole, an-and the, the treasure in the middle is the ra-rabbit."

The Realm

Each of the four players placed one gold piece in the center, and Odie started the game by playing an eight. Being to the left of Odie, Leda set down a seven, and from there, Troy played an eight, and Lars a nine.

"Oh, this is fun!" Odie exclaimed, shaking his body back and forth with delight. "Now, w-we add another tre-treasure piece, and start ro-round two."

Each of them placed another gold piece in the middle. Odie played a ten. Leda placed down a nine, but Troy had a problem.

"I have no eight or ten," the elf said, frowning at his cards.

"Ha! You lose!" Odie shouted with laughter, as he pointed at Troy. "Lars, it is your turn."

Lars stared at his cards. "Well, I will play a ten."

"Nooo!" Odie shouted, upset. "I-I don't have anything to pl-play! This isn't f-fair!"

"Sorry, Odie," Lars replied, trying to conceal a smile. "I had no other cards to use."

"I-I hope Leda wins. She's a dwarf. I love dwarfs," Odie said to Lars, while trying to peek at the leprechaun's cards.

"I won't, Odie, I have nothing to play," Leda said, putting down her cards.

"Then Lars, h-he wins," Odie moaned, while rocking his body, as if in pain. Then, he leaned over to Leda. "I-I think he cheated."

Leda smiled, and knew Lars heard the gneiss. "You know, I think you might be right, but let's play again."

Odie's eyes widened. "Y-you want to play again? Nobody ever, ever lets Odie play back-to-back games of Rabbit Hole."

"I wonder why," Lars mumbled under his breath, and Troy smirked at the remark.

"We will play a second game, but you have to promise to stay calm," Leda said, and Odie nodded his head, obeying her.

Once again, Odie passed out the cards, each player put a gold piece in the middle, and the game began.

"Five," Odie said. "Your t-turn, Leda."

"Four."

"Thank you, Leda," Troy said, placing down a three.

Lars glared at his cards, then to Troy. "Well, I am in a predicament, as I have no cards to play."

"Ha! Ch-cheaters, th-they never win," Odie said, quickly placing down a two.

Leda studied her cards. "One."

Troy frowned. "I have nothing, so I lose again."

Odie looked at his cards. He had a two, but he wanted Leda to be his friend. "I have no cards either, so Leda wins!"

As Odie scooted all the gold to her, Leda could see the gneiss's cards. "Odie, you have a two."

"No, Odie lost. His new best friend won!"

Leda smiled, understanding why Odie purposely lost to her. "Odie, would you like to be my friend?"

Odie gave a bashful smile. "Y-you want to be my friend? Oh yes, I-I love dwarfs!"

"Well, Odie, since it is your Birth Day, I want you to have the treasure from the last game."

"B-but you won."

"True, but it will be my gift to you."

The Realm

"A present for me? Oh, Leda, c-can we please play again? Please! I-I promise to still be good."

Leda pretended to think about it. "All right, only if you are good."

"I will be!" he exclaimed, but then he became serious. "This time, let's all place something valuable, instead of gold."

The companions agreed to Odie's idea. Leda placed two of the emeralds she had received from the troll's hoard. Troy put down the ring of starlight, which he had found in the purslain lair, and Lars had nothing, so he placed down half of the gold he had won. Lastly, Odie placed his treasure down. The gneiss placed his hand inside his mouth and made a vomit-like gesture. When his hand came out, he held three pieces of the precious metal, electrum.

"Six," Odie said, starting the game.

"Five," Leda said. She eyed the treasure, badly wishing to win.

"Four," Troy said. He did not want to lose the ring, and he began to think it was foolish to bet it.

"Five," Lars said.

"Six," Odie boasted, fumbling the card out of his hand and onto the ground.

"I'm out," Leda said, with a defeated sigh.

"Seven."

Carefully, Lars eyed his cards, but shook his head. "Alas, I've lost me gold."

"Eight," Odie said. "What do you have, Troy?"

"I have," Troy paused, checking his cards, "nothing."

Odie threw his cards up. "I have won! I-I love Rabbit Hole."

"Congratulations, Odie," Leda said, while Lars and Troy grumbled out congratulations too.

"Y-you, um, you have all been nice to Odie, and I-I want you to keep your treasures," the gneiss said, scooting the treasure back to them. "And each of you, p-please, take one of the electrum pieces, as a present."

Leda, Lars, and Troy took back their treasure and one piece of electrum, as Odie requested. The gneiss was happy to have his own friends.

***

While Odie and the companions played Rabbit Hole, Dar Caine and Basil returned to the purslain lairs. Hopping down the ledges, Basil reached the floor of the gigantic room first, and the fox began scouting the dead purslains. Carefully, Dar Caine scaled down the wall, reaching the ground and assisting Basil.

"Why was I picked for this?" Dar Caine mumbled under his breath.

Basil looked up at the giant. He hesitated to answer, since Telezzar did not like Basil speaking to others, but he gave in. "I don't know why Telezzar sent you, but since these are creatures, the biggest one will probably have it."

Surprised, Dar Caine stared at the fox. "You talk?"

"Well, of course," Basil replied, smirking, "I'm the familiar for one of the greatest wizards. Does this surprise you?"

Dar Caine grunted. "Yes, but I wish you had revealed this sooner. It was a long journey back here."

Basil laughed at the giant's reply. "Telezzar frowns on my speaking to others. He fears that if the wrong person finds out, I may end up in danger."

"Who would harm you?"

"Telezzar has several enemies, and that is why he and I often use telepathy. When you and your friends found it odd that Telezzar looked into my eyes, he and I were speaking."

"I apologize for interrupting; I should have known better."

Basil chuckled. "You are the only one who doubts Telezzar. Why?"

"It's easier to doubt than trust."

"Then, why do you follow?"

Dar Caine stood silently. He had an answer, but Basil would not understand. "I am the son of a chieftain, and it is my duty to watch over my people. That is why I follow Telezzar, I must make sure nothing happens to the others."

"That is a good answer, my friend," Basil said. "It is good to question authority. In my thoughts, I often do, but Telezzar knows what he is doing."

"I agree. As this quest carries on, I find myself trusting him more and more."

"That is good news, but I have better," Basil said, pawing at one of the purslains. "I have found the key."

Dar Caine trotted over to the purslain, and spotted part of an onyx stone. The giant ripped open the purslain, and his eyes became enchanted by the precious stone, as it lay glittering in the creature's chest. Dar Caine picked the stone up and handed it to Basil.

"Halt!" an unfamiliar voice commanded.

Dar Caine shooed Basil on. The fox was able to slip into the shadows, without the figure seeing, and Dar Caine rose to his feet and turned to the figure.

"Why are you here?" the voice asked. It stepped from the shadows, revealing itself to the giant, and with three other figures.

"Eldred," Dar Caine said aloud, so Basil would know who had stopped them.

The eldred sniggered. "Yes, we are eldred. Now, I will repeat the question, why are you here?"

Dar Caine stood tall, hoping to intimidate them. "My business does not concern you, nor are these your halls."

The eldred laughed. "You are wrong these are the Halls of King Kaulthar, which currently house our eldred prince. That makes these halls, our halls."

Dar Caine grunted, eyeing each one of them. "I have done nothing."

The lead eldred smirked. "I would very much enjoy watching you suffer, but alas, my orders are to take any vagabonds back to King Kaulthar."

"I have done nothing. I am only a weary traveler," Dar Caine replied, making one last effort to escape. "I stumbled across a secret door that led me here."

"How very lucky, or in your case, unlucky," the eldred said. "I know the only secret door is accessible by a pit. Tell me, what happened in there?"

Dar Caine stepped forward into the eldred's face. "I slew your troll and hivitte friends."

The lead eldred swung his bow upward, whacking the giant's head. Dar Caine stumbled back from the blow. Before he could defend himself, another eldred fired a dart, which put the giant to sleep.

The lead eldred stooped down over Dar Caine, whispering in his ear: "The eldred are no friends to hivittes. It is a pity—about the troll—his brothers were fond of him, I hear. Perhaps, when we reach King Kaulthar's dungeon, they will give you a warm welcome."

Quietly, Basil watched as the eldred bound the giant and dragged him off. Using the ledges, the fox scampered up to the purslain lair, and then he hurried off, down the stairwell.

CHAPTER VI

The Secret Plan

asil told Telezzar and the others about what had happened to Dar Caine. Once the fox finished, Telezzar let out a deep sigh. "Surely, they know the secret passage to Kaulthar's kingdom, and they will reach it in three days."

"Odie says it will take one day by elevator," Leda said. "Before Dar Caine reaches Kaulthar, we could—and we could devise a plan."

"Leda is right, and we have the element of surprise," Troy chimed in.

"Oh, how cliché," Basil scoffed. "Surprise or not, you are still outnumbered by the spidermites."

"Basil!" Telezzar snapped, and the familiar became quiet. Instead of returning to his deep thoughts, the wizard looked at the companions. "We have come a long way, but now, if any of you wish to stay, then you may remain here."

"Nonsense, we all must go," Troy said. "We came to save King Claudius; the only difference is we must save Dar Caine too."

"Troy is right," Lars added. He knew that Telezzar's words were meant more for himself than the others. "We all started together, so we will finish together."

The Realm

The wizard nodded his head, happy that the companions decided to go on. "Then, let's be on our way."

Odie showed the group where the hidden elevator was. Telezzar praised the former dwarf king for placing Odie in front of the elevator, and then casting a sleep spell on the gneiss. If the dwarf king had not done so, the spidermites would have surely discovered the elevator.

Odie was upset as Leda boarded the elevator, but she promised him that she would return safely. Telezzar placed the onyx stone into its compartment, and Leda watched Odie's sad eyes, as the elevator slowly descended away.

"Leda, Odie has given you the onyx stone. It was an heirloom for the dwarf family, which he served."

Leda smiled with gratitude. "Telezzar, what happened to the dwarfs?"

"When King Ziklag fell, and Ashturim attempted to seize the throne, some of the dwarfs traveled east. Some settled in the eastern part of the Underground World of Ashturim, while others ventured on. The Mountains of the Blue Dragon became home to some of those dwarf refugees.

"Their numbers were too few, though, and their defenses were crude. The spidermites slaughtered and drove the dwarfs away."

Leda looked at him saddened. "I knew some dwarfs came east, but I did not know any settled among the mountains, save the Mountains of the Great Sea."

"Something else bothers you, yes?"

"Yes, what will happen to Odie?"

"Ah, you wonder whether Odie will let you become his master."

"I do. The thought crossed my mind when we were playing Rabbit Hole. I have grown fond of him."

"There is no doubt that Odie would accept, and serve you well, but it must not happen. Odie is quite valuable—more valuable than I could have foreseen. Surely, evil creatures are hunting him, and that is why he must be bound to no one."

"I don't understand," she replied. She was upset by Telezzar's words, but more confused by his reasoning. She felt Odie should choose his own home.

"Well, gather around, and I will explain," the wizard said, gaining everyone's attention. "Odie has provided each of you with a piece of electrum. These pieces are rare, and yours—surprisingly—have been refined.

"The terebinth, who are the guardians of the Plain of Solarium, once had seven swords made of electrum. Those swords turned demons and evil creatures to stone, but the swords were purposely broken. Each of the broken swords produced seven pieces of electrum, which the terebinth spread across the other plains and Hell.

"From what I have heard, the Bdellium Knights are searching for the electrum. They wish to re-forge the swords."

"They are mad," Troy said, laughing. "Why would they want to re-forge the swords?"

"They hope to reverse the curse and turn paladins and holy men into stone."

Leda laughed now. "Well, it was nice knowing you, Troy."

"It is not amusing," Telezzar replied, "if the paladins and holy men are gone, then more creatures of the darkness will wake from their slumbers, fulfilling the dark deeds of their masters."

"Telezzar, you keep hinting about something evil, as if it were being kept at bay. What is it?" Troy asked.

The wizard gave a wary look. He did not want to tell them, but he realized they were becoming more aware of his thoughts. "It is Dentar. He came to Prixem in search of power and dominion, but he has been held off so far."

"Dentar? You spoke of him earlier," Troy said, remembering their conversation. "You said he has a spy here, following us."

"Yes, he does, though Dentar has found me to be a problem."

"Why aren't your brothers helping us?" Lars asked.

"Because this task was given to me," Telezzar replied with a smile. "You do not think that you three and Dar Caine were accidentally chosen, do you?"

Alarmed, the companions exchanged glances, suspicious of the wizard's words. "What do you mean?" Leda asked.

"I arrived at the tavern, expecting to journey with your kin. Everyone—except William—had come to help me, but William knew Njord, and Njord convinced William to join us. Before I could greet them, though, I spotted you and decided to join you. I am sure that Dentar discovered my plan, and he sent his servants to capture them all."

"Lies! Achren and I were headed for Belfast," Troy snapped.

Telezzar raised his hand, gesturing for the elf to calm down. "The fewer who knew, the better. Your kin were to help me spy throughout the mountains, but when Dentar's servants took them, I knew none of you knew of the plan. Thus, I led you into the mountains anyways."

"How can we trust you?" Troy asked, heatedly.

"Troy, are you not safe? This plan was too important to not see through."

"He is right," Lars said to Leda and Troy. "He has kept us safe, and it was odd that all our kin knew one another. I believe they were going to help him."

"I agree. My father and I were following a bounty, and many people told us our bounty had gone west, to Thracia. My father ingored them all, staying put in Ben-Hadad."

Troy shook his head, still not believing. "We were headed to Belfast. We had no affairs in Ben-Hadad."

"Troy, if you were traveling from Lithia to Belfast, wouldn't Ben-Hadad be out of the way?" Lars asked, picturing a map of Padavona in his mind.

The elf thought silently. "Yes, it is. Achren never had intentions of going to Belfast, did he, Telezzar?"

"Perhaps in the future, but not at the present time," the wizard replied. "Your grandfather, King Azekiel, is a dear friend of mine, and he is the one who reached out to King Dalidon and Njord. He told them of my worries, and in turn, Njord brought Dar Caine and King Dalidon sent Leda and her father."

"My grandfather knew?"

Telezzar placed his hand on the elf's shoulder. "I know this seems odd, and I have felt terrible for keeping it a secret, but I had to, until I gained your trust."

"I wish I had known sooner," Troy said.

The Realm

"I know, and there are no more secrets about this adventure," Telezzar said with a smile. "Now, we should be landing soon. I would advise you all to sleep while you can."

***

Far away, near the trap floor, Crokus and the twins—Caelan and Caneal—walked about. Carlton still hid in the pit, and he could hear his brothers, but something else stirred about.

"Three minotaur princes," an eldred scoffed. He approached the brothers, accompanied by a second eldred and six gargoyles. "What dealings could three minotaur princes have here?"

"That's odd," Crokus said, sarcastically, "I swear, I can hear scum, but I don't see any." Using his size, he gazed over the head of the eldred.

The lead eldred smirked. "Did I say three minotaur princes? I meant two princes and their pet goat."

Crokus snorted, angrily. "Says the pale-faced weakling. At least, I've not lost an elf."

The eldred gave a delightful smile. "Then, you have seen the elf?"

Crokus realized his mistake. "I was making a joke. You are searching for an elf?"

"I will not tolerate this. Where is the elf?"

"Don't know, don't ca—" Crokus did not finish his sentence, for the second eldred shot the minotaur prince in the head.

Caneal and Caelan froze in shock. "Don't be heroes like this goat. Tell me, where is the elf?" the eldred asked.

The Realm

The twins stood silently, staring at their fallen brother. Caneal snapped from his shock and looked to the eldred. "Not here."

Caneal reached for his sword, but the second eldred stepped forward and swung its sword, beheading Caneal. Caelan fell to his knees in disbelief, cradling Caneal's body in his lap.

"Two dead and one remains. Will you tell me what I wish to know?" the eldred asked, softly.

"I know nothing," Caelan replied, spitting at the eldred's feet.

The lead eldred swung his bow, whacking Caelan across the face. "Then, you will travel with us and carry the bodies of your dead brothers."

The eldred took a large blanket and had Caelan place his brothers on it. Then, the eldred led the gargoyles and defeated Caelan away. Carlton—who remained in the pit—wept bitterly for his fallen brothers.

CHAPTER VII

Double Trouble

The elevator stopped with a great *thud*. As the companions rubbed their groggy eyes, Telezzar approached a small hole in the wall and gazed through it.

"I can see six dungeon cells, nothing more," he said, irritably. "How are we to know what's in the room, if we cannot see?"

Lars stumbled to the wizard's side. "Well, this seems like a job for me." His eyes beamed with excitement, and he felt he was about to show his worth.

"Though you are short and somewhat undetectable, we are not risking your life."

"You need me to do this." He reached into his pocket, digging out the Mask of Disguises.

"No, no, no! You are staying here. If the spidermites catch you, they will torture you."

"Yes, but would they torture an eldred?" Lars asked, placing the mask on his face, and shifting into an eldred.

Troy and Leda smiled with admiration, but Telezzar was still hesitant. "I don't think you should take the risk."

Lars huffed. "You had Troy search the purslain lair, Leda become Odie's friend, and you sent Dar Caine to retrieve the elevator key."

"Lars," the wizard replied, chuckling, "Troy was not sent to search that lair, Leda was not told to befriend Odie, and Dar Caine was accompanied by Basil."

"Where is Basil?" Troy asked.

"I had him stay with Odie," Telezzar replied, returning his attention to Lars. "I feel it is imprudent to let this happen, but if your heart is set, then I will let you go."

Lars nodded happily, and he slipped out of the elevator, into the room with six dungeon cells. He scoped the area and studied everything carefully.

There were six dungeon cells against the far wall, just as the wizard had said. The floor was red clay mixed with straw. The cavern walls were a copper color and the wall behind Lars— where the elevator was—appeared the same. To the leprechaun's left and right, there were two giant doorways, but he did not venture towards them.

Lars heard a deep rumbling. He looked about and noticed a hut that sat next to the last dungeon cell, on the far right. Quietly, he tiptoed to the hut, and peeked inside through a window. At a table, there sat two gray trolls, and at the sight of this, Lars darted from the window and into the nearest dungeon cell.

Every so often, one of the trolls emerged to check on the prisoners, and Lars did not dare move from the cell, or remove his mask. Luckily—and he claimed it was his jacket—the trolls never noticed Lars, but fear overtook him each time he saw them, carrying their gigantic wooden clubs embedded with iron spikes and glass shards.

The Realm

Telezzar watched all this from the peephole, and he let out a deep sigh. "Lars has hidden in one of the cells." He turned to a concerned Leda and grinning Troy. "What is humorous, Troy?"

The elf's grin faded. "Nothing, Telezzar, I just...hear someone speaking in the elf tongue."

Troy rushed to the peephole and saw eldred walking by, towards the door on the left. "Telezzar, there are eldred, and they are speaking my tongue. They are complaining that King Kaulthar and Prince Silloweb have called a meeting."

"Get back," the wizard said, rushing to look. The eldred passed the elevator. "Oh, dear!"

"What?" Leda and Troy asked, in unison.

"Lars has left the dungeon cell. He is joining the eldred rank."

"That fool! Telezzar, we must get him. If they find out, they will kill him."

Before Telezzar could reply, Leda perked up. "I hear the dwarf tongue. I think hivittes are passing."

The wizard looked out the peephole, again, and saw a company of hivittes passing. "What are they saying, Leda?"

The dwarf placed her ear against the wall. "They, too, are meeting King Kaulthar, but they are also meeting with King Ziglo of the Hivittes and a Bdellium Knight, Boremon. They are going to discuss gold."

Telezzar nodded, pondering what she said. "I doubt Lars will be caught, but I have a plan. We must be ready for the eldred and hivittes when they pass us again."

Meanwhile, Lars marched with the eldred into King Kaulthar's throne room. The walls and floor were quite different:

carpets and wild animal skins covered the floor, and purple-and-gold tapestries adorned the walls.

The throne was made of gold and silver and bejeweled with gems. King Kaulthar stood at a table with his three guests, the Eldred Prince Silloweb, the Hivitte King Ziglo, and the Bdellium Knight of Death, Boremon.

"Word has reached me, my king, that my eldred spies have captured a prisoner. The prisoner claims to have slain ten purslains in the lairs, as well as defeated the two hivittes and young troll in the pit," Prince Silloweb said, with a smirk towards King Ziglo.

"Your spies have proven themselves useful, but I doubt their prisoner's claim," the spidermite king hissed.

"As do I," King Ziglo grunted. The hivittes and eldred quarreled, just as their dwarf and elf counterparts, and the thought of a prisoner killing two of his guards, only to be caught by eldred, irritated the king.

"Enough about the prisoner," Boremon said, in a tiresome tone. "The behemoth hungers, and the master will not be pleased if his beast is underfed."

"Yes, Boremon, I know what the master wants," Kaulthar said, lethargically. "Once the prisoner arrives, he will be taken to the coliseum, and after he is killed, the behemoth may eat."

Boremon threw his fists down on the table. "Do not belittle my counsel!"

"Last I looked, the master chose me to oversee his business, not you."

Boremon grunted, gnashing his teeth.

"Moving along, what of the electrum?" King Kaulthar asked Prince Silloweb.

"None has been found."

"Pity, I was beginning to think the eldred would be of great value." Prince Silloweb opened his mouth to speak, but King Kaulthar continued: "Ziglo, what of the gold?"

"It has been found," the hivitte king said, proudly. "Soon, we should have enough to pay mercenaries and fund an army."

King Kaulthar smiled. "At least this meeting was not a full disappointment. Ziglo, see that the behemoth assists your workers in retrieving the gold, and have it brought back here."

"Yes, King Kaulthar."

"That will conclude this meeting. Have your servants leave my presence and resume their posts."

After eschewing the spidermite king's orders, Prince Silloweb and King Ziglo dispersed, going about their own business. Separately, the hivittes and eldred trudged from the throne room and back into the dungeon cell area.

When Telezzar saw this, he started his plan. He cast a Friendship Spell on one of the hivittes, and the hivitte veered from the group and into the elevator. Moments later, the eldred emerged, and Telezzar did the same again, but this time Lars joined the spellbound eldred.

Leda donned the hivitte's cape, and Troy slipped into the eldred's cloak. They both left the elevator, following the other servants. Meanwhile, Telezzar started the elevator, needing to retrieve Odie, and Lars relayed everything he had heard and seen.

The Realm

***

Bound in shackles and beaten badly, Dar Caine plodded forward. As if he was full of wine, the giant swayed back and forth while blood trickled from his mouth and down his beard. His scruffy hair was dry and tangled, his arms covered with open wounds, and his clothes hardened by dry blood. The eldred mocked him and beat him more, refusing to believe his story.

***

Disguised as a hivitte, Leda followed the other hivittes to a massive crater, and inside it, there lay a golden stone. Leda and the others began digging around the giant stone; it was a tedious task. Then, after some time, the behemoth arrived. It was nothing like the paintings throughout the mountains. Frightened, Leda and the others stayed away from the behemoth, but it paid little attention to them.

The creature placed its fiery hands on the golden stone. It snarled and heaved. The hivittes watched closely, whispering to one another, save Leda. With one last heave, the stone dislodged from the earth and sat in the behemoth's hands.

"Return it to the throne room," Boremon ordered. He stared at the hivittes with suspicion since he did not trust them. King Ziglo commended his workers, though, and when the hivitte king had finished gloating, he and Boremon followed the behemoth.

***

Meanwhile, the eldred led Troy into a tunnel, and they began searching for electrum. The task was slow and unfruitful, and soon the eldred stopped searching.

"If the king knew how his son was acting," one of the eldred muttered, "he would disown Silloweb. The princeling has done everything but bend the knee."

"Stop complaining," a voice replied, coming toward the huddled eldred.

Troy's hand went to his short sword's handle, ready to battle, but when he saw none of the eldred worry, he dismissed his instinct.

"Ah, well, look who decided to come around," another of the eldred said.

"Quiet," the figure whispered. As it stepped into the light, Troy recognized the figure, with its elongated head and yellow eyes and amphibian-like body of slimy, green skin. It was a jaggeddi. "Have you found any electrum?"

"There's none here," the lead eldred replied.

The jaggeddi shook his head in disbelief. "The master believes that several shards are here."

"Kaulthar is your master?" one of the eldred asked.

The jaggeddi spat at the sound of King Kaulthar's name. "I would not follow that two-tongued spidermite if I were given gold. No, my master is the Lord of Ashdod."

"Ashdod? That's goblin country."

"No more," the jaggeddi said, with a dark smirk. "There is a new lord, and he rules over all dark creatures and beings. He has only shown himself to kings and lords of both light and dark, but I assure you, he exists."

The eldred laughed and scoffed at his words, all but Troy. He had an eerie feeling that the Lord of Ashdod was truly Dentar. As the eldred began to move on, Troy lingered behind.

"I believe you," he said to the jaggeddi. "I believe there is a new dark lord. Who is he? What do you know of him?"

The jaggeddi smiled. "His birth name is unknown, but his new name is Dentar. I have told you all I know, though."

Troy mused for a moment, trying to remember what Telezzar had said about Dentar.

"You know what else I believe," the jaggeddi said.

"No."

"I believe the electrum has already been found. I believe Kaulthar has it."

Troy gave a confused look. "Why not hand it over?"

"He fears Dentar," the jagg whispered. "Word has reached my ear that Kaulthar has found gold to fund an army, too. With gold, an army, and shards of electrum, Kaulthar could rival Dentar."

Troy was surprised, but it all made sense. "If that is true, could Kaulthar truly overthrow Dentar?"

The jagg smirked and turned away, starting back down the tunnel. "Never."

Troy thought of the jagg's words a little longer, before making his way back to the eldred. As he joined them, he realized something: Dar Caine would soon arrive at King Kaulthar's dungeons, and everyone would need to be there. Quickly, Troy pondered for an idea; he needed a diversion, so he could be near his companions.

"I believe Kaulthar is lying," he said to the other eldred, after rehearsing in his mind. They all became silent and stared. "I believe Kaulthar has found the electrum, and we should rebel against him, take the electrum, and place Prince Silloweb in command."

No one spoke, and Troy believed he had succeeded, but then, a hearty laugh changed all that. "As I told all of you, I doubted this one was one of us. He has acted peculiar, and now, he wishes for us to bring treason against King Kaulthar and the master," the lead elded said.

"Prince Silloweb would be a better servant for the master."

All the eldred laughed. "The prince's father cannot tolerate his foolish ways, what makes you think the master would?" the leader asked. "Bind him; we will see how King Kaulthar deals with traitors."

***

The eldred spies and Dar Caine arrived at the main gates. Spidermite servants escorted and directed them to the coliseum, where spidermites, hivittes, and eldred gathered to watch. Everyone knew the claim. Ten purslains, two hivittes, and a troll. Some were impressed, some were skeptical, but all attended.

Chants began to ring out: *Blood! Liar! Troll killer!* King Kaulthar rose from his seat and raised his hand, hushing the crowd. He looked down to Dar Caine, and the two locked eyes.

"You claim to have slain ten purslains, two hivitte warriors, and a troll," the king announced, and the crowd erupted with laughter. "I call your claimed deeds, lies!" The crowd applauded. "Do you have anything to say?"

Dar Caine grunted. "You have no proof against my claims, only that what is done is done."

"Mind your temper," Kaulthar hissed. "If what you say is true, then you should have no problem defeating two trolls—who were, incidentally, related to the troll you claim to have killed."

On the far side, the iron gates were rising. Dar Caine's was not nervous, but he had a bad feeling. Through the iron gates, a pair of heavily built trolls cantered in, raising their spiked clubs, and roaring at the crowd.

Dar Caine grunted. "Come on!"

The two trolls eyed the giant and made their way to him but—since trolls are not very smart—one of them tripped over its own feet. Immediately, Dar Caine charged the second troll.

The two exchanged blows, the troll with its club and Dar Caine with his flails, but the giant was weary. The troll bashed the giant in the face, repeatedly. More blood trickled from Dar Caine's head, but he did not quit.

When the troll raised its club again, ready to finish off Dar Caine, the giant swung his flails upward, into the troll's chest. The creature hunched over, dropping its club. Dar Caine threw down his flails and picked up the club; then, he rammed a shard of glass—from the club—through the troll's head. With a groan and a moan, the troll's body fell limp.

The Realm

King Kaulthar's eyes widened, as he was highly impressed. The crowd roared with pleasure and chanted on, praising the giant, and wanting to see more. Poor Dar Caine only wished to collapse—the grueling match had exhausted him—but he knew one troll remained.

The giant grabbed his flails and dragged them to the last troll. The trolls rolled over, fumbling to grab its club. With a grunt, Dar Caine tossed his fails on the troll's chest, and then, he placed his foot on the troll's throat, crushing it.

The arena filled with shouts and cries of pleasure, as both trolls lay bloody and beaten. King Kaulthar rose to his feet, calling for the eldred spies to bring Dar Caine before him.

King Kaulthar spoke: "You have proven yourself, while gaining the admiration and respect of all." The crowd cheered on. "Take this scepter and keys, which once belonged to those foolish trolls. I name you, my right-hand and second-in-command of my kingdom. You are the true dungeon master!"

The crowd applauded, but slowly, they became silent. A group of eldreds stepped into the coliseum, with one bound in ropes.

"King Kaulthar," the lead eldred announced. "This one bound in ropes—he has spoken ill of you and tried to persuade us against you."

"Is this true?"

Troy looked to the king's angered glare. "Yes, I believe you have secretly taken the electrum, I believe you will use the gold to hire an army, and I believe you intend on overthrowing the master."

King Kaulthar cringed at these words, while the coliseum filled with whispers. "Silence!" he roared to the crowd, as his gaze returned to Troy. "You speculate, young Eldred. Take him away!"

"No! My Prince Silloweb, you must believe me!"

Prince Silloweb stared, torn in two. He did believe what Troy said, but he did not dare make his true thoughts known. Meanwhile, King Kaulthar studied the young prince closely.

The eldred grabbed hold of Troy, but Dar Caine intervened. "I am the dungeon master. I will deal with the king's traitor." Dar Caine pushed Troy to the ground, and then, he grabbed the ropes, dragging off the elf-in-disguise.

Once they entered the dungeon area, Dar Caine cut Troy's bonds. "I am sorry, Troy, I did not want the eldred bringing you here, and I had to convince Kaulthar, too."

"Just hurry," Troy replied, impatiently, "Telezzar will return soon with Lars and Odie."

"What has happened?"

"Too much," Troy replied, following Dar Caine, who planned to free the dungeon's other prisoners. "Odie gave us electrum; Telezzar revealed that our kin were supposed to help him map out the mountains, which is why we are here; and Dentar—the master or Lord of Ashdod—wants to rule all of us."

Dar Caine looked at Troy, wanting to ask several questions, but before he could, the wall opened. Telezzar appeared first, followed by Odie and Lars.

The Realm

"Odie, follow me," Telezzar said, without acknowledging Dar Caine or Troy. The wizard marched straight for the throne room, with the gneiss at his heels.

"Lars, what's going on?" Dar Caine asked, as he freed the last prisoner.

"Well Odie is going to get the gold and Leda, but there is a behemoth, too, so Telezzar plans on taking care of it."

Telezzar and Odie burst through the throne room door. A dark scarlet color lit the room, and it smelled like the foul smoke of Hell. The behemoth—the hideous creature covered in fire and brimstone—snarled at the wizard's appearance, but Telezzar wasted no time. He raised his staff, casting an Immortal Stone Curse, and immediately, the behemoth turned to stone.

While Telezzar cursed the behemoth, Odie plowed over the hivittes, who had been guarding the gold. The gneiss placed the golden stone in his mouth, and then, he propped Leda on his back. As he turned to leave, he charged the stone behemoth and knocked it over, ending the evil creature forever.

Telezzar hurried them from the throne room. "Board the elevator! You are leaving with me and Odie," he said to Lars.

Quickly, the leprechaun scampered onto the elevator, soon joined by Telezzar and Odie. The gneiss placed Leda down, outside, and he smiled at her with a slight whimper, since he did not wish to leave her again.

"Head for Lithia, we will hold a council there," Telezzar said to Dar Caine, Leda, and Troy.

Leda looked at Odie. "I will see you soon," she said. The doors closed and the elevator started for the very top of the mountain, where piles of white snow waited to greet them.

"Now, we wait," Dar Caine said.

"Dar Caine! How are you?" Leda asked, realizing the giant was present.

Dar Caine grunted. "Not terrible, though I blame Troy for this whole mess."

Troy smirked. "At least I showed up to your fight."

"What fight?"

Before Dar Caine or Troy could reply, the elevator returned. Dar Caine, Leda, and Troy stared, surprised. It should have taken the elevator much longer to return to them, but they could only assume that Telezzar had used magic.

"Let them go," Dar Caine said, pointing at two prisoners, an elf, and a man. "I will take them to the spiraling stairwell."

"What of King Claudius?" Troy asked. After all, the king had been the reason the group entered King Kaulthar's kingdom.

"No, I will go last," the minotaur king said.

Without further discussion, Dar Caine boarded with two of the former prisoners. The doors shut, and the elevator began its ascension.

"Will Telezzar's magic speed their trip?" Troy asked Leda, wondering if she knew.

"I did not know Telezzar used magic to speed his own trip," she replied, smiling. "Hopefully, his magic will let us all leave here, quickly. Which I should ask, who goes next?"

"You and the other dwarf," Troy replied, pointing to a scrawny dwarf standing next to King Claudius.

Luckily, the elevator returned. Telezzar's magic was going to speed everyone's trip, and they would all escape King Kaulthar's dungeons before anyone noticed.

Leda and the other dwarf boarded the elevator, planning to join Dar Caine at the spiraling stairwell. The doors shut. Now, whether because of Telezzar's magic, or the elevator being ancient, one of the belts snapped, and the elevator plunged downward into the lowest depths of the mountains.

Troy and King Claudius looked at one another in astonishment. They knew what had happened, and they knew the crash had alerted King Kaulthar's minions.

CHAPTER VIII

The Two Kings

What Troy and King Claudius did not know was that a scuffle had broken loose. While Prince Silloweb did not question King Kaulthar—concerning Troy's accusations—Boremon did. Enraged, King Kaulthar ordered his servants to seize Boremon, but the Bdellium Knight drew his sword, slaying several.

King Ziglo and his escorts rallied around Boremon, and this pitted the eldred against the hivittes and the spidermites. Swords crashed on shields and spears, breaking and clanging. Then, it began. Blood mingled with sand.

The eldred and spidermites battled on—so did the hivittes, though many of them followed the fleeing King Ziglo. When King Kaulthar saw this, he fled for his throne room, thinking it would be the safest place, but Prince Silloweb followed the spidermite king.

Troy's words rang through the prince's head, as he chased after King Kaulthar. "Kaulthar!"

The spidermite king turned, finding the eldred prince behind him. "Have the eldred stand down!"

"No," the prince replied, "my servant was right. Give me the electrum, so I might give it to the master."

The Realm

King Kaulthar saw the prince pull out a knife, but the king only smirked. "You fool. You think I would hold back his ascension?"

"I believe you wish to rival the master. Your withholding only makes you a traitor."

King Kaulthar yelled, angered by Prince Silloweb's delusions and ramblings. At that moment, though, a shadow emerged from the nearest dungeon cell, and with one swing of an axe, Prince Silloweb lost his arm. King Kaulthar stared in horror, not expecting such an event, but he recognized the axe wielder: King Claudius.

"Why!" Prince Silloweb shouted, as he lay curled up in pain. His arm bled profusely, but King Claudius gave no answer; instead, he chased after the fleeing King Kaulthar.

Troy exited the dungeon cell, still wearing his eldred robes. He knelt beside Prince Silloweb.

"My truest servant, forgive me."

"I am no servant of the eldred," Troy replied, pulling back the eldred cloak to reveal his paladin sigil.

Prince Silloweb lay his head back, smiling foolishly. "Though you are a trickster, thank you for revealing the truth about Kaulthar. He only viewed us all as pawns."

Troy reached out and closed Prince Silloweb's eyes. Truthfully, he did not believe that King Kaulthar had any electrum, but the prince had died believing so. The elf lingered for a moment, but remembered King Claudius, and he rushed for the throne room.

The Realm

The two kings dueled and clashed with each other, King Claudius with his axe and King Kaulthar with a double-edged javelin. The minotaur raised his axe, which shimmered in the light, and then hit one of the spidermite's legs. King Kaulthar hissed at the blow, and then lunged forward, causing one of the javelin heads to cut King Claudius's side.

"Claudius!" Troy shouted. He grabbed a nearby hivitte crossbow and took aim.

Kaulthar's wound continued to ooze out onyx blood, down his leg. King Claudius's own blood ran down his matted fur, mixing with the dirt from his old dungeon cell. The two kings exchanged grimacing looks, but neither would defer to the other.

Taking aim at the spidermite, Troy's dart bolted out, lodging itself between King Kaulthar's eyes. Stunned, the spidermite king swayed back, but the minotaur king wasted no time. With a furious swing, the axe cut through King Kaulthar, splitting his man half from the spider half.

King Claudius fell himself, slumping down against the former king's throne. "King Claudius," Troy whispered, coming to the minotaur king's side.

"My sons, where are they?"

"They are here, in the mountains, and they are well."

King Claudius gave a peaceful exhale. "I knew they would never leave me."

Then, a hidden door opened behind the throne. Troy grabbed his short sword, and King Claudius, his axe. They were happy, though, as they were greeted by Prince Caelan and a dozen minotaur guards.

"How is this?" Troy asked, surprised to see the minotaur prince and minotaurs.

"My son," King Claudius said, as he embraced Caelan and began to weep.

"Father, it is good to see you," Prince Caelan said. He looked to Troy and continued: "When we came after our father, we brought our best warriors. We hid them away, out of sight, but when you and the wizard arrived, we called for them."

"Where is Carlton, where are the others?" King Claudius asked.

Prince Caelan gave a solemn look. "Crokus and Caneal fell, Father, while Carlton remained behind."

King Claudius fell to his knees, weeping. "How did it happen?" Troy asked.

Caelan bent down and consoled his father. "It was the eldred and gargoyles that searched for you. They found us, and I would have died, if it were not for our warriors."

Troy's shoulders sunk, somewhat ashamed. The eldred and gargoyles had been hunting him, and he fled with Telezzar, while the minotaur princes remained behind to protect the group. Now, two of them were dead.

King Claudius raised his head, looking up at the minotaur warriors. "You have done well and proved yourselves loyal to the heirs of Ovid."

Each of the warriors bowed their heads, while Caelan helped his father to his feet. "We must go. More enemies are on the way, and it will not be safe here," the prince said.

"I cannot, I must go after Leda," Troy replied.

"It will not be safe, and may be folly," King Claudius said.

"I know, but I must do it."

Prince Caelan reached into his pack and handed Troy three gargoyle horns. "I took these from my captors. Since you are a paladin, I thought they would be best used by you."

Astonished, Troy accepted the horns, and he packed them with the one Telezzar had given him. He exchanged farewells with Prince Caelan and King Claudius, and then, the minotaurs went their own way, while Troy returned to the elevator.

CHAPTER IX

Secrets of the Mountains

Dar Caine led the two freed prisoners up the spiraling stairwell. The elf—Nova—had dirt and mud all over her. She kept brushing her blond hair back from her sweaty face, and her sapphire-blue eyes followed the giant, as he seemed to leap up the steps. The man—Bono Vox—was a bard, which one could tell by his clothing. He had short brown hair and wore glasses with tinted lenses that hid his muddy-brown eyes.

"Where are you taking us?" Bono Vox asked. He gasped for a breath as he trotted to keep up.

"Safety."

"How can we trust you?" Nova asked.

Dar Caine grunted. Now he knew how Telezzar felt when everyone questioned him. "I freed you, and you're going to question me about it."

"I'm sorry. I just...we've been prisoners for so long."

"Why were you taken?" the giant asked.

Bono Vox chuckled. "Well, I attempted to cheat in a game of chance with several spidermites. When I could not pay, I was tortured and brought to Kaulthar."

"You tried to double-cross spidermites? What a fool," Dar Caine said. He looked at Nova. "What of you?"

"I was taken during a raid."

Dar Caine did not know what to say, but he pitied her. They reached the purslain lair, though, and the giant found peace in the den of bloodshed. It was almost over.

"We must descend, and then walk a little way to a pit, but we are almost free," Dar Caine said.

The three began to climb down, but once they reached the bottom, two shadowy figures met them. "Dar Caine?"

"Carlton?" the giant questioned.

"Yes," the minotaur said, approaching the giant.

"What happened? Why are you here?"

"It is a long tale, my friend. After you left, the two eldred and six gargoyles arrived and killed my brothers—Crokus and Caneal. After that, they went back to the fork in the road, and they opened up the runed door."

"What was behind it?"

"Jaggeddi tribesmen. They assisted the eldred and gargoyles."

"Where are the eldred and gargoyles?"

"Dead. My brothers and I hid away a dozen warriors, and when your group and the wizard arrived, we called for them. The warriors slew all of them, freeing Caelan."

"What of the jaggeddi?"

"Nothing, my warriors cannot defeat them all. There is at least three hundred strong."

"Who is this with you?" Dar Caine asked, noticing the figure next to the minotaur.

The figure had an elongated face—much like a jaggeddi—and his slimy, amphibian-like body was a yellowish-green, and his eyes glowed a reddish-yellow. "I am Scioto, a jaggarri."

"Jaggarri?"

"Yes," Scioto replied, with a stern face, "the jaggarri and jaggeddi races are from Tartanzuma. The jaggeddi brought me and other jaggarri here."

"The jaggeddi hunt them for sport," Carlton said, interrupting. "After the eldred and gargoyles left, the jaggeddi released Scioto, planning to hunt him. I saved him, though."

"Why would the jaggeddi do that?"

Scioto smirked at the giant's question. "The jaggeddi have always seen us as the inferior race; their greed will be their poison. Now, with their new master giving them swords and spears, they believe it is their right to rule, and my people suffer.

"Their new master is wicked. He brought the jaggeddi here, to help him rule, but they are tricksters. They have been sowing seeds of discourse, whispering lies between the eldred and spidermites."

Dar Caine nodded in agreement. "The two sides will clide soon. A jaggeddi fooled one of my friends, and he told their lie to an audience of Kaulthar's minions."

Scioto gave a concerned look. "During my time with the jaggeddi, I learned many secrets of the mountains. I learned in the lowest depths, there is a legion of spidermites, who are to sleep until Kaulthar's death. If Kaulthar dies, they will wake from the curse, but there is more. Dentar has hidden black goblins in the lowest depths, too."

"Black goblins," Bono Vox said, laughing. "They are nothing but superstition."

Scioto returned a hard glare. "No, the black goblins are very real and very dangerous. I have seen them. They are vicious half-breeds, descendants of eldred who mated with goblins. They are the champions of all the goblin races."

Bono Vox's smile faded away and the others stood in disbelief. "If this is true, then we must move on," Carlton said.

"No, the others are not here," Dar Caine replied, realizing none of his companions had joined him yet, though they should have.

"We cannot wait much longer, Dar Caine."

"We cannot leave them behind."

"Caelan is waiting for us outside the mountains, with my father and a dozen warriors. We must meet them."

Dar Caine grunted "What of the spidermites? What of the jaggeddi? Will we leave them here, to rule?"

"Caelan and my father will send word to King Dion of Gilon, and they will rid the mountains of all enemies, with the help of Scioto," Carlton replied. "We must go, though."

Dar Caine stared at the purslain lair. He hoped that one of his companions would appear at its mouth, but no one did. Finally, Dar Caine turned away. "Lead on."

CHAPTER X

The Descent

As Troy scaled downward, the light from the dungeon faded away until the shaft held nothing but darkness. He had tied rope to two iron shards and used them to climb down. At first, the iron shards were difficult to place into the wall's rock and soil, but over time, he found it easier.

Not knowing what to expect, Troy left the eldred cloak on. It held a smell that filled the space, and it was heavier than his own. Troy did not know how long he had been descending, and he was unsure how long it would take to reach Leda and the demolished elevator.

Then, fatigue began to settle in. His mouth thirsted for water, as beads of sweat ran down his face. He peered down, hoping to see the elevator wreckage, but none was in sight. Was he mad for attempting the descent?

As he tried to place one of the iron shards into the wall, it broke, and Troy plummeted downward. He grappled and clawed at the wall, as it slid past him, but it was useless. He continued to fall. Then, as it all seemed to overwhelm him, Troy crashed, finding himself atop the destroyed elevator.

For a moment, he gasped. As his senses returned, a stinging pain filled his right hip. He glanced at it and found a jagged piece of wood, embedded deep inside his hip. With shallow breaths, he carefully pulled the wood out, and then, he reached into pack and took out several herbs and his elf cloak. Troy pressed fenugreek and sage against the wound, he tore off a part of his own cloak, and wrapped the strip of fabric tightly around his waist, stopping the bleeding.

With a wince of pain, Troy rose to his feet and looked out of the wreckage. Terror seized him; he was not alone. High walls stretched upwards, and he could not see the ceiling, but carved crevices covered the walls, like a catacomb. Quickly, he realized these crevices were not for the dead, but for a vast number of spidermites, which now stood between him and Leda.

"Who are you?" one of the spidermites asked, noticing the elf.

"An eldred messenger," Troy replied. Before he walked out to the spidermites, the onyx stone—the elevator key—caught his eye, and he stooped down and slipped it into his pack.

"We were placed under a spell by King Kaulthar. We are only to wake if the king is dead."

Troy gave a respectful bow. "Yes, I fear the king has passed. A rebellion broke out between the hivittes and spidermites, and apparently, the hivittes allowed two dwarfs into the kingdom. I have been sent to recapture them."

"Filthy hivittes!"

"I agree. If you will permit me to pass, then I will return the escaped dwarfs to the dungeon."

"Hold," the spidermite said. "Who is your lord?"

Troy stood still, hesitant to answer. "Well, I do not serve any hivittes. My allegiance is to the eldred, Prince Silloweb, but we all serve the master, do we not?"

The spidermite grinned at the answer. "Pass, my friend, through the army of wickedness."

Troy did not need to hear the invitation twice. Swiftly, he made his way through hundreds of spidermites. They each glanced at him and spoke to one another, repeating the tidings he had brought. Troy feared them, though. They stood tall, were well-trained soldiers, and highly disciplined. He was glad when he passed the last of them, and journeyed on, venturing deeper into the mountains.

The tunnel was dim. Though he was tired, Troy did not dare to stop. He knew dark creatures with mischievous deeds lurked in the shadows. He did pull out a pizzelle and snacked on it to help pass his hunger.

Should have invited Caelan, Troy thought, *but he would have stayed with his father. Of course, a dozen minotaur warriors, and I did not bother to ask for any to accompany me. At least the spidermites are far behind; cruelty and malice rule their minds.*

Troy's thoughts stopped, as his ears perked up. Someone or something was moving through the dark and attempting to surround him. He briskly stepped aside, peering into the darkness, and catching sight of one of his hunters.

Dire wolves. There must be a pack down here. While his mind raced with fear, he quietly stepped along the wall, hoping to elude the wolves. Then, a heart-wrenching howl cut the silence, and Troy knew they were closing in.

As he placed his hand on his sword's handle, the wall next to him opened. He looked to find a short-hooded figure. "Come with me."

Without hesitation, Troy followed and entered the hole in the wall. He found himself in an undersized, quaint room—and gladly away from the dire wolves. As his eyes glanced around, he found gold, gems, and magnificent armour all around the room.

"May I ask who you are?" the hooded figure asked. It returned to the stove, where hot tea was boiling.

"Troy," he replied, immediately regretting his foolish slip. "And you?"

"No name, I am a knocker."

"You are a spirit of good?" Troy asked, feeling some relief over his fortune.

"Indeed, Master Eldred. Care for some cakes and tea?"

"No, just water please."

"Quite sure?" the knocker asked. Troy nodded his head, politely. "Very well, here's some water."

"Thank you," he said, taking a sip. "You haven't seen two dwarfs pass by here, have you?"

The knocker mused. "No, can't say I have, but that doesn't mean they haven't. Those dire wolves are nasty creatures."

"Yes, they are. The path I was traveling, does it lead to an exit from the mountains?"

"Oh, yes, but the path is dangerous," the knocker replied. "As you have seen, there are dire wolves, but there are ghouls, banshees, and even a rumored behemoth."

Troy scowled at the news. "Is there a safer path?"

"Of course, but to know the way will cost you a bag of gold," the knocker replied, pausing, "and the brounie, too."

"Brounie?" Troy asked. Unsheathing his short sword, he rose to his feet and swept about, glaring.

The knocker chuckled. "Not a friend of yours, eh?"

"No," Troy said. He turned back to the knocker, short sword still drawn. "You will show me the safer path."

"Tsk-tsk, don't be so loud," the knocker said. It set a cup of tea down and went to the doorway.

Troy followed, thinking the knocker was going to reveal the safer path, but he was mistaken.

"You rang for us?" a deep voice asked.

"Yes, masters," the knocker replied. It took off the hooded cloak, revealing it was not a knocker, but a snottling, servant to goblins.

"What is this?" the voice asked. A giant figure stepped into the room, and Troy saw it was a black goblin.

"The present, master," the snottling said. "He is an eldred, and those dwarfs are his friends."

"An eldred who is friends with dwarfs?" the black goblin asked, laughing. "That is a new low for the eldred."

"Yes, master, but there was a brounie, too."

"There is no brounie," Troy said.

"Lies, master! He lies!" the snottling squealed.

"Where is the brounie?" the black goblin asked.

"It disappeared, master."

The black goblin growled. "How am I to prove this eldred lies, if you have no brounie for me?" The snottling became nervous, and with one swing, the black goblin beheaded his servant. "No one makes me appear as a fool."

"What do we do with it?" a second black goblin asked.

"Bind it. We head home."

Two black goblins stepped up and tied Troy's hands behind his back. Then, the dozen black goblin warriors escorted him away. They moved swiftly and did not speak. Troy wondered if they believed the snottling's story, but he did not dare to ask them.

On and on they ventured. The black goblins prodded him through the darkness, until they came near one of the mountain exits. Troy could not believe his eyes. There were thousands upon thousands of black goblins, all eating, drinking, and playing games of chance to pass the time.

"Shaagaz," the lead black goblin said, approaching a table where some of the black goblins rolled dice. "Shaagaz."

"What?" the largest black goblin roared.

"An eldred."

"Eldred? What of him?"

"He was found by a snottling spy."

Shaagaz rose to his feet and looked to Troy. "Why are you here?"

Troy had already planned his words. "Shaagaz, is it? I apologize for intruding. You see, King Kaulthar is betraying the master."

Angrily, the black goblins that heard the news snorted at it. "Speak," Shaagaz said.

"King Kaulthar possesses electrum, and he recently unearthed gold. He is attempting to create an army that will rival the master, and the hivittes have joined his side, releasing prisoners. The eldred are loyal to the master, and I have been sent to reclaim two dwarfs."

The black goblins grunted at one another, believing Troy's words. "Shaagaz, we must defend the master."

Shaagaz roared back, and then looked to Troy. "We serve the master. Why has he not warned us?"

"This betrayal just occurred. The master knows all, but surely, it would take time for him to warn you. The eldred are trying to keep the master's plan intact."

Shaagaz nodded his head. "I believe you for one reason. My spies have reported legions of spidermites entering our part of the mountains. Kaulthar must have learned the master placed us here, and now, he wishes to sneak up and destroy us all."

Troy bowed his head. "The eldred will fight by your side, Shaagaz. We serve the same master."

"So be it. The dwarfs will be released into your custody," Shaagaz said. He turned to his host, glaring at them. "Kaulthar is rebelling against the master. He is sending spidermites here, to battle us all. Ready yourselves, we will give them a black goblin welcoming!"

Immediately, the black goblin prison guard handed Leda and the second dwarf—Torrok—over to Troy. Leda recognized Troy, but she remained silent, going along with the plan. As the black goblins readied for battle, Troy led the dwarfs away, slipping out of the mountains.

"Troy," she said, hugging his neck. "I was worried that we would be there forever."

Troy removed his eldred cloak, placing it in his pack. "I was not going to leave you behind." He pulled the onyx stone from his pack and handed it to Leda. "You'll probably want this."

Leda smiled, taking it. "Thank you." She glanced back at the mountains, musing for a moment. "I wonder who will win."

Troy shrugged. "It will be a battle between black goblins, the reckless half-breeds, and spidermites, well trained and disciplined."

"Not that battle, Troy," she replied. "Dentar has many minions and followers, and if we continue following Telezzar, then we will battle them all. I was wondering if we can win in the end."

CHAPTER XI

Loyal Demons

In the Land of Ashdod sat a vast mountain known as Mount Abyss, and atop the mountain sat the Tower of Heathens where Dentar and his minions resided. Inside the mountain, though, the joining stalagmites formed Dentar's hidden chambers and throne room. On his throne, he sat, facing his quivering brounie, but his mind was burdened, brewing over his foiled plans.

"Why didn't you stop them?" Dentar's cold voice asked.

"My Master, who would you listen to, a brounie or one of the eldred?" the brounie replied fearfully.

"But it was an elf."

"Indeed, master, but he claimed loyalty to you. My people are known for being tricksters, but I would never trick you, master."

"Of course not, Geshur," Dentar replied, rising from his throne. He slowly strode about, circling the brounie. "That leaves us with a problem, though. How did the battle end?"

Geshur crouched back. "The black goblins were crushed, master, but the spidermites have very few numbers left."

Dentar lashed out, striking Geshur. Then, he closed his eyes, taking counsel with himself. "If I am to start a war, it must start with taking Gilon, and to destroy Gilon, we must have those mountains."

Geshur whimpered and approached Dentar, minding the distance though. "I know my Master looks to himself for advice, but may I make a suggestion, master?" Slowly, Dentar's eyes found the brounie, waiting. "What of your home servants, master?"

Dentar gave a crafty grin. "Demons," he whispered. "Dear Geshur, you may have redeemed yourself, for now."

He sped hastily to a nearby table, where maps and documents lay strewn out, across it. "If the Nine grant me what is rightfully mine, then we will not need the Mountains of the Blue Dragon—or any other mountains."

"No mountains, master?" Geshur asked, confused.

"Yes," Dentar replied, studying the maps. "You see, demons are more powerful than any servant I have. I won't need mountains to hide them, though I will continue to hide the black goblins through them."

"Ah, then war will begin immediately!" Geshur screeched with enthusiasm.

Dentar laughed. "Don't be a fool. The electrum is still loose, and I will not send out my demons until I have reversed the electrum curse." He looked down at the brounie. "Where are the Bdellium Knights? Why have they not brought any electrum?"

Geshur slunk back, jerkily. "M-master, I don't know where they are, or why they have failed you. I know Boremon was with King Kaulthar, but I also know th-that Telezzar and his companions have found electrum."

"What?" Dentar stared at Geshur, an irritable flare lit his eyes. "Call the Bdellium Knights out of hiding. I wish to speak with them, especially Boremon."

"Yes, master," Geshur said. The brounie did not hesitate to transform, camouflaging with its surroundings and disappearing from Dentar's presence.

Wasting little time, Dentar left his throne room and walked about the lonely halls. He reached the stable, where several gremlins brought his beloved creature—the lammasle, a creature with the head of an elk, body of a lion, and wings of an eagle. Dentar mounted his war-beast and departed for Hell.

He descended from the Plain of Prixem. He had not made the journey since he left Hell and settled on Prixem. The first plain he passed was Aquilla, the water plain; the second was Thermidor, the desert plain; and lastly, he passed Delirus, a once prosperous plain turned into an asylum. Then, it came. The Gates of Hell sat looming before him, and as always, Geryon the Dragon lay guarding them.

Geryon grinned. "Dentar the Wretched," the dragon bellowed, eyeing him.

"Geryon the Slime and Waste of Hell, itself," Dentar replied, as the lammasle landed on the basaltic ground of Hell.

Geryon's grin widened, as a chuckle escaped. "At least I still have a spot in Hell, and the devils do not despise me."

"I would enjoy bantering with you, but I have important business with the Nine. Open the gates."

Geryon threw back his head in laughter. "Why? Do you wish to die, or just come close to Death?"

"Open the gates."

"You committed a heinous sin, Lord of Ashdod." Taken aback, Dentar stared at Geryon, but the dragon only laughed. "Oh, yes, word travels fast. I know what the good people of Padavona call you. Nonetheless, you wish to see the Nine, and I will grant that."

The dragon turned. "Open the gates!" he roared, to the wraiths and spelts. He looked back to Dentar and continued: "Enjoy your visit, and try not to get killed, Lord of Ashdod."

Dentar did not reply; he only entered.

Hell, such a barren wasteland. Ash and brimstone filled the air, making it difficult for any creature to breathe, but the worst part was the constant screaming. Screams of never-ending agony. They fueled the laughter of the devils and demons, who abused the damned souls. Damned souls that had shown no mercy in life, thus knew none in death.

"My prince," the voice of an imp said, happily, "how good to see you again."

"Arxy, it is a pleasure," Dentar replied, conjuring a fake smile. "I hardly missed the place, due to the screaming."

"Ah, my prince, you know what is written in the old chronicles. The screams are forever a reminder of our bond with Death."

Dentar rolled his eyes, dreading the oncoming lecture. "Of course, everyone knows." He started to walk toward the Nine's council chamber, hoping the imp would not follow.

Arxy cleared his throat, and began reciting, "DeAth, the eldest son of Balor, left the Void and changed his name to

Death, and Death longed for love. He found himself a lover and they lived contently, until she gave birth to thirteen daughters, the Virgin Valkyrie. The birth of the thirteen daughters also brought sorrow, as Death's love left her mortal being."

Dentar sighed, lethargically. "And Death was never the same. Now, when someone dies from the Seven Plains, the Virgin Valkyrie escort the soul to the House of Death, and there, the souls of the fallen await judgment. After judgment passes, good souls enter the House of Balor and evil souls come here, to Hell.

"As I said, I know the chronicles, Arxy."

"Indeed, my prince," the imp replied, impressed. "Here we are. The council is already in order, and I suggest you look for no friendship, my prince." The imp looked at the door, sadly. "They've changed, all of them, since that rebellion."

A corner smirk stole Dentar's face. "Thank you for the warning, Arxy."

"It is my duty, my prince. Farewell, until our next meeting."

Dentar gave a nod, as he pushed open the door. On the other side sat nine thrones, and upon the nine thrones sat the Nine Rulers of Hell.

At the head sat King Abaddon. He was a colossal compared to the other demons and devils of Hell, and his brute strength and cunning wit made him deadly. Around his neck hung a chain with his father's femur and engraved on the bone was scripture that read: *Devour All Flesh.*

To the right of King Abaddon sat Abigor, Baalzaphon, Leviathan, and Lilith. Abigor, General of Hell, was a terrifying devil who possessed a cruel temper. Baalzaphon, Captain of the

Guards, was Abigor's cousin, and since he could control his temper—unlike Abigor—Baalzaphon was one of the wisest strategists. Leviathan, Grand Admiral of Hell, despised Abigor and between the two devils was a never-ending rift for power and pride. Lastly, there was Lilith, daughter of the king and Princess of Hell. Unlike most of the demons and devils, she was prudent in her thoughts and showed compassion for those she cared for.

To the left of King Abaddon sat Murmur, Meldon, Anneberg, and Beelzebub. Murmur, a Count of Hell, had a melodious voice that sang whenever he spoke, but some on the council disliked the count, mistrusting him. Meldon, Treasurer of Hell, was Murmur's brother, but—unlike his brother—Meldon had bought his way onto the council, by giving the king glorious treasures. Anneberg, Demon of the Mines, was the newly elected member, replacing the late Belial. Lastly, there was Beelzebub, the king's eldest son and a Prince of Hell. Much like his father, Beelzebub was a brute with cunning wit, but he used his talents only to help further his father's agendas.

"Ah," King Abaddon whispered, with a smile. "Greetings, my son, Belial."

At these words, Dentar's heart churned with anger. "I am no longer Belial. He is dead." He stared at his father. "I am Dentar."

"What mockery is this?" Meldon asked. "You changed your name? The one your father gave you. What shame—"

"Continue counting your coins, Meldon," Dentar replied, which brought smirks and chuckles from several of the council members.

Leviathan sneered, though. "Changing your name will not change who you are."

Dentar smiled. "If you ever try it, I'm sure most in here will hope that your claim is not true." His eyes then went to Anneberg. "Congratulations on replacing me, as one of the Nine."

The Demon of the Mines bowed his head. "Thank you, Belial."

"Please, Anneberg, call me Dentar, for Belial is dead."

King Abaddon chuckled. "It is a pity you created a rebellion, my son." This caught the attention of Dentar and everyone else. "You have such eloquent manners, which would have made you a great king."

"Ah, yes, but there's one tiny detail you overlook, dear Father, and that is Beelzebub and Lilith are older." The king opened his mouth to reply, but Dentar continued: "And the only true pity here, Father, is that you did not die during Belial's rebellion."

Most of the council fell into an uproar, while Dentar stood silently, amused by the pandemonium he had created.

"Silence!" King Abaddon roared. The fury in his voice burned, like hot coals tossed into a fire. "Why have you come, Belial?"

Dentar sighed. "Once again, Belial is dead," he said, lazily, but still amused. "As for my being here, is Hell no longer my home?"

"You gave up that right, with your petty rebellion," Abigor replied, enraged by Dentar's attitude.

"Abigor, please reserve your anger for the lesser demons," Dentar said. "Besides, my question was directed at your king."

"You've answered your own question," King Abaddon said, leaning forward from his throne. "You recognize me as everyone's king, but not your own. Thus, Hell is not your home."

"Very well," Dentar replied, with a cunning grin. "If there is no place for me in Hell, then there must be no place for my former servants. Perhaps Hell would like to be rid of them, too?"

Murmur laughed aloud. "You were a Prince of Hell, so everyone was your servant."

"I meant the demons who served directly under me."

"Now, why would a former prince desire his servants?" King Abaddon asked, rhetorically. "Perhaps it's to use them in his quest to control Prixem?"

Most of the devils laughed. "The mighty have fallen, indeed," Baalzaphon said.

"I agree," King Abaddon replied, "I must revoke your privilege of commanding demons."

Dentar shook his head in disbelief, but Lilith's calm voice cut in: "Father, he is still your blood. The rebellion that Belial created has allowed us to find and conquer many traitors, while also striking fear into our servants."

"Giving him servants would be beneficial to all of us," Meldon said, thinking of the money that Hell would save.

Meldon's words did not move King Abaddon, but Lilith's reasoning persuaded him. "Very well," he replied, glaring at his son, "at the beckoning of your sister, I will allow you to take your servants and leave."

"Thank you, Father," Dentar said, giving a respectful nod.

"Never return," King Abaddon snapped. Many of the Nine grunted in approval, while others smiled, but Lilith sat still, upset with her father's words. "Never return, Dentar."

CHAPTER XII

The Yak Folk

Lush, green grasses swayed back and forth as Dar Caine, Carlton, Nova, and Bono Vox made their way north. The Mountains of the Blue Dragon were far off now, somewhere to the southeast, and the Mountains of the Green Dragon were on the horizon.

"We are not far from the mountains," Dar Caine said, looking ahead. "Once we reach them, we will continue north, until we reach the border of Nethinims."

Huffing and puffing, Carlton reached the giant's side. "We need to be careful," he said, exhaling heavily. "The Green Dragon is said to not fancy visitors, so it would be wise to avoid the mountains."

"I understand." Dar Caine ran his hands through his dark hair several times, contemplating. "The mountains provide us cover, though, and will lead us safely to the border."

Carlton snorted. "We won't make it to the border, if we are caught. The dragon is dangerous, and we just escaped one mountain infested with evil. Who knows what servants this dragon has?"

"Myths and fairy tales," Dar Caine replied. His words bolstered his spirit. "We will not enter the mountains, and I will not be frightened away."

The minotaur shook his head, disagreeing, but said nothing more about the matter. Dar Caine took up his flails and continued leading the group on.

There was not much around the mountains, only jagged rocks jutting upward, boulders crushed in half, and slippery piles of pebbles. At first, Dar Caine swung his flails, clearing a path, but soon, the rocks became too many. Nova and Bono Vox struggled to climb through the terrain, even with Carlton's help.

Dar Caine glanced ahead, but he caught sight of something strange. "Carlton," he called back to the minotaur.

Carlton jogged up to the giant's side. "What is it?"

"We're not alone."

"What did you see?"

Dar Caine glanced around. "A figure with fiery eyes and wild hair."

Carlton snorted. "Wildermenn," he whispered, irritably. "I told you this was a bad route."

"Wildermenn?"

"Wild men of the mountains," the minotaur replied. "They are savage beings. They are mutes who communicate by the tapping of stones."

"Maybe they didn't see me." The giant looked around, gesturing for Bono Vox and Nova to hurry along, quietly. Silence hung in the air...until little taps echoed across the terrain.

"Or maybe they were waiting to surround us," Carlton said. He grabbed Bono Vox and Nova and threw them to the ground, hovering over them and protecting them.

Suddenly, the taps ceased, and a scuffle ensued, as several wildermenn appeared with spears. Dar Caine met them head-on, swinging his prized flails, and taking out the closest wildermenn.

"Stay here," Carlton said to Bono Vox and Nova. He leaped over the boulders in front of him and joined Dar Caine.

Bono Vox peered over the boulder. "Not sure about you, but I'm tired of taking orders."

Nova smiled back at him. "Give me a little time, and I will cover you."

Bono Vox unsheathed his sword and went to meet the wildermenn head-on, and Nova scampered from her spot to a boulder, surrounded by jagged rocks. She could see the wildermenn charging toward Bono Vox. She took out a crossbow, which she found in the mountains, and began firing darts.

Now, as the four held their own, an unexpected party arrived to aid the small band of travelers, having seen the skirmish. The wildermenn, seeing their numbers fall, fled back into the Mountains of the Green Dragon, fearing the party of yak folk.

"Hail, warriors, you have my greetings," the yak leader said. He wore a kilt and carried an axe, just like all his followers.

Carlton snorted at the sight of the yak folk. While the yak folk and minotaurs had similar traits and beliefs, the two races were still quite different, with the mintoaurs viewing the yak folk as lesser folk. "Greet yourself, half-breed," Carlton replied, establishing the hatred.

"Carlton, they just saved us," Dar Caine said, highly unimpressed.

"We had it under control."

The yak leader grinned. "Yes, Goat, listen and obey your master. Remember who saved you." Laughter ensued from the other yak folk.

Carlton became angry. "No one is my master! I am Prince Carlton of Ovid, son of King Claudius."

"Ah, a prince," the yak leader replied, broadening his chest. "I am a prince, too. Prince Ishtar."

"I am Dar Caine Condorian, son of Njord McAdoo. These are my friends, Nova of Elhanan, and Bono Vox of Thracia."

Ishtar glanced over them. "Strange band, aren't you? Word has spread that a war broke out in the Mountains of the Blue Dragon. Perhaps you know something?"

Dar Caine grunted. "I will not let you invade our matters."

"I do not mean to intrude or overstep boundaries," Ishtar replied, bowing slightly. "Messengers from all over are telling how a band of misfits overthrew Kaulthar, and I merely observed that you are a band of misfits."

"We are traveling to Lithia," Dar Caine said. "Now if you don't mind—"

"I do," Ishtar interrupted. "You are no war party and will surely be killed by nightfall. Rest with my people for the night."

"We have orders."

"Orders from Telezzar, no less. He told me and my people that we might find some of his misfits, and indeed we have!"

Even after hearing Telezzar's name, Dar Caine remained hesitant. "The prince is right, Dar Caine. It will soon be dark, and the wildermenn will return," Bono Vox said.

Dar Caine looked at Carlton, who was not happy, but the giant felt there was no choice. "We will accept your invitation, good prince."

Ishtar and the yak folk led Dar Caine and the others away from the field, closer to the mountains. The giant did not like this and neither did Carlton. Tales of the Green Dragon filled their minds, and the minotaur brooded over the fact that Dar Caine had not listened to him. Nonetheless, they followed the yak folk into the mountains, to a secluded chamber.

Once everyone had filed in, Ishtar gave a nod. "Sack them." Immediately, the yak folk grabbed Dar Caine, Carlton, Bono Vox, and Nova and placed sacks over their heads.

Dar Caine grunted, struggling with them. "What is this?"

"Be calm. We're blinding your view, so you cannot see where we go from here."

Dar Caine tried to find Ishtar, but it was useless. The yak prince tapped several stones, scattered about, and after a moment of silence, the stone wall divided, revealing a doorway.

Ishtar went through the doorway first, followed by everyone else. Once they were inside, Ishtar closed the door. "Remove the sacks."

"I'm going to skin your fur off," Carlton threatened. He approached the yak, enraged by the treatment.

Dar Caine grabbed the minotaur, though, and held him back. "Don't be foolish."

The yak prince smiled. "Let him go, maybe I can teach him not to underestimate the strength of a yak."

"You're mad. I've seen Carlton in battle, and I would choose him over you and all your folk, here."

The yak folk stared at Dar Caine, and then looked at Ishtar. The yak prince was embarrassed and somewhat heated, and he stepped forward. "Take back what you said," he whispered. "It is tradition for yak folk to fight over such insults."

Dar Caine smirked. "I meant what I said."

"Let us break him, Ishtar," one of the nearest yak folk said.

Carlton stepped up, readying himself. Ishtar was hesitant; he had no wish to fight the wizard's friends. "No, we should admire the giant's loyalty to his friend, for that is how we are with one another," Ishtar said to his people, and they nodded in agreement.

Carlton snorted. "Wise words."

Ishtar smiled back, and then turned away to continue leading the group on. After traveling a little way, the yak folk met young ones, who took their armor so they could clean it. Yak women soon appeared, bringing water. Lastly, the yak elders and yak chief arrived, but the sight of strangers troubled them.

"Why do you plague our people, Ishtar?" Asher, the yak chief, asked, with worry and fear.

"The wizard, Telezzar, requested that we take care of them," Ishtar replied, bowing before the chief.

Asher gave an angry scowl. "There is a minotaur."

Dar Caine stepped forward. "Please, I am Dar Caine, grandson of High King Draul, great chief. My company and I are not enemies, and if you ask us to leave, we will."

"The High King," Asher whispered, musing. "Yes, you, grandson of the High King, are most welcome in my village, as are the elf and man—but the minotaur must go."

Carlton snorted. "I am Carlton son of—"

"Do not speak!" Asher snapped. He harbored a strong bitterness against the minotaurs.

"Father, the wizard asked us to protect the minotaur, too," Ishtar said. "I will unarm him, but he must stay."

Though he was disgruntled with his son, Asher nodded. "Very well, I will oblige on behalf of your word to the wizard."

Ishtar and several of the yak folk led Dar Caine and the group away. The village was small and tight knit. The homes of the yak folks were chisled into the mountain, and instead of stony ground, it was sandy.

At last, they reached a deserted stockroom, which the yak folk had converted into a resting place. As the group settled in, yak women arrived carrying four bowls of broth and two jugs of water, and after the four had eaten their fill, the yak women took the bowls and jugs and left. Ishtar bid them all goodnight and left, as well.

"I'm going to rest," Nova said. She had forced herself to eat the broth, though she was not hungry.

"Who can sleep here?" Carlton asked, looking about.

"It could be worse," Dar Caine replied.

Carlton snorted. "I still think they treated us unfairly. Who sacks guests' heads?"

Bono Vox smiled. "Lighten up, my furry friend. They didn't kick you out at least."

"Furry friend? I've fought goblins bigger than you."

"I didn't mean anything by it."

Carlton looked at Dar Caine. "Why do we trust them?"

"Telezzar sent them, and they gave us food and shelter. We'll leave in the morning."

Carlton rose from his spot. "I can't wait," he replied, shuffling off to a corner to lay down.

Bono Vox and Dar Caine continued sitting by the fire, staring at it. Slowly, it danced while the flickering flames died, and the crackles became silent.

"Legends of old say that fire can tell the future," Bono Vox whispered to the giant.

Dar Caine grunted, not believing such tales. "Those same legends say that fire drives one mad with deception."

"It's true. I've also heard the best way to have a fire reveal the future, is for a bard to play the fire's tune." Bono Vox's eyes stared at the dying flames. "If one could learn the future by fire, they could learn a day or even a lifetime."

Dar Caine looked at the fire. "All happiness would be gone. If one knew the revelations of life, then they would never know how to spend their days. Death would consume their mind, entrenching itself in their thoughts."

The Realm

Silence fell on the room. Finally looking away from the fire, Bono Vox rose from his spot and found a place to rest. The room grew darker. Dar Caine shuffled his furs and fell asleep.

CHAPTER XIII

Leda's Parting

Leda held a piece of fur and examined it closely. "Matted fur and it appears to be minotaur."

"I hope it is," Troy replied, with a yawn.

Leda threw the patch of fur down. "We've traveled far enough. Let's set camp."

"Oh, yes!" Torrok exclaimed. "It is unwise to travel much farther. Darkness is almost here, and the Green Dragon is near. Oh, its wrath is cruel!"

Troy rolled his eyes. "Thank you for your advice," he replied, before adding in a whisper, "you crazed fool."

"Troy," Leda said, with an appalled smile. "You cannot say things like that. He might hear you."

"What's he going to do? Complain as he has been this whole journey?"

"We don't know what he has been through," Leda replied. "I'll start a fire and you ration out what food we have."

Troy looked over to Torrok and smirked, as the dwarf darted his head about and twitched at every strange sound. "Can we eat his portion to feed our patience?"

"The food, Troy."

The Realm

Amongst the dwarfs and himself, Troy divided some salted meat from Leda's pack and pizzelles from his own. When the fire was ready, and everything set, the three sat down and ate in silence, enjoying their small meal.

Torrok wolfed his food down, and when he had nothing left, he scampered off to an area of solitude, wrapping himself in his cloak, and falling asleep. Troy and Leda sat next to the fire, watching the embers flicker and fade out.

"I cannot lie," Troy said, rummaging in his pack for his pipe. "After our stay in those damp, dreary mountains, I have longed to see Lithia."

"I have seen the Woods of Eliel and of Elhanan, but I've never ventured north of Ashturim," Leda replied, cleaning her pipe. "I've not fancied either of the woodlands."

Troy pulled out his ivory pipe, carved by the short elves of Bucklin, who were renowned for making exquisite pipes. "Nethinims is much different, and Lithia is the crowning jewel."

Leda crushed up some tobacco from Thracia and put it in her pipe. "Are you famous in Lithia?"

Troy—who had just inhaled a lungful of his own herbal smoking blend—coughed vigorously and looked taken aback. "Well, not really. I'm one of the king's grandsons, but my brothers—especially Achren—are better known."

"Oh," Leda replied, somewhat awkwardly. "I did not mean to embarrass you."

"No, it's fine," Troy said with a deep sigh. "I wanted to train animals, but my father saw it as weak. His dying wish was for all his sons to become great, and greatness to my father is achieved by wielding a blade."

"So, you became a paladin?"

"No choice. All in my lineage take the oath and become a paladin."

"Do you like being a paladin?"

Troy mused for a moment. "Sometimes I feel that I have to prove myself. I feel that I'll never escape this choice, or my father's lingering shadow."

"You're a noble paladin, Troy," Leda replied, attempting to console him. "My skills as a ranger are undeniable, but there are times that I feel it's not my calling."

Troy smirked. "At least you're good at what you do. Have you seen me in battle?"

"You are on the reckless side," Leda said, laughing.

"I prefer daring."

Leda grinned back. "Do you have any lovers back home?"

"Why, are you interested in daring, reckless elves?"

Leda blushed. "No, but I do like intelligence, which you lack."

"Ah, then Torrok must be high on your list as a suitor."

"Troy, that's not funny."

Troy laughed, as he began cleaning his own pipe out and Leda did too. "I have a lover back home, but I am not interested in her. She is from Elhanan. Through an arranged marriage, I am to marry her to keep an alliance between Elhanan and Nethinims."

"Why?"

"Tradition," Troy replied, as he wrapped himself in his cloak. "If there is no marriage, then Elhanan is not bound to aid my people. The alliance has become more important now, with the threat of Dentar."

"Why wouldn't Elhanan help you?"

"Elhanan is traditional. Nethinims is too, but not as committed. Elhanan frowns on intermarriage between elves and other races, and they believe they are better than those of us in Nethinims and Eliel—especially Eliel."

"Oh," Leda replied, unsure of what to say. "We should rest now, Troy, it's getting late."

"I agree. Goodnight, Leda."

"Goodnight, Troy."

The black night had a short claim on the sky, or so it seemed that way. As daylight began to break, the shadows of night scattered away.

Torrok was the first to wake, and his mumblings soon woke the others. Troy was unhappy about this, but he kept his complaints quiet. They each ate two pizzelles for breakfast, and then resumed their journey. It was a short way, until they stumbled onto a disturbing sight.

"What could have done this?" Troy asked. His hand went to the handle of his short sword, as his eyes swept about the area. He was unsteady at the sight of the gathered dead bodies.

Leda bent down, studying. "They appear to be wildermenn of the mountain."

"The Green Dragon did this! It will eat us!" Torrok exclaimed, frightened.

Troy grabbed Torrok and covered his mouth. "Stop! You will get us all killed with your yelping."

Leda stood and looked at Troy. "No dragon did this. Some of these bodies have been bruised by flails."

"Dar Caine. He must not be far ahead."

"Quick, we must catch them."

Using her skills through the terrain, Leda led Troy and Torrok after Dar Caine and his company. Anticipation overcame Leda and Troy, as they felt they were narrowing the gap. Then, something unexpected happened.

"Halt!" a thunderous voice called out.

"It's the Green Dragon!" Torrok cried, jumping to the ground.

Troy and Leda looked at the giant minotaur-like creatures. "Who are you?" she asked.

"Leda? Troy?" a familiar voice asked.

"Dar Caine!" they both exclaimed, simultaneously.

The giant appeared, and within moments, the three were hugging and clasping hands.

"I wanted to wait and find you, but Carlton urged me to lead Bono Vox and Nova away."

"We managed to escape, thanks to Troy," Leda replied. "He fooled spidermites and black goblins by saying he was one of the eldred, working for Dentar. Then, the spidermites and black goblins battled each other, believing they were enemies."

"True, but we only found you because of Leda's tracking skills," Troy chimed in.

Dar Caine smiled at them. "I'm just pleased you're both well. Come, we will eat and rest with the yak folk, and then at midday, we will leave and continue for Lithia."

Ishtar escorted the group back to the yak village, where Carlton, Bono Vox, and Nova greeted them. They all sat down and ate one last meal before departing.

"The dwarf is mad," Troy whispered to Dar Caine. "We should release him."

Dar Caine grunted. "For once, we agree on something."

"I will take him," Leda said.

"Where are you going, that we are not?" Dar Caine asked.

"Odie's brother was brought to these mountains. I want to find him and reunite him with Odie."

"You're just as mad as Torrok," Troy said.

Dar Caine shook his head, not liking her intention either. "Leda, you don't know if Odie's brother is alive."

"True, but I will never know unless I go and search."

"We need to go to Lithia," Troy pressed. He did not want Leda wandering the mountains alone with Torrok.

"I must do this. What if Odie's brother has some electrum?"

Troy looked at Dar Caine, who mused silently over the dwarf's words. "She is right. Odie's brother needs to be found."

"Then, I will go with her."

"No, Troy," Leda said. "Not this time. You need to go to Lithia with Dar Caine and the others."

"Troy is right, though. You should not go alone."

"I am taking Torrok."

"You need me," Troy said, upset.

"Troy, you are needed in Lithia," Dar Caine replied. He looked to Leda and continued: "I will speak with Ishtar and see if he will accompany you. It will ease my mind if he does."

"All right," Leda said.

With a soft, *ahem*, the three turned their attention to Bono Vox. "Not meaning to interrupt, but if you are releasing people from this group, then I would like to leave for Thracia."

"If that is your wish, then so be it," Dar Caine replied, not truly caring if the bard stayed or departed.

"Thank you, my friend. I will leave when you depart for Lithia."

"Then, I hope you're ready," Dar Caine replied, rising to his feet. "We're leaving now."

"Now?" Troy questioned. "We've not told Leda to come with us."

Dar Caine shook his head, with a smirk. "She's not, Troy. Her story's going to be different from ours, but in the end, our journey's will lead us there, to Lithia."

CHAPTER XIV

Mountains of the Green Dragon

Filled with darkness, the mountain reeked, and bones of dead creatures lay covering the ground. Leda and Ishtar pushed on, holding their breaths.

Torrok blamed the Green Dragon for it, and under his breath, he cursed Leda for bringing him along. "My lucky coin will save me," he whispered, as his fingers rubbed a counterfeit gold coin.

"Quiet, you," Ishtar said. He too was nervous about the mountains' atmosphere.

"Curse the furry one."

"You must be quiet, Torrok," Leda said, covering his mouth. The three stood in silence, listening for any movements through the darkness, but nothing happened.

Ishtar grabbed Torrok by the shoulder, slinging the dwarf against the wall. "If you get us caught by some dark creature, I will cut out your tongue."

"He cannot help it, he is not in his right mind, so you must be kind to him."

The yak released Torrok and remembered what Troy said. "This dwarf is mad and will get us in trouble.

"The Green Dragon will eat you," Torrok replied.

Ishtar snorted, quite annoyed. "Stop speaking of dragons."

"The truth is painful to hear," Torrok whispered, with a demented, jovial smile.

Ishtar threw down his pack and readied his axe. Whether Leda approved or not, Torrok had to be silenced for good.

"Quiet," Leda said. She motioned Ishtar to be still, as she placed her ear against one of the walls. "There's movement coming our way."

All at once, a bloody, ravenous scream cried out from the dark depths, and then a second and then a third, until there were many. "Goblins," Ishtar whispered.

"Run!" Torrok exclaimed, as he scampered off into the unknown darkness.

"No, Torrok," Leda said, but it was too late. "We must go after him, Ishtar."

The sound of the goblins grew nearer. "No, he's on his own. We must hide."

"Where?"

"I don't know," Ishtar replied, looking around. He sighed, knowing there was no way out. "Run, Leda."

"Where?"

"After Torrok. Go!"

She realized Ishtar had no intention of following. Gradually, she stepped away from the yak, and then, as if in a footrace, she sprinted into the darkness. Bones cracked under her feet; wild, hostile cries rang out all around her; and her breaths became heavy and her sweat thick as blood.

"Torrok," she panted. Tears streamed down her face, as she wandered aimlessly. "Torrok!"

Panicked, she tripped and fell to the ground. She stumbled to get up, but her strength failed her. Her mind told her to rise and run, but she lay motionless on the stone floor.

"Torrok," she whispered, again. Her tears filled with frustration and fear, as no answer came. "Curse you."

"No," came a demonic voice, "curse you."

Through the darkness, Torrok's outline emerged, but he was not how Leda remembered him. He no longer seemed naïve or dim witted; his appearance was threatening by how he both spoke and approached her.

"Torrok?" Leda asked, somewhat frightened.

"You spoiled the master's plan," Torrok said. "The Blue Mountains were almost his. He began to suspect King Kaulthar's allegiance, so he sent me as a spy."

"A spy," Leda replied, finding her strength, and rising to her feet.

"Yes, and killing you will bring me much joy," Torrok said, as he pulled two rusted short swords from his back.

Leda huffed. "I could have butter knives and still beat you."

Torrok chuckled. "Are you trying to buy time so the yak princeling can save you? Shame, I always thought you could do everything alone."

Leda gritted her teeth, but before she could speak, another voice answered: "But we all need a little help." In terror, Torrok whipped his head around, but saw no one. "I'd send you back to your master's hoard, but I'm bored."

Torrok wasted little time. He threw down his short swords and started running away, but emerging from the shadows, the unknown figure snapped her fingers. Piercing upward from the stony ground, vines and roots grasped and wrapped around Torrok, pulling the dwarf into the earth.

Gazing horror, Leda looked at the figure. "Who are you?"

"Do not fear me, Leda. I have been watching you and your group, ever since my brother told me of you and them," a beautiful woman replied, stepping toward the dwarf. She wore a white gown with golden fringes, her hair was lush and gold, and her smile was kind. "I am Gwendolyn."

Leda was unsure of what to say. "H-how do you know my name?"

"There are many things I know and many things I do not, but you have questions that need answers. Please, come with me."

Without hesitance, Leda followed the woman away from Torrok's grave. Neither spoke to the other, but Leda's mind raced with questions.

Why am I trusting her? I do not know her, and I do not know where she is taking me. However, her thoughts were conflicted: *She did destroy Torrok, and at least she knows her way through the darkness. Oh, if only I had brought Troy.*

"Esther, open the door," Gwendolyn said, breaking Leda's thoughts.

The wall before them started to part, and it reminded Leda of how she met Odie. Once the doorway was open, a quaint creature appeared and climbed onto Gwendolyn's shoulder.

"This is Esther, a quokka," Gwendolyn said, as she pet the creature, which looked like a cat-sized kangaroo.

"I did as you instructed, Gwendolyn. I led the yak prince to the leprechaun village," Esther said, with a soft squeal.

"Ishtar is alive?" Leda asked, happily. "And you speak?"

"Yes, the prince is alive, and don't all familiars speak?"

Leda smiled at Gwendolyn. "You're a witch."

"Yes, though I take up the title wizard as my brothers, one of whom is Telezzar."

Overcome with relief, Leda followed Gwendolyn and Esther into their home. The home consisted of one room, arranged perfectly and nicely. In the middle of the space sat a round table, overflowing with a banquet of food. Paintings of a different land hung on the walls, and numerous shelves displayed old books and weapons.

"Leda, please eat," Gwendolyn said, as she prepared a plate of cut and diced fruits.

"Thank you." She had not eaten well since leaving the yak folk village, and the stress and worry had famished her. "Your home is very nice, Gwendolyn."

"Thank you," Gwendolyn replied. "After you eat and rest, I will take you to Ishtar."

"Where is the leprechaun village?"

Gwendolyn mused for a moment. "Right now, in the lower levels. The leprechauns' magic changes the village's location every sunrise and sunset, so only those who know where the doorway is located can find it."

"I've never heard of any village doing that."

"I believe it is the only one to do so."

"They have to, though. I mean, think of all the enemies and creatures lurking in these mountains. I've heard the Green Dragon is violent and ruthless," Leda said, devouring her plate of fruit.

"Who said so?" Gwendolyn asked, curiously.

"Torrok—the dwarf you killed. He feared the Green Dragon, as well as many of my companions." Leda began making a second plate, but then she realized something. "Gwendolyn, if the Green Dragon is your friend, I apologize for offending you."

Gwendolyn gave a soft smile. "Well, yes, she is a dear friend," the wizard replied. "You see, I am the Green Dragon."

The dwarf dropped her plate, and her body went numb. "Y-you are the Green Dragon?" she asked. "How? You don't look like a dragon."

Esther giggled. "I am the Green Dragon," Gwendolyn replied, "and I do not appear as a dragon because I do not wish to, right now."

Leda was lost for words. She looked at her plate and then at Gwendolyn. "Explain."

"All ten wizards are shapeshifters, and each of us represents one of the ten dragons, including Telezzar the Blue."

Leda took a sip of her hot tea, still surprised. "Why did Telezzar not tell us?"

"Well, we do not reveal our shape-shifting ability, so not many people know. We have grown more cautious, too, since the arrival of Dentar."

"Telezzar spoke of Dentar. Who is he?"

The Realm

"To explain Dentar—and my brothers and I—I must go back to long ago, when all lived in the Void.

"I was born in the Void, before being sent here, to Prixem. In the beginning of the Void, there were many different clans and peoples wandering about. The two most important were Dunbar and his wife, Rhea, and the Thebian Triad. The triad consisted of three brothers: Birog, the eldest, and the twins, Elcmar and Del Baeth.

"Now, Dunbar created races of giants to serve him, and one day Birog went to the House of Dunbar and took a maid to be his wife. Dunbar did nothing for many couplets, until he learned that the maid had given Birog two sons, Ogma and Balor.

"Dunbar—needing and loving the taste of battle—made war on Birog's home of Formorian. During the battle, Ogma was slain. Birog was heartbroken and he ordered Balor to kill Dunbar, but instead, Balor crept into his father's chamber and killed him, so that the war would discontinue. Balor became King of Formorian, and he took up his father's place as part of the triad.

"Now, many couplets passed, and all was quiet until two strangers appeared. These strangers proposed a competition, which would determine the ruler of the Void. The test was to see which of the four greatest leaders—Mankato, Segomo, Balor, and Dunbar—could create the perfect race.

"Mankato created the eagle carnai, and Segomo the huns—both races have died out. Dunbar created the first demons, and Balor created man. The strangers named Balor, Lord of the Void, because he made man dependant on one another.

"Dunbar was furious. He made war against Balor, but it was the demon king's undoing. His twisted ways caught up to him, and he cast down to a dark and evil place, now called Hell.

"Balor—with Mankato and Segomo—created the Seven Plains and placed their races on them. They made other races, but the elves, Children of Balor, were given charge to rule over all the creations and keep them safe.

"Alas, the elves failed. Dunbar lay quiet for some time, but when loosened for three days, he attempted to defile the Elf Queen Eden of Elhanan, and he killed the Elf King Kota of Nethinims. Balor was angry, and he had Dunbar bound and brought to him in Formorian, where Balor ended Dunbar's treachery forever.

"Seeing that the Seven Plains needed new leaders, Balor—my father—entrusted the powers to me and my nine brothers. My father sent us here, to keep the plains safe, but times have changed. Dunbar's son, King Abaddon, had three children, and the youngest has come to take and rule the Seven Plains for himself."

Leda sat stunned. Telezzar and Gwendolyn were the children of Balor, and Dentar was the grandson of Dunbar. "Why don't you attack Dentar?" she finally asked.

"No," Gwendolyn replied, somewhat upset. "Dentar—or Belial, if you wish to know his demon name—is much more powerful. There is no proof, but Telezzar believes that Dentar has killed our brother, Lorcan the Black."

"Why? How?"

"Lorcan was one of us, one of the ten. You could argue, he was the most powerful of us, too," Gwendolyn said. "Telezzar has no proof, but he believes that a brounie servant of Dentar's was Lorcan's familiar."

Leda's eyes widened. "What's going to happen to our plain?"

Gwendolyn shook her head. "Telezzar wants to reforge the seven electrum swords, but I do not believe that will be enough. I urged him to go a different path."

"There's another way?"

"Yes, there is three ways, possibly, but he wishes to pursue the electrum swords, though he did heed my advice, regarding an heir of King Kota."

"What's special about his lineage?" Leda asked, listening intently to the wizard's every word.

"As King Kota died at the hands of Dunbar, he cursed his lineage to forever be at war with Dunbar's seed. Every heir in King Kota's line has been a paladin."

"Wait! Telezzar heeded some of your advice, so he went after one of King Kota's heirs. Is Troy a descendant of King Kota?"

"Indeed, though I believe Telezzar recruited Achren Red-Dragon, who is an honorable and renowned blades man," Gwendolyn replied, sipping some hot tea. "Nonetheless, their grandfather, King Azekiel, is one of the greatest paladins, so I am sure Troy is a worthy paladin too."

Leda remembered her conversation with Troy, and now pitied him even more. "I still do not understand. How is King Kota's lineage helpful, besides being dedicated to the paladin-code?"

"They can wield the Sword of Kota. The sword was a gift to the king from Queen Eden, but the sword has been lost."

Leda mused, silently. "I believe both yours and Telezzar's plans are wise."

"Probably," Gwendolyn replied, with a yawn. "Telezzar is the one creating an army, though, not me. He can do as he wishes; my role will come to be when the time is right."

"Gwendolyn, I have one last question."

"Ask, dear Leda."

"Well, I entered these mountains searching for a gneiss named Arthur. I've been told you have him."

"I do," Gwendolyn said, with a smile. "Telezzar told me you might come inquiring about the gneiss, and you may have him, only if you reunite him with his brother."

"That is my intent!"

"Then, Leda, I will place Arthur in your care, but first, let us rest."

Leda rose and went to a small bed. She wrapped herself in a bulky, soft quilt, and as she drifted to sleep, Gwendolyn played a reed pipe and hummed a yak folk lullaby.

CHAPTER XV

Council in Lithia

"I know what Gwendolyn believes—I read her letter—but now is not the time," Telezzar said, perusing the shelves upon shelves of history books.

"Should we not look into everything, though?" King Azekiel of Lithia asked. His aged-hazel eyes held doubt, and he brushed back his silvery-grey hair—often a tell for when he was worried.

"Azekiel, you of all my friends should understand. I wanted to use the sword of King Kota, but I couldn't find it. Our best hope is to hunt the electrum."

King Azekiel sighed. "My scouts are reporting that demons have joined Dentar's army. Now, it is true the electrum swords can turn demons to stone, but what of Dentar's other minions?"

"My dear Azekiel, do you no longer trust me?" Telezzar asked, laughing aloud. "Many armies here, on Padavona, will not sit idle and let Dentar destroy their homelands. There is a plan set in motion."

"What of the chess set?"

Telezzar stood quietly, suppressing his initial words to the king. "I would not worry about the chess set. There is no proof that Dentar has it."

"We should not wait to find out. It would surely be our downfall."

The wizard nodded his head, agreeing. "You should not worry about such things, I assure you."

"I hope you're right," King Azekiel replied, still not comforted by the wizard's words. Then, a knock came at the door, and the king rose from his seat.

Telezzar's eyes roved away and out the library window. The couplet of Tau had finally settled on Padavona, meaning autumn had arrived. Across Lithia's beauty, leaves of red and yellow began to flicker in the wind and fall one by one, and the flowers of many colors started to fade. He dreaded the coming couplets. He was even unsure if his plan would work, but he knew Dentar's strength was growing, and shadow spreading.

"If you are done daydreaming, then you should read this note from Gwendolyn," King Azekiel said, laying the note on his desk.

"Ah, but it is good to be a dreamer," Telezzar replied, slipping over to the desk, and reading the note. "Very good, Leda has left Gwendolyn's home with the gneiss, Arthur."

"She will not be present for your council?"

Telezzar shook his head, as he folded the note and tucked it into his satchel. "There is no need. She is on her own journey, and soon, we all shall be."

"Where will you send Troy?" King Azekiel asked, interested in Troy's fate, in Telezzar's grand scheme.

The wizard chuckled, though. "I thought we agreed you would not meddle in my business with him."

"Come now, Telezzar, he is my grandson. I only wish to know he will be safe."

"Safe? Is that why you had him become a paladin? To keep him safe?"

King Azekiel gave an offended look. "It was his father's dying wish. Besides, all Red-Dragons become a paladin or serve the order."

"You know his father never cared about anything but battle."

"It brought honor, and that is all he wanted for his sons. He loved them, especially Troy."

"No, of them all, he loved Troy the least." The king had no answer, so the wizard continued with his cunningness. "You are continuing his father's madness by forcing Troy into this arranged marriage."

King Azekiel smirked. "This is what you've been building your argument up to. You know that the marriage will create a covenant between Elhanan and Nethinims."

"And that is more important than Troy's free will?" Telezzar asked. "He has eyes for another."

King Azekiel sighed. "I know. He has grown quite fond of Nova."

"Indeed," Telezzar replied. "Don't force Troy into an unbreakable bond."

The king pondered silently. "I will consider your counsel. It has been hard. Ever since I heard Dentar killed Lorcan, I've been concerned about keeping Lithia safe."

"Azekiel, you are a wise friend. Elhanan and Nethinims will fight side-by-side against Dentar, regardless of some arranged marriage. Let Troy dictate his own path."

King Azekiel poured two glasses of red wine, handing one to the wizard. "I will consider it, Telezzar, but I will not answer you now, binding my words one way or another," he replied, raising his glass. "Now, let us drink to your plan, and then be on our way to the council."

***

Sculptured bushes towered overhead, birds chirped in unison with pleasure, and colorful leaves flew about. In one of Lithia's gorgeous gardens, Nova lay, letting the sun beat down on her face, while Troy talked to her and weaved flowers into a crown.

"Here," he said, "a beautiful crown for someone just as fair, if not fairer."

Blushing, Nova accepted the gift. She marveled at it, enjoying the colors of red, yellow, and white. "Troy, these past few couplets have been enjoyable with you."

"I've enjoyed being with you, too," he replied, laying down next to her.

She smiled. "Tell me again how you outwitted the eldred."

"You don't want to hear that story again. I've told you before, and it never changes."

"Please, Troy."

"All right," he replied. "I've told you about the jagg, and how he warned me that Kaulthar had electrum. Well, I leaked this belief to the eldred, but one of them did not believe me, so we went to Kaulthar. He tried to intimidate and persuade me to be quiet, but I did not fear him. I boasted to his people what the jagg told me, and Prince Silloweb believed me. Because of my distractions, the others and I were able to free you and escape."

Nova stared at him with admiration. "But I've heard from other friends that you were afraid—maybe even terrified—of Kaulthar," she said, with a giggle.

"True, I was scared." Troy conceded with laughter.

"You should ask Dar Caine for his version. It's much more amusing."

Before Troy could reply, a voice called out from within the garden: "Troy!"

He lay stunned for a moment. "We must go; she's here," he whispered, slowly rising to his feet.

"Oh, not again, Troy. This always happens. Can't we confront her about all this?"

"Confront her? No, she's mad in the head and terribly jealous."

"I can defend myself," Nova retorted, feeling Troy's words were a slight at her.

"I didn't say you couldn't. I would rather avoid the ordeal, though."

Nova smirked. "She's expecting to marry you. Where are you going?"

"The kitchen, come on," Troy replied.

The two slipped away from the garden and to the kitchen. In the middle of the enormous room, a table sat with various foods and wines. Pans of bread were stacked next to the oven, meats and cheeses sat in buckets of ice, and the cook stood over tomatoes, dicing away.

"Ah, Troy," the cook said, cheerfully. "It is good to see you."

"And you, Easton," Troy replied, "I need a place to hide."

After entering the kitchen, Nova closed the door and Easton gave a giddy smile. However, another voice answered Troy, "Give me a reason to help you, little brother."

Troy turned around, finding Gilead, who looked like an older version of Troy. "Gilead, not now. I want to be alone with Nova, but you-know-who keeps interrupting."

"Oh, the trouble of love," Gilead mused. "Get into the cupboard, but don't forget that Telezzar's council begins soon."

"This is why you're my favorite brother, Gilead," Troy replied, grabbing a handful of cubed cheeses, and slipping into the cupboard.

The cupboard was barren, save the presence of the two elves. While Troy lit a lantern, Nova sat down and waited for him.

"Is there someone you find interesting, if you are not interested in her?" Nova asked. It was no secret; she hoped to hear her name as the answer.

"Possibly, but I'd rather not discuss it."

"Oh," she replied, her feelings crashing like a ship against rocks in a harbor. There had to be some explanation. "Do you fear commitment?"

Troy smirked and looked at her. "Yes, the elf who joined the Paladin Order fears commitment."

"I was only asking."

"No, you wanted to know my thoughts, and once I gave an answer you didn't like, you questioned my character."

Infuriated, Nova jumped to her feet and stared at him, enraged. "How dare you! I asked a simple question. I did not question your character."

"You wouldn't understand," Troy replied, disgruntled. The two stood, staring at one another; her blue eyes as a boiling sea, and his hazel as fire-sparked wood. The tension grew tighter, until he cut it: "We should not have come here. The council will be starting soon, so we should be on our way."

The pair stormed out of the cupboard, as Easton and Gilead stared oddly and exchanged shrugs. Troy and Nova marched from the kitchen and to the council chamber, neither speaking to the other during the lengthy walk.

Everyone was already assembling for the council, save Leda. After entering the vast, circular chamber, each member sat on a throne hewn from marble stone. Linens of purple and blue hung on the walls, and in the center of the chamber, golden stones lay arranged in the cigil of the Paladin Order.

As everyone settled in, Telezzar stood before them. "Greetings and salutations, my companions, and friends. Today we meet to discuss our means of stopping Dentar." Everyone listened intently. "Dentar has claimed Ashdod, and it is believed his army is massive, filled with goblins, dire wolves, and even demons. However, I believe there is hope."

"Hope is good, Telezzar, but even the paladins have struggled keeping him at bay. As you have confided in me, there is belief he has slain Lorcan," King Azekiel said. He did not wish for his hope to lie in the hands of Telezzar's inexperienced misfits.

"My dear Azekiel, it is rude to interrupt," Telezzar replied. "Besides, everyone has seen battle, even if it has been mere glimpses in the mountains."

Dar Caine sat high on his throne. "King Azekiel, I will remind you, not all of us are young and with little battle experience."

"Battling kinsmen over land does not constitute as giving one much battle experience," King Azekiel replied.

"We are not here to quarrel amongst each other," Telezzar said, intervening.

Dar Caine grunted, and King Azekiel answered, "My apologies, Telezzar, please continue."

The wizard reached into his satchel, revealing three pieces of electrum. "Leda, Lars, and Troy received this electrum from the gneiss, Odie. The electrum is what we must use to defeat the Demon Prince.

"Long ago, Balor, Lord of the Void, had seven guardians known as the terebinth. Each of them possessed an electrum sword, but for reasons unknown, the blades were shattered and scattered across the plains. It is time to reforge them."

"Telezzar, you cannot possibly find every electrum piece. There will not be enough time either," King Azekiel said.

"The electrum could be anywhere, but I believe I know where most of the pieces are," Telezzar replied, pulling a faded map from his satchel. "I have devised a plan, too, to retrieve the electrum, but it will involve us traveling in smaller groups."

"Is it wise to use a divide-and-conquer method?" Dar Caine asked.

"There is no need to worry, my friend. We are not the only ones fighting Dentar; there are many others—living on other plains—who realize his hunger for power will spread. We are not alone."

Lars jerked nervously. "Still, you want us to separate?"

"I'm quite certain it will work, and, Lars, you will be coming with me," Telezzar replied, calming the leprechaun's nerves.

"How will you separate them, Telezzar?" King Azekiel asked.

"Dar Caine and Carlton will accompany Scioto back to Tartanzuma and retrieve the electrum. Lars and I will stay here, on Prixem, and Troy and Nova will go to Hell for the electrum, there." Immediately, the wizard regretted revealing the plan too quickly, as everyone shouted in an uproar.

"Hell!" Troy exclaimed. "You want us to waltz into Hell to find the electrum? This is mad!"

"Yes, and must I go with Troy?" Nova asked, heatedly.

Troy kept quiet, embarrassed by Nova's reply to the wizard's plan. Telezzar eyed them both, wondering what had happened. "Hell may be evil, but there are some who will help, though they don't know it yet."

"Telezzar, you cannot guarantee this. It is dangerous," King Azekiel said. He did not agree with the plan, especially since it sent a paladin into the depths of Hell.

"I trust Troy and Nova, and I will hear no more about this," the Blue Wizard replied. "Now, we have other business to discuss."

"My brother?" Dar Caine asked, looking at the wizard.

Telezzar gave a nod. "Yes. Dar Caine's youngest brother, Ehud, has traveled here with grave news. Apparently, other malobathron chieftains are plotting to overthrow Njord McAdoo as the head chieftain. Dar Caine, you are the rightful heir, so you must return and revive order."

"What of our hunt on Tartanzuma?" Carlton asked.

"You should return home, too, Carlton. I fear I have heard nothing out of Ovid in some time," Telezzar replied. "Besides, Caelan will not return here, from the mountains, for another three couplets. When he does you and Dar Caine must meet Scioto at the border of Res Publica and Dagon. From there, you will carry out the hunt."

"Three couplets is not much time," Dar Caine replied to the wizard.

"I understand, but that is when Scioto will arrive. I believe it will be enough time for you to return home, set order, and meet at the border." Telezzar was pleased; everything seemed to be falling into place.

"When should I leave?" Troy asked, finding the confidence to speak again.

Telezzar mused for a moment. "You have the most dangerous task, but there is nothing hindering an early start. After dining on a homemade meal and a fresh night of sleep, you should leave tomorrow, at sunrise."

Before Troy or Nova could reply, Lars asked, "And us, Telezzar?"

"Three couplets," the wizard replied. "Ehud has offered to watch after Odie, but I must accompany them, since we are moving Odie to the Castle of Dalian, in Gilon. Afterwards, I have business to attend to."

"Will I be coming with you?" The leprechaun had been longing to return home, to see it one last time, and the wizard could sense this.

"No, you should return home. When the time is right, I will fetch you." Telezzar smiled and looked at each of them. "If there are no further questions, I think it is best we prepare for our journeys. Time is of the essence, and Dentar will not rest."

Part II

Hunt for Electrum

Table of Contents

CHAPTER XVI

The Way to Hell

Riding on horseback, Troy and Nova neared the Port of Winged Wooly-Rhinos. They needed to buy a winged wooly-rhino to carry them from Prixem to Thermidor, and Troy wanted to fly a different creature from Thermidor to Hell, since winged wooly-rhinos were bulky and slow.

The port was located near the border of Nethinims and Gilon. Many travelers at the port were journeying to other plains, too, while some needed transportation to far parts of Prixem. Sellers were abundant, some with winged wooly-rhinos, but many with goods such as spices and silks.

Troy and Nova walked about the stalls. There were many winged wooly-rhinos, all covered in ruddy, flaxlike hair, though there was an occasional black-coated one. Troy studied their wings, inspecting for the best.

One of the stall owners sat, old and lethargic. He sold no winged wooly-rhinos, though he owned many. The reason could have been his grimacing face, his surly outlook, or his churlish attitude. Indeed, those reasons may have played a part, but it was his race—goblin—that kept his business low.

The Realm

Nova noticed him first, but she looked away. Troy pitied him. "We would like to buy one," he said, approaching the goblin, and speaking in the goblin tongue.

The goblin looked up and smiled. "An elf speaking Goblin? That is funny," he replied, laughing until it broke out into a harsh cough. "Where are you going?"

"That is private."

"If you don't trust me, then I can't trust you."

Troy looked away. There were many other sellers, but he turned back to the goblin. "Thermidor."

The goblin grinned. "Five gold."

"Three gold."

The old goblin grunted. "Fair enough."

After finishing the exchange, Troy and Nova picked out their winged wooly-rhino and were on their way. As they left, Troy glanced back at the old goblin, who sat back down and returned his face into a hideous sight. With that, the two mounted the winged wooly-rhino and left.

Time seemed lost. The winged wooly-rhino flew downward, leaving Prixem far behind. The stars surrounded the two elves, flickering like torches in the night. They could see the golden sun and ashen moon, but the darkness stretched out like a vast sea of black.

Aquilla lay in their path first. The blue, majestic waters tossed back and forth like wind through a lion's mane, and most of the plain's creatures and races lived underneath, in the waters.

The Realm

Nova gasped, worried. She wrapped her arms around Troy's waist, hoping not to fall. He glanced at her, noticing her beauty against the deep waters below. *We should have never argued*, he thought. He stole a second glance, and this time at her sapphire eyes. *They sit as two pools, where I wish to drown for eternity. Oh, I am foolish for angering her. She is all I ever wish to know.* His thoughts ceased for a moment, but one creeped up. *I cannot, though; I am due to another, for the greater good.*

Meanwhile, Nova's own thoughts conflicted. *It has only been a couple couplets, which is not enough time to truly know someone.* She mused for a moment. *It does not matter. He made his view clear in the cupboard.*

The two continued this silent journey, as their thoughts screamed in their minds. For five days, it went on this way, until they finally reached Thermidor.

The sandy, barren wasteland was home to scavengers and raiders, and few kingdoms flourished since most of its inhabitants were nomadic. The sand of the plain stretched far-and-wide, as stars in the sky.

Troy guided the winged wooly-rhino into—what appeared to be—one of the few thriving kingdoms of Thermidor. Beings of different races walked to-and-fro, admiring the jewels, spices, and other goods of the market. All seemed oblivious of the elves.

They stayed in the market, attempting to sell or trade the winged wooly-rhino, but they had no buyers.

"How are we going to reach Hell?" Nova asked, as she gently stroked the winged wooly-rhinos mane.

"We must keep trying."

Nova pointed, as her eyes lit up. "He appears to be a scribe, of some sort. Perhaps he could help conduct some proposition?"

Troy nodded, and Nova led the way. The folks of Thermidor began to take notice of the winged wooly-rhino, as it bumbled through the market, but Troy flashed glares at anyone who stared too long.

"I don't care what you owe. You will pay it, or I will have you imprisoned!" a large, stocky fellow shouted, wagging his porky fingers.

"But he knows," the other man pleaded.

The fat man grunted, as he combed back his thinning gray hair. "Once again, I don't care."

Guards took hold of the man, as he pleaded more, and they carried him off. Nova approached the heavy fellow, who scribbled and scrabbled fiercely into his notebook.

"Sir, may we have a word?" Nova asked.

"Be quick," the fellow replied, lethargically flipping through the notebook, and jotting down more notes.

"We are from Prixem and are looking to trade or sell our winged wooly-rhino—for fair value," Troy said, catching the fellow's attention.

He looked up from his notebook, with a cheeky smirk. "Why should I be interested?"

"You work for a king, or someone of royalty, so you have connections. We want your assistance."

"Well, if it is a council with the king you seek, then let it be done," the fellow replied, with a pompous laugh.

The Realm

From the market, the fellow led the two back to a beautiful palace, belonging to King Salar, and as they walked through the gigantic stone doors, they marveled. Columns and pillars of ivory stretched high above their heads; silks of purple and scarlet, embroidered with jewels, wrapped about the ceiling fixtures; and in the middle of the room sat a throne of pure gold. Troy's eyes roamed the room, but at the sight of the king's statue, he became frightened.

As the court horns summoned the king, a scribe waddled before the throne, crying out: "King Boremon, he who overthrew King Salar, will now take the throne."

Troy's stomach twisted with fear, and Nova gasped. "It's him. It's Boremon from Kaulthar's kingdom," she whispered.

Troy looked down, not wishing to lock eyes with the Bdellium Knight. "I know. He knows both of us. I will speak, but he may recognize me."

With a delightful grin, Boremon sat down on his throne. "Come, pay tribute to the King of Saladin!"

Troy bowed as he stepped forward. "If it pleases the King of Saladin, we would like to sell or trade our winged wooly-rhino for a creature from the royal stalls."

Boremon cringed. He felt insulted having to oversee and answer such a petty request. "Surely, you jest?"

"No, my king."

"Guards!" Boremon shouted. "Send them back to the streets. I have no time for such insolence."

The Realm

Troy and Nova let the guards escort them through the stone doors. Once outside, the two fled. They did not dare stop, as Boremon had struck fear in their hearts.

When they finally reached the outskirts of Saladin, the sun was setting, and the stars were coming out. They entered the desert, searching for shelter, and Nova spotted a cave, which was good enough.

"I thought he would recognize us," she said, still shaken from the experience.

Troy smirked. "I could have taken care of him."

"He's a Bdellium Knight; he would have killed us both." She had never feared anything as she feared Boremon.

"You still doubt me," he replied, shaking his head. "I battled with Telezzar, I have fooled Boremon twice, and you still doubt me."

"I never said that. You believe I doubt you or I think lesser of you, but I do not."

Troy stared at her, puzzled. He did not know what to say, but she waited silently. "I think we should eat," he said, digging into his pack.

"What do we have?"

"Not much."

"What will we give it?" Nova asked, looking at the winged wooly-rhino.

"Nothing, we can hardly feed ourselves."

"Troy, it has been faithful."

Troy sighed, as he pulled out some vegetables. "Here, give it this."

The Realm

Nova took the vegetables—a mixture of carrots and cabbage—to the winged wooly-rhino. The creature snorted happily and ate. She smiled and returned to her own share of food, eating in silence, while Troy restlessly sharpened his weapons.

"I think I will sleep now," she said. "Will you sleep?"

"In a bit," he replied, looking to the mouth of the cave. He did not intend to sleep, and she knew it.

"I have never been so far from Padavona. Would you stay by my side throughout the night?"

Surprised, Troy slowly nodded. "Yes, if you would like."

Exhausted from the day's events, Nova laid down and fell asleep with ease. Troy lay next to her; his eyes stared at the smoldering stones and dying flickers of the fire. With weary eyes, though, he soon succumbed to sleep.

The night slipped away, like grains of sand in an hourglass. At the coming of dawn, the sun rose up as a golden emblem in a sea of blue. Troy woke, as the first sunrays hit his face, and after stretching, he took the winged wooly-rhino out for a walk.

As he stepped out with the creature, he found a lengthy caravan passing by. Lines of camels and elephants stretched far forward and far back, carrying spices, silks, pottery, and an abundance of other goods. One of the passing caravan leaders—a turuk giant or sun-giant—approached Troy.

"Greetings, my friend!" the giant cried out, hoping to sell Troy some goods.

Troy gave a nod. "Salutations, my giant friend. What brings you this way?"

"We are traveling south, for Saladin, to trade."

Troy shook his head. "You will not find any welcome there. Saladin has fallen to a new king, a Bdellium Knight."

"Then, the rumor is true," the giant replied, sighing. "We heard of this, but we thought other merchants were spreading lies, attempting to hoard Saladin's ports."

"No, they did not lie. I tried to trade this winged wooly-rhino, but I found no success."

The giant gestured with his hands in excitement. "A winged wooly-rhino? Come, I have spices, precious stones, and silks of exotic realms. I will trade with you."

Troy looked over the goods, but he fretted at their sights. "I'm not sure."

"A slave, perhaps?" the giant asked, pushing for an agreement.

"I need a creature that can take me to Hell."

The giant stared, bewildered. "Hell?"

"Can you help me?"

The giant thought for a moment. "I do have a gryffin, which can make the trip. Are you sure that you do not wish for a slave, though?"

"I am quite certain," Troy replied, growing giddy inside at the thought of a gryffin. "I will trade my winged wooly-rhino for your gryffin."

The giant and Troy traded the two creatures, and parted ways, with the giant disappearing in the caravan's endless numbers. Troy returned to the cave with the gryffin, where he found Nova awake and divvying out breakfast.

"You traded it," Nova said, somewhat surprised and somewhat saddened.

"Yes, the giant took it for the gryffin."

She petted the gryffin, marveling at it. "How will we enter Hell?" She was beginning to worry about not having a plan to enter or escape the wretched place.

"I do not have one," he replied, sitting to eat. "Hopefully, there is a secret way, since the main gate will be guarded."

"Troy, we need a plan. We don't even know where to go, once we enter."

"Do I sense doubt?" he asked. "Everyone is an enemy to everyone else in Hell. I hope to find a demon or devil who is willing to betray the others and help us."

"Dentar is one of them, though."

"Dentar was a prince, and now, he has been cast out because he betrayed his father."

"He will still have friends."

"He has no one. He has more enemies than friends," Troy said, finishing his pizzelles. "Come, we should be on our way."

After gathering their belongings, the two mounted the gryffin, leaving Thermidor. The journey of the next five days to Delirus was much like the five days from Aquilla to Thermidor. Silent. Both thought of speaking to the other; both had thoughts crashing in their minds; but neither could find the right words or put them in order.

Then, Delirus lay in front of their eyes. A chill overcame both, for they had reached the land of shadow and death.

The Realm

They did not know where they were. Empty buildings sat next to one another, and towering over the deserted city, was a beautiful castle. *It must have housed a great king*, Troy thought, staring at it.

"What happened here?" Nova asked.

"In the texts that I have read, it is said a plague invaded the land, corrupting everyone. Common folk slaughtered one another, high lord waged war against high lord, and the king lost his sanity." Troy looked around, as he guided the gryffin on. "We must be careful. Goblins and other foul creatures roam here now, fulfilling dark biddings. It is even said, the Bdellium Knights visit often, imprisoning anyone they can and creating alliances with greed-driven races."

"Will Boremon follow us here?"

Troy smirked. "He seemed too comfortable with his new surroundings. I do not believe he will remain there long, though."

Nova slumped against a wall, as they took a break for some water. "What other creatures lurk here?"

Troy looked around. "Mugworts. Long ago, devils and demons sold many mugworts to slave traders, but the traders—being greedy—stole more mugworts. Angered, the devils and demons slaughtered the deceitful traders, and with them dead, the mugworts escaped to here."

"Why would they stay here?"

"They are a stubborn race and not clever. Some did move on—"

The Realm

Gruesome howls pierced the air. Troy unsheathed his sword and pushed the gryffin to lie down, while Nova armed herself with a spear and shield. *Boom! Boom!* Goblin drums beat aloud. Troy and Nova maneuvered through the shadows, only to find a heartbreaking sight that served to solidify the plain's madness.

Troy, what is that?" Nova asked. She stared at a massive hole filled with fire.

"A sacrificial pit," he whispered, watching the orange and red flames jump like wild dancers.

Black smoke billowed high over the surrounding buildings, but the sight became more horrid. Goblins appeared, prodding captives toward the pit. The women wailed for mercy and the children cried for their mothers, but the goblins gnashed their teeth. Then, with one push, the goblins forced them forward, and as one body, the captives fell into the fiery pit.

Courage filled Troy and he thought of slaughtering all the goblins. This was fleeting, though. With a swallow of humility, he realized his urge was foolish, and his body felt numb.

The elves crept away, returning to the gryffin. No words were spoken, but the two mounted the gryffin and flew off. Nova held Troy tightly, silently crying. Meanwhile, he sat speechless. He— the great paladin, the protector from evil—had let goblins burn innocent people to death. Three words filled his thoughts: *weak...heartless...failure.*

CHAPTER XVII

Nine Lords and Seven Pieces

The black gates loomed high. Troy and Nova stared at them, never seeing anything quite monstrous and intimidating. At the foot, Geryon slept soundly, while basilisks crawled about, and wraiths glided along the outer walls.

"Do you have a plan?" Nova asked, awed by the sight.

"We enter through the front," Troy replied, hesitantly. "When the next group of spirits arrive, we may be able to blend in, slip past the dragon, and enter."

Nova shook her head. "The dragon will see us. If we are caught, then we will remain here forever and no one—not even Telezzar—will be able to save us."

"No. Right now, the dragon is sleeping, so when the next group of spirits arrive, it won't bother to pay attention."

"We will stand out. Even if the dragon does not notice, what of the wraiths?"

Troy readied the gryffin. "We could keep this debate going, but a group is nearing, and we are going to enter."

As the flock of evil spirits passed them, Troy spurred the gryffin into the pack and followed them to the gates' entrance. Geryon—having woken to their cries—roared at the wraiths, and they opened the gates. Tired, the dragon returned to his slumber.

Orange fires of torment lit Hell in a bold brightness, while red lava spewed up from the ground and landed on the working slaves. The slaves gnashed their teeth, howling like banshees, as their skin ripped away from their bodies—though they were already dead. The bitter agony and never-ending darkness should have been for none, save those who had forged Hell and made it their home.

It was all quite surreal to Troy, but he came to his senses, steering the gryffin toward some gigantic fallen boulders. "We will be safe here," he said. "Let's make a plan."

Nova smirked. "Well, go ahead. I have wanted to make one, but you keep ignoring me."

"Nova," he replied, pausing sorrowfully, "I'm sorry. I have not been listening to you, but we are here, now. What should we do?"

"Why should I believe you care?" she asked. "I thought you cared, but you made your stance quite clear in the cupboard. And ever since the day of the council, you have been different."

"I have," Troy replied, a mixture of anxiety and anger pounded through him. "I'm sorry for shutting you out, but it's hard. I do not want to lose you, not here, not anywhere. I love you."

Silence ensued. Troy stood speechless, surprised by his own words, and Nova smiled, dumbfounded.

"I have more demons than Hell as a whole," he finally whispered.

Nova raised her hand to his face, guiding his eyes to hers. "Then let me be the star to guide you."

Troy turned a bashful red. He knew what words he wanted to say, but they had no order. "Let's get this over with," he said, gazing away from her.

Disappointed, Nova nodded her head. "You are right."

The two looked out. Mugworts slaved about the main gates. They were beaten to the bone, for their masters were relentless with punishment. Wraiths floated around with whips in hand, and when bored, they would screech at the mugworts, forcing them to cover their ears from the hideous pitches. The wraiths enjoyed it, and made a game out of it, to see who could beat the most mugworts each day.

"Spelts are coming," Troy said, nervously, as he watched the humanoid creatures with long, sky-blue hair and ghost-white complexion appear.

Nova had never seen a spelt. She watched them, as their red eyes glared about. "What is a spelt?"

"A lower breed of vampire," he replied, "while vampires are cunning, diplomatic, and finesse on the battlefield, spelts are not. It is said, spelts are half-golem, too, which is why they thrive on brute strength."

"Why are they here?"

"I do not know, but we will have problems if spelts are one of the main guardians of Hell."

Gliding toward the spelts, one of the wraiths shouted at them, "What are you doing, you filthy scum!"

The spelts hissed back, and their leader drew his sword. "The business of our master. If you were not busy playing games, then you could do what the master desires too."

"Games? We do not play games. We work hard, and our slaves work hard for us."

"It was only an observation," the spelt said, giving a devious grin.

"Leave us be, you half-wit!"

"Let me show you my blade."

"Show them pain!" the wraith shouted to the other wraiths, and a scuffle broke out.

Supremacy and bloodshed filled their minds, and the spelts and wraiths clashed. Using their whips, the wraiths forced the spelts to fight from afar, rendering the spelts' swords useless. The half-vampires grew angry, though, and using their shifty speed, they attempted to cut down the wraiths. As the brawl hit its climax, three spelts and one wraith fell dead. It may have gone on longer if it had not been for Citron.

"Troy, who is that?" Nova asked, noticing Citron. He held an air of authority about him. His hands clenched a pair of massive flails; chains draped around his belt, and he wore black-and-bronze armor.

Troy's eyes widened, shocked. "That is Citron, leader of the Bdellium Knights."

Citron stepped between the spelts and wraiths, looking to each side. "What is going on?"

"These half-wits mocked us and attacked us, master," the wraiths replied, in one accord.

"No!" shouted the lead spelt. "These floating fools play their games, screaming at the slaves and forcing them to fall down, only to beat them for falling."

"Enough," Citron replied, a cold chill ran through his voice, as his unseen eyes glared at them all. "I should slaughter all of you for causing this petty interruption."

The spelts huddled together, while the wraiths were still. "Forgive us, master," the wraith said. "We do not want your wrath turned against us, as it is with Boremon."

Citron swung his flails, crushing the wraith. He looked to the other wraiths and asked, "Who knows of Boremon?"

A second wraith—the new leader—floated forward. "This one flaunted knowledge of Boremon, master. We know nothing, save you are the leader of the Bdellium Knights."

Citron marched away with disgust. After exchanging heated and frightened glares, the wraiths and spelts parted ways.

"Citron sounds upset with Boremon," Troy whispered.

"Upset? He sounded infuriated," Nova replied. "Do you have a plan?"

"No."

"I do. Opposite of the front gate is a stairway, but it seems there is an elevator next to it."

Troy looked to where she pointed. "The stairway must be to the Thousand Spiral Stairway Abyss. We may find the electrum in the abyss, or at least help."

"We make for the elevator, then?"

Troy gave a nod. "Quickly, while the wratihs are still shaken up by Citron's anger."

The Realm

Troy and Nova slipped to the front of the boulder, and then scaled down a rocky platform, using rope from Troy's pack. Once at the base of the platform, the two bundled themselves tightly in their cloaks and moved as shadows toward the elevator.

Troy was right. Shaken by Citron's anger, the wraiths did not see the elves, and concentrating on their work, the mugworts did not either.

Nova was the first to reach the elevator, but she waited for Troy before opening the doors. Tightly pulling her cloak about herself, she stood stiffly against the obsidian doors, tensely holding her breath.

Troy did not take long. Once he reached her, they opened the elevator doors and slipped aboard. They were safe, or so they thought.

"Elves?" a deep voice mumbled. It was the elevator conductor, who appeared as a troll but was not one.

For a moment, Troy's hand went to the handle of his short sword, thinking to draw it. Nova raised her hands, though, gesturing that they meant no harm to the conductor. "Please, do not report us."

"Elves do not belong in Hell, so why are you here?" the conductor asked, as it shifted its kilt to fit more comfortably.

"None of your business," Troy replied.

The elevator shook, as the conductor rumbled with laughter. "You are aboard my elevator, so your business is mine."

"Dentar wishes to take over our homeland, Padavona, and we have come to retrieve the electrum pieces to stop him," Nova replied. Perplexed with her, Troy closed his eyes in distress, ready to cut down the conductor before it alerted Hell of their presence.

"Dentar?" the conductor questioned, and Nova nodded back. "I hate that swine dung. He is the one who brought me to this place, and I have sworn vengeance against him."

Surprised, Troy and Nova stared at the conductor, speechless. Perhaps Telezzar was right, perhaps Hell had more allies than enemies. "Will you help us?" she asked.

"Of course," the conductor replied, cheerfully. It grabbed hold of a steer and shifted it to descend. "My name is Timuluk, and I am a pygarg from Solarium."

"I am Nova, and this is Troy. We are from Prixem, under the guidance of Telezzar the Blue."

The pygarg nodded its head, but Troy cut in, "If you are from Solarium, then why are you here?"

Timuluk sighed, with a bitter look. "I distate the tale." The pygarg stroke its beard, rememerbing some distant memory. "Before Belial was an outcast, he had many of his demons capture pygargs and other races, so he could use us in his rebellion. My three daughters and I were out searching for food, when they ambushed us, and Belial—himself, mind you— butchered my little girls, as if they were nothing but wild sport."

"Oh, Timuluk," Nova whispered, wishing to hug and console the pygarg.

The pygarg cleared its throat, attempting to shed no tears. "I want justice. I want Belial's head or Dentar's or whatever he calls himself these days."

"He calls himself Dentar," Troy said.

With a powerful jolt, the elevator came to a halt, and the pygarg opened the doors. "There is a piece on this level. I saw it once, but that was long ago. While you are finding it, I will alert others who hate Belial, and they will help you."

"Who will you alert?" Troy asked, unsure of the pygarg's plan.

Timuluk grunted. "If I tell you, you will not like it, but I know they can be trusted."

"Timuluk—"

"Trust me. I will take care of the business and then be back. Good luck with your search."

Troy and Nova watched as Timuluk disappeared behind the closing obsidian doors. Turning away from the elevator, the two found themselves facing a sandy, barren land with nothing but soft, whisking winds and an occasional monolith. With no other choice, they ventured forward.

CHAPTER XVIII

The Abyssal Brothers

As Troy and Nova roamed the plain, they did not speak with each other. The silence cut them both. Troy was unsure of what to say, while his feelings of duty and love waged war in his heart. Nova knew of these conflicted feelings; he was due to another, but he claimed to love her. Still, she was uncertain.

"Will you talk to me?" she finally asked.

Troy's pace slowed, as he looked at her. "About?"

"You know what. Before we met Timuluk or developed our plan, we were having an important conversation."

Troy stared at her, mesmerized. "Your face is smudged with smog."

"Troy—"

"Nova, I have spent every waking moment with you for almost five couplets. I enjoy being with you, but we know it cannot happen."

"Why?"

"I have been promised to another."

"I know. I know your promise and your duty, but when does it end?" She stared at him, heartbroken. "I beg you not to follow that path."

Troy smirked. Everyone else had always made the decisions for him, he knew the path he was to take, but at this crossroad, it was different. "I realize what I must do, and there is no other path."

"But there is—"

"No," he replied, "I have already chosen the path to be with you."

She smiled back. "You choose me?"

"My heart always has."

As the two embraced one another, a sharp howl cut the air. The elves looked to where the howl had come from. Bounding along at an alarming rate, a pack of hellhounds were making their way to the elves.

"We must hurry," Nova said. "We cannot defeat them."

Troy debated whether to flee or fight. "No, we must fight," he said, unsheathing his short sword.

Confused, Nova snapped: "What are you trying to prove?"

"Nothing, but we cannot outrun the pack. It's better to fight now, while we have strength."

Nodding, Nova readied her spear-and-shield. "Then I will fight by your side."

Caught in the moment, he looked at her. "Will you for eternity?"

"Always," she replied.

Nervous but exhilarated, the two met the hellhounds head-on. Nova buried her spear in the chest of the first, forcing her to pull out her crossbow. Troy raised his short sword, slashing at one of the hellhound's sides, but the beast jumped back, avoiding any further blows.

Slowly, the hellhounds began to form a two-ringed circle around the elves. Their ash-black and fiery-orange eyes remained focused on the elves, while their iron-like teeth snapped.

Nova fired aimlessly, while Troy jabbed without success. Then, something unexpected happened. Three demons appeared—like a puff of smoke—and using whips and spears the size of gate poles, the three merry demons drove the hellhounds off.

"That's right!" the first demon shouted, with joy. "Run your fury pup hides back to your lairs!"

"Yes! Let it be known that Abyssal Kidron kicked your puppy loins out of here!" a second demon cried out, joining the first demon.

"Oh, my," a third demon said, realizing Troy and Nova were present, "we have company, brothers."

"Not just any company, Abyssal Grihorn," the first demon said, looking the pair over. "We are playing guests to two elves."

"You decided to honeymoon here, with us?" the third demon asked, happily. "I am Abyssal Grihorn."

"Do you think anyone—in their right mind, mind you—would come here, after being married?" Kidron asked. Then he added with a loud whisper, "Besides, look at him, do you really think she would be with him?"

"Yes, we are elves. No, we are not married," Troy said to them.

"I knew it!" Kidron shouted.

"Can we please hear their story?" the first demon asked.

"I don't know, can we, Abyssal Kishon?" Kidron replied, mockingly.

"I am Troy, and this is Nova. We are from Prixem, and we came here to retrieve electrum."

Kidron playfully dropped his jaw. "By Abaddon's beard, that's a journey!"

"Kidron, they don't want your remarks," Kishon said.

"Yeah, besides, Abaddon does not have a beard," Grihorn chimed in.

"Oh, Grihorn, you have no wits," Kidron sneered.

Troy huffed. "Can you help us or not? We need to get back to the pygarg and his elevator soon."

The three demons glanced at one another. "Of course, we can," Kidron replied, with a hearty laugh.

"Here," Kishon said, holding something out to them, "this is the electrum piece you want. We give it to you freely since you have provided us with amusement."

Bewildered, Troy slowly reached for it. "You are giving this to me because we amuse you?"

The three demons broke out into laughter. "Of course not! Why would we give you this?" Kidron replied.

Troy glared at them. "Because Telezzar the Blue sent us to get it. We need to defeat Dentar."

The rumbles of laughter ceased from the brothers, as they stared. "You are taking on Dentar? The one who was Belial?" Kidron asked.

"Who else proclaims to be Dentar?"

"This changes everything," Kishon said, looking to his brothers. They each nodded, and Kishon continued: "Before

Belial left, he did many evil deeds, which included framing us. That is why we are here, in the abyss. We happened to find the electrum and have kept it since."

"Then, you will help us?" Troy asked. He was becoming hopeful. "We need the electrum."

Kishon held the electrum, tightly, but Kidron nudged him. "Tell him the truth, Kishon."

Kishon sighed. "This is not the real electrum. I once had it—it was my prized possession—but I bet it against the gargoyle king and lost it to him."

Troy smirked. "We're in a hurry, and you are trying to trick us with a replica?"

Kidron intervened, gesturing for Troy to calm down. "We can still help. It will take you many days to reach the gargoyle king, but by our magic, my brothers and I will take you there in mere moments."

Troy looked to Nova, who gave an approving nod. "We will accept your help, but can you return us to the pygarg, when we are finished?"

"Consider it done."

The three Abyssal brothers began drawing signs in the sand. The elves stared, mesmerized, as the demons made strange symbols and spoke aloud in strange tongues.

"Kishon, Grihorn, take hold of them," Kidron said, pointing to the elves.

The younger Abyssal brothers grabbed Troy and Nova, holding them tightly, as Kidron's chanting grew louder and louder. Then, a portal opened before the demons and elves.

"Do not let them go," Kidron said to his brothers. He looked to the elves and continued: "Do not leave our sides."

The five stepped through the spiraling, greenish portal. On the other side, they found themselves in the gargoyle king's kingdom. Troy and Nova had never seen so many gargoyles. They bustled to-and-fro, most not noticing the demons or elves, but those that did shot evil glares.

"Can we pick up gargoyle stones before we leave?" Grihorn asked his brothers. "They are my favorite snack."

Kidron looked at his brother sharply. "Stay focused, Grihorn."

Troy had been staring about the city, while listening to the brothers. Buildings towered all about, taller than any monument he had seen. "There," he said, pointing to the tallest. "He lives there?"

"Not even close," Kishon replied, chuckling.

"No, the gargoyle king sits atop a large wall, so he can oversee his people," Grihorn said, pointing to a wall.

The five hurried to the wall, weaving through the crowded city streets. The king's dull, yellow eyes peered down, catching sight of the demons and elves. He could not resist grinning, while he picked at his razor-sharp teeth.

"Abyssal brother," the gargoyle king said to them, with a mocking tone. "What brings you here?"

"I bring guests, King Gargouille," Kidron replied.

"Guests?" The gargoyle king rose from his seat, standing almost as tall as a giant, and he looked down at the elves. "Well, why have you come?"

Troy was nervous, and in his eyes, King Gargouille's gray skin seemed to darken, as if he was angry at Troy for not answering quickly. "I come on behalf of Telezzar, the Blue Wizard. He has sent me to find the electrum of Hell."

King Gargouille gave a hearty laugh, as he arranged his peculiar ring, which was half-onyx and half-marble. "I will not hand over anything, and the wizard is a fool to think otherwise."

The king's answer did not surprise Troy, but the elf remained silent for a moment. "Telezzar is wise," he replied to the king, developing a plan. "He sent me for a certain reason."

"What reason is that?"

Troy reached into his pack, digging around. "I will trade you this unicorn horn for the electrum."

King Gargouille and his people gasped. They knew Troy had not slain a unicorn for its horn. No. The horn had once belonged to a living gargoyle. "You slaughtered one of my own and now demand I give you my treasure for the horn?"

"No, I did not slay any gargoyle. I offer this horn to you, knowing it means much to your people. I only wish to have the electrum."

King Gargouille's face grew ill tempered, and he gnashed his teeth, but he could not let Troy walk away with the horn. "I would have your head on a pike, if you were not friends with the Abyssal brothers," he replied. "I will accept your trade, but none of you are ever to return here."

Troy traded one of his four gargoyle horns for King Gargouille's electrum piece. Afterwards, Kidron wasted little time summoning a portal, and he led the others through it safely, taking them to the elevator.

Timuluk was glad to see the elves, they boarded the elevator, and the pygarg happily let the Abyssal brothers aboard, too. Then, the elevator raced upward.

"I have spoken with my contacts," Timuluk whispered to the elves, as the elevator neared the top.

"And?" Troy asked.

"They will help us."

"Who are your contacts?"

Before Timuluk could answer, the elevator's doors opened and three devils stood at the entrance—Abigor, Beelzebub, and Baalzaphon.

"So, you are the ones overthrowing Belial?" Abigor asked.

Astonished, Troy and Nova stood speechless. "Y-yes, we plan on battling Dentar," Troy replied.

"My brother is powerful, and you will have no chance, but I do not want him coming back here, to try and usurp my father. We will help you," Beelzebub said, bitterly.

"We will win, if we re-forge the seven electrum swords."

Abigor grunted. "We know why you are here. We will go and retrieve the five pieces from the Nine Levels. Since you have the piece from the Thousand Spiral Stairway Abyss, you must go and retrieve the last piece from the Council Chamber of the Nine."

"Take the pygarg, too," Baalzaphon ordered, "and remember, if you are caught by anyone, then we do not know you."

The three devils turned away and left, followed by the Abyssal brothers, who would be scapegoats if anything went wrong.

Waddling on its stumpy legs, the pygarg followed Troy and Nova as they slunk toward the council chamber. Soon, the sandy pathway led to a brick stairway, going straightway to the council chamber. They hurried up the stairway, coming to a large door. On the outside, nine different black banners draped above the large door, and each bore a symbol for one of the Nine.

Troy pushed against the door, but it would not budge. "Timuluk, can you break it down?"

"Of course." The pygarg grabbed hold of the door, ripping it from its hinges. The three entered.

Torchlights lit the chamber in a yellowish-green glow. The three glanced about. The chamber was set up as a throne room, with a large throne carved into the wall, opposite the door; and to each of the giant throne's sides, sat four lesser thrones, each also carved into the wall. Above each throne, sat a giant dial with miniature, evil creatures etched on them.

"There," Troy said, pointing to the dial above King Abaddon's throne.

Troy started for it, but Timuluk jerked him back. "It is too simple. There must be some trap."

Troy looked around. "We must get it."

"I will."

Waddle by waddle, Timuluk edged toward the giant throne. Nothing happened. Once Timuluk reached the giant throne, the pygarg looked back. Troy grinned, knowing the pygarg would succeed, but Nova held her breath, concerned. Timuluk smiled at them. The pygarg climbed atop King Abaddon's throne and grabbed hold of the electrum piece in the dial.

"I have it!" Timuluk exclaimed.

"Don't move," Troy replied.

"Why?"

"Oh, Timuluk, look down," Nova said, bursting into tears.

Timuluk looked down, finally noticing the spear. The pygarg turned and smiled at them, tossing the electrum. "Go, there is nothing you can do."

"Timuluk," Nova whispered, but the pygarg fell dead.

Nova sobbed heavily. Troy picked up the electrum, as he stared at the pygarg; he felt helpless again, as he—the anointed paladin—could not save anyone from evil. It was not over, though. He shook his pitying thoughts away, pulling Nova to him.

As they fled the council chamber, horns started ringing out, alarming and alerting all of Hell that intruders were afoot. The barks of hellhounds grew louder, as Troy and Nova dashed towards the gryffin.

"Elves!" Abyssal Kishon cried out, meeting them. "Here is the last five pieces, but you must hurry!"

"What happened?" Troy asked. He did not believe that Timuluk stealing King Abaddon's electrum had sent all of Hell into a frenzy.

"We were betrayed. Abigor set off the alarms, hoping others might catch Baalzaphon and Beelzebub."

"Why?"

"If caught, they could be banished or killed."

"Were they caught?"

"I do not know. After setting off the alarm, Abigor killed my brothers and injured me," Kishon replied, revealing a gash to his side. "Hurry, though! The hoards of Hell will be here soon, and you cannot be caught, too, or this will all be in vain."

"The front gates are closed," Troy said, as he and Nova mounted the gryffin.

"I will take care of it," Kishon replied.

Abyssal Kishon bounded from the hiding spot, straight for the front gate. With all his strength, he slashed through the wraiths and forced the front gate up.

Troy urged the gryffin on. The front gates were still open, but all of Hell was gathering towards the entrance, many confused by what was happening.

"We're going to make it!" Nova exclaimed, happily.

She spoke too soon, though. A fiery problem loomed in the gateway, and Troy's eyes glared. "Geryon," he whispered. "We will never escape if the dragon is loose."

"Abyssal Kishon will take care of it," Nova said.

"No," he replied, shaking his head, "you must take the reins."

"No, Troy!"

"Take them," Troy said, shoving them into her hands. He took his pack off, placing it in her lap. "This contains all of the electrum. You must take it to my grandfather."

"Troy—"

"Good-bye," he said, giving her a farewell kiss.

Geryon's talons slashed at Kishon, the dragon was livid with the demon, but his sights slowly turned to the approaching elves. Troy jumped down from the gryffin's back, and with short sword in hand, he rushed the dragon head-on, hoping his diversion would allow Nova and the gryffin to escape.

Geryon growled, he sensed the electrum with Nova, but he knew Troy was a paladin. Conflicted, Geryon glanced back and forth, but in the end, it was a simple choice. After all, who was this paladin to charge him?

CHAPTER XIX

SinGoth

Relief flooded Troy as he watched Nova and the gryffin escape. It was not over, though. He glared at Geryon, and behind him, the hoards of Hell made their onslaught. *If this is my end, then what an end it will be*, he thought. His grip tightened on his sword's handle, and the blade appeared ablaze, reflecting the fires of Hell.

Geryon's spear-like talons grasped for Troy, but the dragon only took hold of several mugworts, yelping. More mugworts arrived, though. They carried reapers and instruments of stone, but they charged the elf prince.

Troy extended his blade, cutting off the forearm of the nearest mugwort. The mugwort cried and howled in pain, and the other mugworts were leery of charging the elf.

"Get him! Kill him!" Geryon roared. The dragon spread his wings, preparing to fly over the gate, which stood between him and the paladin.

The spelts and wraiths stared at Troy and then at one another. Though they bickered, neither were foolish, nor did they intend to meet the sword so quickly. Instead, they began taunting one another over being too fearful to battle one elf paladin.

Geryon came flying down, talons spread, but once again, the dragon only grabbed mugworts. "Grab him!"

Confused, Troy looked around, and only Geryon was trying to catch him. This emboldened Troy, he did not fear these creatures or servants of Hell, and he slashed at those that stood too closely. He had to escape—that had to be the plan. He began plotting, but before he could act, someone unexpected appeared.

"Descendant of Balor, surrender to me."

Troy looked to find Citron, loosening several chains from his belt. "I may go where I please," Troy replied.

Citron smirked. Holding onto one end of a chain, Citron threw out the other end, which bound Troy by his wrist. "Bow to me, elf."

Troy fought, wrestling to free himself. "Fight me!"

Citron slung out a second chain, catching Troy's free hand, and he threw Troy down, disarming him. "Come on!" Troy shouted, trying to pull Citron towards him.

Citron snarled, as Troy pulled and began to rise to his feet. "Bow to me," Citron said again, throwing a third chain, which bound Troy by the neck. Citron swung the three chains about, tossing Troy to-and-fro until he lay limp.

The Bdellium Knight approached Troy, standing over him and nudging him, but Troy lay unconscious. "Imprison him."

The spelts rushed to Troy, grabbing him. They dragged him away, through coal-dark tunnels and smoldering hallways, to one of the lowest parts of Hell's dungeons.

Time passed on. When he woke, he found himself chained to a wall, unsure of how long he had been inside the dungeon.

"Hello?" Troy asked, unsure if anyone was nearby.

A rustle came in the darkness. "My spirit has been broken this day."

Troy squinted into the darkness. "Who is there?"

"Kishon is dead, or you would not be here."

"Kidron? Grihorn?"

"It is I, Abyssal Kidron."

"How? Kishon said you died."

"No, I survived, just as you," Kidron said. "Now, we will be tried as traitors, and no doubt, they will hang us both."

Troy shook his head, as he took a deep breath to clear his thoughts. "No, Hell is made of tunnels and darkness. We can escape."

Kidron snarled. "My brothers died to help you, and we face the same fate."

"You are not dead yet, but you make death your choice."

Kidron jumped out of the darkness, lunging for Troy. Immediately, wraith guards entered the dungeon, shrieking and bringing the demon to his knees. Kidron wept bitterly, and as the wraiths tightened his chains, he screamed in anger. The wraiths shrieked again. Kidron threw back his head, howling, but the wraiths drew out their swords and all fell silent.

The wraiths floated off, taking Kidron's body and slamming the dungeon door. Troy was alone. He looked around the dungeon, inspecting his surroundings, and immediately, he formed a plan.

In the midst of the floor, there was a large hole, and there was a large hole in the ceiling, directly over the one on the floor. *A sewer system*, he thought to himself.

With all his strength, Troy pulled his bonds forward, hoping the old, rusted chains would give way. He pulled and fought, until *Snap!*

Troy stumbled to the ground, almost falling into the hole. His heart beat fast as he backed away, but he was happy the chains had given away.

He crept to the dungeon door, peering outside. "Guard! Help!"

A mugwort came bursting through the door. Troy flung himself forward, swinging his chains, and hitting the mugwort across the face. The mugwort lurched back and snarled. Furiously, it jumped at Troy, hoping to overpower the elf.

The two exchanged blows, with the mugwort clawing and beating, and Troy swinging his chains. The two stumbled and bumbled about, as the skirmish came to the center of the dungeon.

Then, it happened. The mugwort grabbed Troy's throat, pinning the elf down. Everything was going black. Troy fought back, trying to loosen the mugwort's grasp or swing his chains. Nothing was working, and all was going black. The mugwort threw back its head, howling with delight, but Troy slipped his feet up, aligning them with the mugwort's chest. With one desperate kick, Troy pushed the creature, and the mugwort staggered backwards, losing its balance, and falling into the giant hole.

It was over. Troy lay on his back, choking and breathing heavily. His eyes roved about the dungeon, making sure no one had heard the scuffle and come to investigate. His grip tightened on his chains, as he rose to his feet.

He slowly made his way to the hole. Gazing downward, it was an endless-black abyss, and looking upward, it was a dark ascent into the unknown. With a heavy sigh, he contemplated, but something caught his ear. He looked back up the hole in the ceiling, listening carefully. Something was coming.

Troy dashed into the shadows, trying to breathe calmly, so as to not give himself away. He waited. He could hear it was growing closer and closer. Then, it appeared. A deranged-looking creature with yellowish-green skin. Faintly, Troy thought he recognized it.

It began sniffing the air, as if it were hunting prey. "I smell you, Elf. Come out, there aren't many places to hide."

Troy knew it was right. Hesitantly, he crept from the shadows, but he kept the chain hidden. He found the creature odd. It wore armors of men, elves, and goblins, and it carried a strange axe.

"Ah, an elf," the creature chuckled, scratching its frizzled black hair. "There's no need to fear me. I'm elf born, as you—or at least half."

"Half elf, half goblin?" Troy asked.

"An outcast, indeed," it replied to Troy, "Hell is my home and imps are my friends."

"Imps?"

"Yes, they told me about you and that you were here," it said. "The imps also told me of a great trial, which we shall attend in secret, if you wish to join me."

"Why should I trust you? Why do you want to help me?"

The creature shrugged. "You're not from here, and by all rights, neither of us should be. If I free you from this dungeon, then I want you to free me from Hell."

Troy smirked. "Why don't you just leave on your own?"

"Where would I go? I do not know the outside world."

Troy pondered, staring at the creature. He did not have many choices, so he nodded his head. "All right, we will do this together."

"Thank you."

"First, help me retrieve my belongings," Troy said, pausing. "What is your name?"

"I am SinGoth, SinGoth the Half-Breed," the creature replied, bowing. "Now, let us get your belongings and be on our way."

SinGoth slipped from the dungeon, finding Troy's short sword and pack in a large pile of prisoner belongings. With his short sword returned, Troy hacked at the rusted chain, until it finally fell off.

Instead of using the hallways, SinGoth took Troy through the sewage system. They climbed the half-breed's rope up, passing many empty dungeons and storerooms, and at the end of their ascent, they came to a wide lair.

"Follow closely," SinGoth said.

"Where are we?"

"The hellhounds are kept in a massive labyrinth, and we are in one of the lairs."

"What?" Troy snapped.

"We are in a hellhound lair," SinGoth repeated. "We will follow this trail for a little while and meet Arxy, and he will show us to the hidden passage, to the council chamber."

The two sprinted from the lair, down a much smaller tunnel. Troy struggled to keep up, but he did not want to lose SinGoth, not in the hellhound labyrinth.

"Arxy?" SinGoth whispered. "Arxy?"

"Here," a voice replied, appearing before the half-breed and elf. "What took so long?"

"The elf," SinGoth said with a sly smile.

"Come on, we must hurry. The council has already commenced."

SinGoth and Troy followed Arxy. "Have you made an escape plan?" the imp asked the two.

Troy gave an odd look. "No," he replied, looking at SinGoth. "Do you not have a plan?"

"I'm still making it."

"What? Why are we going to this trial, if we do not have a plan?" Troy asked.

Arxy gave a cunning grin. "My offer still stands, SinGoth."

"What offer?" Troy asked.

"I told SinGoth, I can provide a means of escape. I can free some of Hell's prisoners, starting a riot, and provide a creature to escape on."

SinGoth grunted and looked at Troy. "Yes, but in return, you and I would have to go to the library—on the Thousandth Level of the Great Abyss—and erase his name from the records."

Arxy stopped and turned to SinGoth. "Is it wrong that I desire my freedom, just as you?"

"I'm not doing it, Arxy."

"Yes, we will," Troy said, interrupting. Arxy was surprised, while SinGoth was baffled. "We will erase your name, but you must have our escape ready by the end of the council meeting."

"What?" SinGoth whispered, irritated and bewildered by Troy's agreement.

Arxy smiled. "Very well," the imp replied, "continue down this path, and you will find the secret passage to the council. I must go and see that everything is prepared."

The imp vanished from their presence, leaving Troy and SinGoth in the middle of an unknown path. SinGoth's eyes burned with anger.

"What have you done, Elf?"

"My name is Troy."

"You have promised something beyond dangerous."

"And we will see it through," Troy replied. "Now, lead on to the trial."

SinGoth gnashed his teeth, slowly turning and leading the way. Just as Arxy said, the secret passage was visible to them, and they entered it, finding a staircase before them. They crept up it, all the way to a small balcony, which overlooked the council chamber.

"Why do you plague me?" King Abaddon roared. "What reason do you have for betraying me?"

Troy peered out, expecting to find Baalzaphon, Beelzebub, and Abigor on trial, but instead, Anneberg stood in Abigor's place.

"Father, I have done nothing," Beelzebub answered, strongly. "We have already killed three demons of the abyss and a rebellious pygarg, and an elf is currently imprisoned. Do you believe I would use such followers to start a rebellion, as my brother?"

Lilith rose up. "Hear his words, Father. If he meant to start a rebellion, he would not have used such lowly beings. He has gained nothing."

Whispers filled the room. King Abaddon growled. "Why does part of my flesh wish to hinder me? My own offspring!"

"My King Abaddon, Belial's wild spirit does not roam in Beelzebub," Murmur's melodious voice chimed in. "I taught all of the royal children, and Belial was the most wretched. Lilith's reasoning is most prudent, here, and Beelzebub has been ever loyal."

Murmur's words calmed the king's heart, and King Abaddon looked to Lilith, who gave a trusting nod. "My son, Beelzebub, take a seat. I find no crimes or faults."

As Beelzebub took his seat, Baalzaphon looked to King Abaddon. "I am Captain of the Guards. Why would I use three outcast demons, a pygarg, and an elf to betray you, my king?"

"I lead the legions," Abigor spat back.

Levithan laughed at Abigor. "Baalzaphon has been loyal to the king. He is the reason that Belial was defeated, not your *legions.*"

Beelzebub applauded. "Truer words have never been spoken. Baalzaphon has been loyal, and when Belial threatened to take the throne, Baalzaphon stopped him. It is absurd to believe Baalzaphon would go against his loyal ways, only to create his own rebellion."

The other demons and devils whispered amongst themselves. Not all were sold on Leviathan's and Beelzebub's statements, but they did speak truthfully. King Abaddon stared at Baalzaphon.

"My king, I live to serve."

King Abaddon nodded his head. "Take your seat, Baalzaphon, I find no fault."

Baalzaphon bowed his head and took his seat. All eyes turned to Anneberg.

"My king, I have always been loyal to you. I know nothing of this rebellion, and I beg for your mercy," Anneberg pleaded.

"Someone must pay. Let the blood of Anneberg be spilt to appease the crime," Lilith said.

"I agree, my king," Meldon chimed in, "the mines have not been prosperous as of late. It could be that Anneberg has been holding back, hoping to fund his own rebellion."

"Silence you serpents!" Anneberg snapped. "My king, I would never betray you! The mines have been dried of goods for some time. I have no ties to this rebellion!"

King Abaddon rose from his seat, unsheathing his broad sword. "Belial betrayed me and was exiled. If that was not good enough, then perhaps shedding your blood will be. Bend the knee!"

Anneberg fell to his knees. "My king, I bend! I am your servant!"

SinGoth touched Troy's shoulder. "We should be on our way. There is nothing else to see."

"Anneberg is innocent. Why?" Troy asked, confused.

"They want bloodshed, not justice," SinGoth replied, watching King Abaddon swing his sword, "that is Hell's sin."

Troy stared, lost in thoughts. SinGoth grabbed him, though, and the two crept away, down the staircase, through the tunnel, and to the hellhound lair. Thoughts still swam in Troy's mind, dumbfounding him. *So, this is what happens when beasts have power and make laws. Bloodshed rules over justices, and betrayal is stronger than faith.*

"Here," SinGoth said, throwing a pack to Troy. "Arxy has started our plan. Quickly, follow me."

"What about the library?"

SinGoth ignored Troy's words, but the elf sprinted after him. They came to the main courtyard, almost a stone's throw away from the elevator.

"I don't see Arxy," Troy said.

"I trust him."

"He trusts us. What about the library?"

Before SinGoth could answer, the elevator door opened and prisoners exploded out, armed with swords and spears. The mugworts, wraiths, and spelts in the courtyard rallied and met the prisoners head-on, though they did not understand what had happened.

"There," SinGoth said, pointing. He dashed to Arxy with Troy behind him.

"Quickly, before Citron arrives!" Arxy shouted.

The imp handed over the reins to a giant hawk. "Arxy, you have been a wonderful friend," SinGoth said, mounting the giant hawk, and helping Troy up.

"As you, my friend. You kept our bargain?"

SinGoth smirked. "Hell's sin, Arxy. We owe you a debt, and we will return someday to fulfill it."

"What?" Arxy asked, angrily. "No! You must finish what you promised."

"Never promised," SinGoth replied.

SinGoth urged the hawk off. Arxy reached for the reins to stop them, but the hawk's wings spread out, knocking him back. The imp shrieked, shouting for Geryon to stop them from escaping, but it was too late. The hawk flew off, fading away from Hell's view.

CHAPTER XX

Malobathrons and Minotaurs

A brown pack swayed back and forth as it exited a meadow of tall grasses. Carlton stared at the faint lights of Ovid, happy at their sight. It had been over a couplet since the council in Lithia, and he was ready to be home. With a hearty snort, his weary legs continued trudging on, knowing the journey was almost at its end.

Though the journey would end, the task would just be beginning. Carlton knew the minotaurs would go to war against Dentar, but the difficult part would be convincing others to join. Some would join the minotaurs, like the Free Goblins, Amarog the Dire Wolf, creatures of the forests—bears and foxes—and beasts of the field—oxen and bison. Carlton's greatest concern was the centaurs. The rift between the centaurs and minotaurs was no secret, but would it stand between the centaur's decision? If the centaurs went to war, then others of Res Publica would, too.

Carlton's mind eased on thoughts of alliances, as he reached Ovid. Something seemed wrong, though. *This is not the great city I left*, he thought, peering down the empty streets and watching the flickering torchlights.

"Who are you?" a furious voice asked.

Carlton's hand clenched his axe, and he turned to the voice. "I am Prince Carlton, son of King Claudius."

From the shadows, a guard stepped forward, bowing before Carlton. "My prince, forgive me; I did not know it was you."

"Rise," Carlton replied. "What has happened?"

"You must come with me, my prince, for you are not safe here, in the open. If they find out you have returned, they will kill you."

"Who?"

"Come, my prince."

"I have no time for games or ruses."

The guard looked about and whispered, "Your father's brother, Caelix, has come home, and he has claimed the throne."

Carlton snorted. He remembered his father's brother well, for when Carlton's grandfather passed, Caelix attempted to poison Claudius and gain the crown. "Caelix is here?"

"Indeed, my prince, and he brought mugworts."

"Mugworts?"

"Yes, my prince, they feast in your father's halls and Caelix leads them," the guard replied. "The story of mugworts is true, too. Their bluish-purple skin, long black hair, and gangly hands like lion paws."

Carlton snorted, angered by Caelix's actions. "I am going to pay my respects to Caelix. Rally the guards on duty; we are taking back Ovid."

The guard rallied a dozen minotaurs, and they marched with Carlton to King Claudius's throne room. Word reached Caelix's ear of Carlton's return, though, and he decided to meet the young minotaur head-on, at the stairway of the king's throne room.

"Ah, my brother's son, welcome," Caelix said, mockingly, as he caught sight of Carlton and the guards. "I trust your well?"

Carlton smirked, as he continued marching to the stairway. "Quite well, and much better than my father's brother, who—if I remember right—was exiled from here."

Caelix gave a hearty laugh. "Your father and brothers were presumed dead, so I took it upon myself to return and restore order."

"In another world, I would let my presence serve as a warning for you to leave, but now, I would much rather take your head."

"Death!" the mugworts cried out, in unison.

"Silence!" Caelix shouted. His attention returned to Carlton, but the mugworts were right. "If that is how it must be, dear Carlton, then so be it. Kill them all."

Immediately, the mugworts leaped forward, charging the minotaurs. The minotaurs took rank, readying their axes. The two sides clashed. The mugwort's spears pierced the armor of several minotaurs, but the other minotaurs swung their axes, delivering heavy blows against the armor-less mugworts.

Caelix unsheathed his sword, one made of dragon bone. He stepped down from the stairway, slaying the nearest minotaur, but his eyes never left Carlton's.

Carlton snorted and stepped forward. He knew there was no other answer to end the madness, so he charged Caelix. The two thrust about, taking turns dominating, but neither overtook the other.

"Give up, boy," Caelix grunted. He was older and wiser, but his heavy armor slowed him.

"I can't. My father did not raise a quitter or a traitor," Carlton answered. He held his own against Caelix, but his weapon proved useless.

As the sword and axe crossed, Carlton weakened his stance, knowing his blade would break. The young prince slipped one hand down to his thigh, taking hold of his dagger, and as his axe blade cracked apart, he spun around Caelix's side and thrust the dagger downward. The blade found its mark, piercing through the back of Caelix's throat.

Carlton looked out, seeing the mugworts fearful stares. "Rise up, Minotaurs of Ovid, kill them!"

At Carlton's cry, the minotaurs turned on the mugworts. The mugworts tried to flee or fight, but the minotaurs overwhelmed them, killing all present.

As the last mugwort fell, the minotaurs cheered, having reclaimed Ovid, and over Carlton's return. Carlton found no joy, though. He bent over Caelix's body, picking up the dragon-bone sword and examining it.

"We are victorious, my prince!" the minotaur guard said to Carlton. The minotaurs prince nodded his head. "What is wrong?"

Carlton gave an uneasy look. "Caelix is no one. How did he come by this sword, and how did he convince mugworts—two-hundred strong at that—to follow him?"

"He is a minotaur, and we are a proud and stubborn people, my prince."

Carlton snorted. "Too true," he replied, but he did not believe the guard's words to be the answer. He looked down at Caelix's body, pondering, *Did you truly act on your own, or were you a pawn for a greater enemy?*

***

Creeping as a shadow through Dagon, Dar Caine's journey was winding down. He had missed the mighty oaks and pines, and he had longed to hear the cry of elk and running rivers, but he knew much had changed in his father's absence.

"Chief McAdoo?" one of the malobathron guards questioned, as Dar Caine neared.

"No, it is I, Dar Caine."

The guard met Dar Caine and bowed his head. "It is good that you have returned, but where is your father?"

"He is not here."

"Then you must hurry, the others have taken council with your brothers, and they are attempting to take control of the clan."

"Curse them," Dar Caine whispered. "Who has gathered?"

"All of the malobathrons—McConnell, McGleish, Dakin, Durand, Wycuff—but the cordorians were invited too, though I don't know which malobathron did so."

"Cordorians? It must be those filthy McConnell's or Wycuff's, only they would dare defy the malobathron way and lay in bed with our neighboring enemy."

"True, but do not speak evil about the cordorians, not now. With your father gone, the McConnell and Wycuff clans have grown bolder, and I do not trust the loyalties of the other clans."

"I trust the Dakin's for their proven loyalty, and I trust the Durand's for the same, and because they are my mother's kin. The McGleish can be bought since they are nothing but followers."

"The McGleish have grown close to the McConnell's. I would not look to them for support."

Dar Caine grunted. "I will go to them."

The giant's steps held anger and fury. As he passed through the fortress, the other giants were pleased to see his return, though he only grunted as they whispered his name with happiness.

It was not the first time some of the malobathron clans disrespected the McAdoo's. While they were within their rights to hold council, they exceeded that right by looking to replace Njord McAdoo as the High-Chieftain of the Malobathron Clans, especially with four living heirs.

Dar Caine entered his father's hut, finding the council in a heated debate. "Your father has not returned, surely he is dead," a cordorian leader said.

"When have we given our enemy the right to lead us?" Dar Caine asked, making his presence known.

The elders and chieftains looked at Dar Caine, many surprised, but few relieved of his coming. "Dar Caine, son of Njord, welcome," the McConnell Chieftain, Coalton McConnell, replied. "We did not expect you here, or we would have waited."

"Would you?"

"Indeed, you are Chief Njord's eldest."

"What of the cordorians?"

"We have been at peace with them, since your father left," one of the Wycuff elders answered, with a sneer.

Dar Caine nodded his head; his eyes glared at each of them, sharply. "What decisions have we made?"

Some of the chieftains and elders exchanged worried glances. "None, Chief Condorian," the Dakin Chieftain, Drabog Dakin, replied, rising to his feet, "and none will have to be made."

"True," a Durand elder chimed in, "with Chief Condorian's return, there is no need to worry about the McAdoo clan's leadership."

Coalton McConnell smirked. "Chief Condorian? He is no chief."

Dar Caine charged him, but several Dakin's and Durand's held him back. "I carry that title to remember."

"Carry it all you want, it does not make you one," Coalton McConnell answered. "If the McAdoo's want this boy to lead them, so be it, but Chief Njord is not here to lead the six clans. He must be replaced."

"How dare you sulk about my father's halls, like a dog seeking scraps!" Dar Caine shouted.

"I am hurt by your father's absence, too, but we need a new malobathron chieftain," the Wycuff Chieftain, Abner Wycuff, said.

"We can tell that you are torn up by Chief Njord's absence," Drabog Dakin replied. "As for me, I say no change is needed. I will follow his heirs, just as I followed him. The Dakin's are with the McAdoo's."

"If it's a vote, the Durand's stand with you."

"Ah, stand all you want, but we need proven leaders," Coalton McConnell said. "If it's a vote, then you know mine."

Abner Wycuff forced a regretful smile. "I'm truly sorry, but I must back the McConnell's."

Everyone looked at the McGleish Chieftain, Magnuson McGleish. The McGleish's had always been known to act or vote last, even in the early days when Draul was High-King of Prixem. "For now, I will back the McAdoo's."

The McConnell's and Wycuff's exchanged glances. "What of the cordorian's vote?" Coalton McConnell asked.

"This is malobathron business, not cordorian," Dar Caine replied, angrily. "They are lucky I do not practice my grandfather's teaching: *the only good cordorian is a dead one.*"

"Hear me—" the Cordorian Chieftain started saying.

"Hear me, be gone," Dar Caine said. "Be gone, all of you."

Hurriedly, the McConnell's and Wycuff's rose and left, followed by the cordorian giants. The McGleish's gave Dar Caine false smiles and left with their heads hanging.

"It is good to have you back," the Durand Chieftain, Urijah Durand, whispered to Dar Caine, as he led his people out.

"That it is, Chief Condorian," Drabog Dakin chimed in, hugging Dar Caine. He added with a whisper, "This will not be the end; they will attempt to replace your father again. If you leave, you need to name a brother as the acting chieftain."

"I will heed your advice," Dar Caine replied.

"Good, now rest," he said, leading his people out. "And remember, the Dakin's are always with you."

As the Dakin's left, the Halls of Njord McAdoo fell silent. Dar Caine looked to his brothers, Orion and Saul.

"What would you have done?" Dar Caine asked, curious to know his brothers' plan.

"Called on the Dakin's, Durand's, and McGleish's to battle with us, just as before," Saul answered.

Dar Caine smirked. "McGleish's? They would have sided with the McConnell's and Wycuff's had I not been here."

"The Dakin's and Durand's are the strongest," Orion said.

"True, but we are stronger, though you let that image slip by letting cordorians in here," Dar Caine replied.

"Enough of this bickering and lecturing, Dar Caine. Where is father?"

Dar Caine sat down at a table, pouring himself a glass of heavy wine. "There is an evil growing in the east, a fallen Demon Prince, named Dentar. He took father."

"Took him? We must call on the clans and rescue him," Saul said.

Dar Caine grunted. "After what all just happened, you believe the clans would help us? The McConnell's and Wycuff's would rather he stay there, and the McGleish's would quickly change their allegiance."

"Then what are we to do?"

"I am helping a wizard, Telezzar—the same who called for Ehud—and he will try to save father."

"What of us?"

Dar Caine chuckled. "You two will be here, watching and protecting our people. Saul, you will be the acting chief, while I am away."

"What if another council is held?" Orion asked.

"Then both of you will go, and Saul will remind them that I have made him Chief Saul, while father and I are away on business," Dar Caine said, downing the rest of his wine. "Now, if neither of you mind, I wish to rest. Tomorrow, I will speak with the chieftains and elders of the Dakin and Durand clans. I will also speak with the McGleish's and commit them to our side." Dar Caine rose from the table and gave his brothers a wild glare. "And if either of you ever let a cordorian in this hall, again, it will be the last mistake you make."

CHAPTER XXI

To Tartanzuma

Couplets passed, changing the seasons, and soon the time came for Dar Caine to fulfill Telezzar's quest. He left Saul in charge, naming his brother Chieftain of the McAdoo Clan and High-Chieftain of the Malobathron Clans. With nothing else to do, Dar Caine journeyed off to the border of Dagon and Res Publica, waiting for Carlton.

The couplet of Nu was nearing its end, meaning winter was almost over. Already spring's touch was close, as Upsilon patiently waited its turn; some flowers already started to blossom, filling the chilled air with sweet perfumes.

Dar Caine reached the border, well before Carlton. The giant sat on a fallen, hollowed-out tree, passing the time with a smoke. As he settled in for a wait, something caught his attention. His eyes glanced around; he was not alone.

"What is your business, Giant?" an eldred asked, accompanied by a dozen others, all armed with swords and crossbows.

Dar Caine grunted. "I could ask the same, considering you're trespassing on my land."

"Your land? This land belongs to all giants, but it is also known that the elves—our kinsmen—are keepers of the woodland realms."

"Your kinsmen?" Dar Caine asked, laughing aloud.

The eldred's face hardened. "You will remove yourself, or we will take you prisoner."

Dar Caine rose from his seat, towering over the eldred. "This is my forest."

"I told you—"

"I will not repeat myself," the giant said.

The lead eldred nodded to the others, and they readied themselves, but something unexpected happened. From the forest, a woman emerged. She had rigid, bark-brown skin, was lovely to the eyes, and her eyes sat shining like glittering green emeralds.

"Why have you brought evil to this forest?" the woman asked softly, as she approached the eldred.

The eldred glared at her. The woman was no true woman, she was a dryad, but her mystical—yet deadly—beauty did not easily subdue them. "Who are you?" the lead eldred asked.

"I am Tamarisk," she replied. "I felt your presence, and I know you bring evil and mischief. You must leave."

The eldred smirked at her. "We were going to take the giant prisoner; you wish to join him?"

"Don't do anything foolish," Dar Caine warned.

The eldred did not listen, though. At once, two of them charged towards Tamarisk, but Dar Caine, pouncing like a panther, caught them both. As the giant wrestled them, Tamarisk strutted toward the leader.

The other eldred followers charged her, but from the ground, vines shot up, gagging, and dragging them into the earth. The leader's eyes widened, and he turned to flee. As he ran away, he slipped on a root and fell to the ground, and Tamarisk—in no hurry—made her way to him.

"No!" he shouted at her, fumbling for his sword's handle.

She leaned down, bestowing a kiss on his cheek. Immediately, his hand went to where she had kissed him, and he screamed, as if it burned. The eldred began coughing and choking, until he fell back, silent and stiffened as a stone.

"I would have preferred to put an axe-head in him," Dar Caine said, walking to Tamarisk's side.

She returned a devilish grin. "I could have handled all of them."

"What fun would that have been for me?" he bantered back, with a wink. "Thank you, though."

"Anytime," she whispered back, strutting away to the nearest tree. With a smile, she placed her hand on the tree, becoming one with it.

The forest fell silent, again. Dar Caine returned to the hollowed-out tree, passing the time with his pipe. He watched as the ice cycles cried their tears, and the snow began to melt, from the sun's heat. Then, his ears perked to another coming host.

"Where is he?" Dar Caine asked, noticing Carlton was not among the minotaurs.

"Prince Carlton has fallen ill. He sent word to the wizard, and the wizard instructed us to bring the jagg here," one of the minotaurs guards replied.

Dar Caine grunted. "Why is he bound?"

"Why not?"

"He has done nothing wrong. Cut his bonds and be on your way."

The minotaur guard cut Scioto's bonds, releasing him into Dar Caine's care. Without further words, the minotaurs departed. Dar Caine slumped back onto the hollowed-out tree, though, considering a new plan.

"What bothers you, my friend?" Scioto asked.

"I did not have a plan, aside from getting to Tartanzuma, and with Prince Carlton not coming, I feel we need one."

"Our plan should stay the same. Get me to Tartanzuma and I will speak with the jaggarri council, and then we will worry about dealing with the jaggeddi."

Dar Caine nodded his head. "Fair enough."

The giant cleaned his pipe quickly and gathered his pack. Then, the two struck out. It was a twenty-seven-day journey to the Port of Winged Wooly-Rhinos, and they had good luck, making good time and coming across no foul figures.

When they finally reached the port, they found it overcrowded with business—it was almost mid-Upsilon, after all. Scioto had never seen such controlled madness, whereas the giant was used to trading ports. As they walked amongst the stalls, Dar Caine spotted one merchant who carried a careless scowl.

"We're looking for a winged wooly-rhino," Dar Caine said to the goblin merchant. "Are you open to business?"

The goblin smirked and cackled. "First an elf speaking Goblin and now a giant with a jagg. What will be next?"

Dar Caine looked at the goblin, oddly. "When was the elf here? Were there two?"

"I don't reveal information—unless you wish to propose a nice price."

Dar Caine grabbed the goblin by the throat, pinning him against a wall. "Were there two elves?"

"Yes!" the goblin gasped, with a muffled cough. "Two elves and he spoke Goblin. They were my last customers, long ago."

Dar Caine released the goblin and smiled. "If Troy and Nova trusted you, then I do, too."

"I charged him eight pieces of gold."

Dar Caine grunted. "Lower it."

"Take your business elsewhere."

Dar Caine thought of pinning the goblin again, but another idea struck him. "Your sword is rusted, and that armor has seen better days, yes?"

"Yes, but if you're going to propose a duel, then I'd rather spit on you and be forced to chew nails."

"That can be arranged," Dar Caine said, laughing aloud. "No, where I'm going, I could use an old fighter like you."

The goblin stared in disbelief. "Instead of paying me, you're offering me the chance to retaste battle and the closeness of death?"

"It's what you want."

The goblin cackled back. "I will join whatever lost cause you're up against."

Hastily, the goblin merchant cut all his winged wooly-rhinos loose, save two which he, Dar Caine, and Scioto would use to reach Tartanzuma. Once they were ready, they mounted the winged wooly-rhinos and were off.

"You're name, my goblin friend?" Dar Caine asked.

"Groith," the goblin answered. "Ah, I have not battled for many couplets. Long have I yearned for the old days when I could use my blade."

"I knew you had a fighter's heart."

"Indeed! I was once a goblin of high rank, one of the best, but that was long ago."

"What happened?"

Groith shook his head, as sorrow painted his face. "That is a tale for another time."

CHAPTER XXII

The Parley

A thick, green jungle met Dar Caine, Scioto, and Groith. The trees' sticky, thick leaves hung high over their heads, muddy rivers slowly ran upstream, and jungle creatures ran off, at sight of the winged wooly-rhinos.

"The jaggeddi live up stream, in the rich, fertile lands," Scioto said, as he watched the river rush that way.

"And your people?" Dar Caine asked.

Scioto pointed deeper into the forest. "We live in fear, hiding from the jaggeddi."

"Why don't your people fight back?" Groith asked.

"The jaggeddi have always seen us as inferior, but Dentar's poisoned words have made them act out. He disestablished our ways of life, rebuilding a puppet society that he may govern from afar."

"Stick a knife in them all," Groith replied, cackling.

"Enough chatter," Dar Caine said, interrupting, "we need to reach your village before nightfall."

"There is no need to rush," Scioto replied.

"What do you mean?"

Scioto did not answer the giant. From the jungle, several jaggarri hunters emerged, quite happy to see Scioto. He met with them, speaking in the jagg tongue, and explaining all that had happened. The hunters eyed the giant and goblin, hesitant to accept them, but they struck a deal with Scioto, nonetheless.

Scioto returned to Dar Caine and Groith. "They do not trust you, but I have convinced them to take us to the council."

"Then let's go," Groith said.

Scioto placed his hand on the goblin's chest, not letting Groith pass. "You both must surrender your weapons and be bound. That is the only way this works."

"I will not be bound like some wild animal," Dar Caine retorted, heatedly.

"If we wish to speak with the council, then you will do this thing."

"I will not be bound."

"Ah, let them have their way," Groith said, handing over his sword to Scioto. "They are binding all of us."

Scioto smirked. "They are not binding me."

"Wait a moment," Groith replied, in disbelief.

"If we must be bound, then you must be too," Dar Caine said. "After all, we are here to fight for your people and your freedom."

Scioto pondered the giant's words and nodded his head. "I will be bound."

The jaggarri hunters tied the three's hands together and led them away. Each of them felt humiliated by the act—and for their own reasons—but none of them complained aloud. Instead, they followed silently, as the hunters tracked and followed the signs. They had been away from the village since the beginning of spring, hunting to restock the stores used over the winter.

After some time, the hunters brought the three to the village's location. The jaggarri met the hunters with joy, and the council members were among them.

"Is that Scioto?" one of the council members asked.

"He was taken in a raid," another answered.

"I have returned," Scioto said to them.

"It is Scioto!" another exclaimed. "Quickly, cut their bonds!"

The hunters untied the ropes, freeing Dar Caine, Groith, and Scioto. Scioto spoke with the council members, and he told them his tale, and he urged them to listen to the giant. The members exchanged weary glances, but they agreed and called for a meeting.

"I am Dar Caine Condorian, son of Njord McAdoo. I have been sent here, under the orders of the Blue Wizard, Telezzar, to bargain with the jaggeddi and restore balance."

"Bargain?" one of the members sneered.

"You can do nothing!" another shouted.

Dar Caine grunted. "The jaggeddi will agree to my terms, or I will bring war to their doorstep."

Sneers and chidings fluttered through the crowd. "Giants. All of you think alike, believing you can solve any problem with a blade."

"Silence, Jolon," an elder replied. His eyes were aged, but they looked at Dar Caine and he trusted the giant. "We have little hope against the jaggeddi. We should be thankful that he has come to deliver us."

Dar Caine stood tall, proud, and somewhat intimidating. "Show me the way to the jaggeddi, and I will speak with them."

"They will not listen," Jolon replied, and many agreed with him.

"No, they will not," Dar Caine said, "but while I am parleying with them, you will gather your hunters, your warriors, and those that can fight; and be ready for my return."

The council members looked at one another, seeming to debate through the glances and glares. "Give him the map, Jolon, and let him be on his way," the elderly member said.

Jolon rose from his seat and handed the map to Dar Caine. "I do not believe this will work, Giant, but we will rally, as you have asked."

Dar Caine returned a nod, and then turned his own way, meeting Groith outside. "Where is Scioto?" the giant asked.

"Gathering fresh supplies for our trip to the jaggeddi."

"I will need him here, and you will stay with him."

"Why?"

"The jaggarri trust him, and I need their three pieces of electrum for Telezzar," Dar Caine replied, as he walked with Groith to find Scioto. "I do not wholeheartedly trust the council. I believe some would put a knife in all three of us if it meant no war against the jaggeddi."

"Why? Are they not tired of this oppression?"

"Dentar has many spies, and some on the council may be bought."

"How did it go?" Scioto asked, meeting the giant and goblin.

"Well," he replied, "I am going to speak with the jaggeddi, and I have urged the jaggarri to rally and wait for my return."

"I have readied a boat."

"You will not be coming."

"Why?"

"I need you here, to speak with the council on surrendering their electrum to me. I am leaving Groith, too, and as I told him, I do not trust the council."

"You do not know the way, let me come."

Dar Caine shook his head. "I need you here," he replied. "As for the way, I only need to sail upriver, and I will reach the city."

Scioto did not argue, though he did not agree. He and Groith remained behind, with Scioto trying to claim the electrum and Groith keeping an eye out, while Dar Caine left the village.

The giant decided not to use the jaggarri boat, which Scioto had secured. Instead, Dar Caine saw a jaggeddi port on the map, and he made his way for it.

Dense shrubbery filled the lush, green jungle. Massive insects buzzed and crawled about, and monstrous lizards roamed the riverside. The giant watched every step carefully, but in no time, he reached the port.

One rundown shack and a lonely barge made up the port. The jaggeddi bargeman—and port owner—had slimy, green, amphibian-like skin, and he only wore a purple loincloth and had a black patch over one of his yellow eyes.

"I want passage to the city," Dar Caine said.

The bargeman did not understand the common tongue, and he spoke heatedly at Dar Caine in the jagg tongue. The giant grunted and pointed upriver; then, he pulled out two gold pieces, and the bargeman smiled.

With no further words, the bargeman and Dar Caine boarded the barge, and they began to sail up the murky river. The bargeman chanted and sang in the jagg tongue. What he said and sang, Dar Caine could not guess, but he kept a lookout for any foul figures.

The barge sailed on and on, slowly arriving at the jaggeddi city. As they neared, Dar Caine marveled silently, quite impressed with the wealth and display of the jaggeddi. A majestic stone temple loomed over the market square, where spices, silks, and eccentric foods enticed the eyes and filled the nose.

Once at the river's edge, Dar Caine tossed the gold coins to the bargeman and hopped off. The giant weaved his way through the market, admiring it, but the jaggeddi shot evil glares and stares at him. Nonetheless, he made his way for the ruler's home.

The home was not difficult to find. Aside from the temple, there was only one other large and grand-scale building. Dar Caine studied the stones, which made up the home, as many were larger than he was.

"Halt!" one of the royal guards exclaimed.

"I must speak with your ruler."

"You are?" the royal guard asked.

Dar Caine grunted. "I was sent by the Blue Wizard."

The royal guard sent a messanger to the ruler, asking whether to let Dar Caine in or not. In the meantime, the royal guard stood silently, watching the giant's every move. Almost immediately, the messanger returned, though, escorting Dar Caine in.

"Welcome, Malobathron Giant," the ruler said, greeting his guest. His yellow eyes stared at Dar Caine, as his lips smiled, preparing to speak lies, but he did not forget his manners. With a bow, he continued: "I am Chief Ohanzee, and it is a pleasure to be in your presence."

Dar Caine bowed his head back, studying Chief Ohanzee. He wore silky, ocean-blue pants, displaying his wealth, and a robe of wild animal furs, attempting to show his power and fearlessness. "I am Dar Caine, son of Njord and grandson of High King Draul."

Chief Ohanzee raised a hand to his chest, faking an awed expression. "Grandson of the High King? I did not know we entertained such a guest."

"It is I who am entertained, Chief Ohanzee."

Chief Ohanzee smiled, despising the slight. "What may I do for you, Grandson?"

"I am here on behalf of Telezzar, the Blue Wizard."

"Ah, the Blue Wizard," Chief Ohanzee said, musing. "What does he desire of the jaggeddi?"

"Peace. He wants the jaggarri and jaggeddi to be at peace, as they once were, before Dentar's dark magic corrupted your hearts."

Chief Ohanzee smirked and strolled to the window of his chamber. "Come here, Grandon," he said, and Dar Caine walked to the window side. "See how peaceful it is? It has never been this way. Before, it was chaotic, but Dentar has given us the opportunity for peace."

"How is this peace? The jaggarri live in fear."

"A small price, Grandson," Chief Ohanzee replied. "Dentar has shown us the weak link—the jaggarri—and they have been subdued. Tell the Blue Wizard, if he wants the jaggarri free, then he must come make them the rulers of Tartanzuma."

Dar Caine grunted. "I'm afraid you do not understand, Chief Ohanzee, that's why he sent me."

The giant turned away, walking from the throne room, but Chief Ohanzee bantered back, "If you were not here to parley, I would have you slain, Grandson, but when you bring those inferior jaggarri, I will have you then."

CHAPTER XXIII

Second Civil War

"What do you mean, they denied?" one of the jaggarri councilman asked.

"Dentar has given them power, and they see you and your people as a problem. They believe they will win any war that comes," Dar Caine replied, tiredly. He had answered the same question many times, but the jaggarri continually seemed upset.

"We cannot win. We should disband our gathered numbers and go further into the jungle, before the jaggeddi come here," another member advised.

"Before I left, many of you claimed my going to speak with Chief Ohanzee was vain. Why has that changed?"

"We do not answer to you!" a member shouted back.

Dar Caine smirked. "No, but I am your only hope. They want a war; let's take it to them."

"We do not have the means to raid their city," Jolon said, finally speaking up. Many other members agreed, and their chatter swept the room.

"My brothers and friends," Scioto said, stepping before them, "if not now, when? This giant has battled trolls, spidermites, and many others; he is a mighty warrior who I would readily follow. I have not lost faith, and you should not either."

"Your words are good, but careless, Scioto," Jolon replied. "I do not trust the giant."

Dar Caine hung his head. "I was sent here, to claim the electrum of Tartanzuma. I have taken it upon myself to help free you and your people. If freedom seems unkind, then hand me your electrum and I will be on my way."

Jolon and the others exchanged shocked looks, as fear grasped their hearts. Scioto waved his hands, disbanding the giant's invitation. "We need you," he said, looking out to the council, "some of us are just unwise."

"I know," Dar Caine replied, staring at Jolon.

Jolon rose from his feet, pointing at Dar Caine. "You threaten to leave!"

"The jaggeddi do not fear Telezzar; thus, they do not fear you. Dentar has placed them in a lofty position, which means war is inevitable," Dar Caine replied, stepping closer to the council members. "Will you not let me lead you?"

"We are trying to return to our ways of life, to peace and traditions."

"You will never be at peace, so forget your traditions," Dar Caine replied. "The time for war is now, and I am from a warring people, and I will lead you, if you let me."

"Leave us, so the council may discuss a decision," Jolon said.

Dar Caine and Scioto exited the council hut, meeting Groith outside. "We will march soon," Dar Caine said to them, as they made their way to their hut.

"Indeed," Scioto replied, picking up a small bag and handing it to Dar Caine. "This is the electrum. Jolon gave it to me."

Dar Caine opened it, looking at the pieces and smiling. "I need the jaggeddi's."

"What is your plan?"

"We will go ahead of Jolon and the army, sneaking into the jaggeddi city. We will take out the guards and find the electrum."

Before Scioto or Groith could comment on Dar Caine's plan, the hut door opened, and Jolon entered. "We have found two traitors on the council, and if there were any others, they will flee or have a change of heart."

Scioto nodded his head. "This is good news."

"I was worried some had been bought," Dar Caine replied. "Well played, Jolon."

"We cannot thank you enough, Dar Caine."

"I do not need it," the giant replied. "Are your people ready?"

"Yes, we have gathered all hunters, warriors, and those that can fight. We are ready to follow you."

"Good," Dar Caine said. He picked up his pack and looked at Scioto and Groith. "We need to start now."

"Now?" Scioto questioned. "That is not wise. It will be dark soon, and creatures of the night will be hunting."

"It is true, Dar Caine, wait for the morning," Jolon chimed in.

Dar Caine shook his head. "When night comes, the army needs to march, so they may move unseen by jaggeddi scouts. We must attack at sunrise, but the guards must be dealt with before then, so we must leave earlier than the army."

"It is not wise," Scioto argued.

"I'm going," Dar Caine replied. "What are you doing?"

Groith cackled at the question. "I came here to battle, not sit around a village full of jaggs."

Scioto looked at Jolon. "Go with the giant. I can lead our people safely," Jolon said.

"Very well, I will travel with you," Scioto said to Dar Caine.

The three departed from the jaggarri village, into the lush jungles of Tartanzuma. Dar Caine suspected the electrum would be in the great temple and he told Scioto and Groith of his suspicion, and they agreed.

As they traveled farther upriver, they crept through the brush, fearing to walk openly next to the river. None of them spoke to each other, and all was silent. The silence discomforted Scioto. He had grown up hearing stories of the night creatures, and he believed the old tales. Groith seemed ready to fire his crossbow, glancing around at each sound he heard, but Dar Caine breathed easily and listened carefully.

Then it happened. Rushing from some underbrush, two monstrous jungle spiders appeared, screeching, and charging at the giant. Dar Caine spun around, swinging his flails, and seeing him in danger, Scioto and Groith quickly rushed forward to his side.

At first, they struggled to land blows, for the spiders were quick, and their bodies camouflaged with the jungle trees. The first spider attempted to go around them, while the second charged, again.

"Keep your guard," Scioto said. "Their legs are coated with poison."

Dar Caine grunted, swining his flails and landing a blow against the second spider. "I fear nothing!"

Surprised by the blow, the spider fell to its side, and Dar Caine charged it. It stumbled to escape, and the giant raised his flails again, crushing the spider's front legs. Then, he swung again, finishing it.

Groith took aim and shot at the first spider, blinding one of its eyes. Scioto stepped forward, thrusting his spear at it, but it jumped back, avoiding Scioto's attempt. Scioto raised the spear up and threw it, hitting the spider in the side. It shrieked. Groith charged the spider, unsheathing his sword, and he swung at the spider, hacking at its legs.

"Look out!" Dar Caine shouted.

The first spider rose on its hind legs, jutting its stinger towards Groith, but Dar Caine pushed the goblin aside. Then, grabbing the stinger, the giant forced it upward, making the stinger pierce the spider's own chest. The spider stepped back, writhing in pain, and retreated into the jungle.

Dar Caine smirked, as he helped Groith up. "Not bad for an elder."

Groith cackled at the joke. "Don't mock me, or I'll do worse to you."

Scioto stared at the dead spider, shaking his head, and looking at the others. "We should not have come alone. We should wait for Jolon and the others."

"We have wasted enough time battling these spiders; we must hurry ahead," Dar Caine replied.

"There is worse out here, Dar Caine."

"I do not disagree, but if we wait here, then it may find us."

Before Scioto could argue back, Groith pointed to the river. "What is that?" he asked, interrupting them.

Dar Caine and Scioto peered towards the river. "A barge," Scioto said. "Perhaps, we could take it to the city, instead of walking openly or in the jungle brush."

Dar Caine was not as eager. "I believe that is the barge I sailed on to the city." He stared at it, feeling uneasy. "Wait here, while I go search it over."

Scioto and Groith hid back in the shadows, while Dar Caine dashed to the riverbank. He was wrong, it was not the same barge, but he found a gruesome scene aboard it. Quickly, he returned to Scioto and Groith.

"The bargeman is dead, but there is a dead panther, too."

Scioto gave a grave look, but Groith began sniffing the air. "The wind carries something besides the sweet smell of flowers."

"What is it?" Dar Caine asked, readying his flails.

"I was a scout in my warring days, and I have not smelled such a scent since."

"What is it?"

Groith locked eyes with Dar Caine. "A werewolf."

"No," Scioto replied, "the creature does not live on Tartanzuma."

Dar Caine grunted. "This is not your Tartanzuma, it is Dentar's."

"We need to move on," Groith urged. "Make for the barge."

"No, we can take it," Dar Caine said.

"No, Groith is right, make for the barge," Scioto said, rising to his feet, and planning to run it. Then, everything happened at once.

"No, Scioto!" Groith shouted.

The werewolf tackled Scioto to the ground, drooling with delight. Before Dar Caine or Groith could react, the creature tore off Scioto's left arm, leaving the jagg in a pool of blood.

"Scioto!" Dar Caine shouted. Without any thought, he charged the creature, and the two began to circle one another, slinking-like.

Meanwhile, Groith rushed to Scioto's side. "We're losing him, Dar Caine."

At those words, the giant swung his flails wildly, cornering the werewolf against a tree. The creature desired the taste of blood, though, and it leaped forward at Dar Caine, who swung his flails, delivering a blow that would have crushed any man.

"Give in to me," the werewolf barked, in a gravelly voice.

Swiftly, Dar Caine swung his flails, again, crushing the werewolf's head. The creature slunk back, howling in pain and anger. Dar Caine grabbed it, hugging it tightly and breaking several bones, and Groith picked up his crossbow, firing all his darts at the werewolf, until its head hung lifelessly.

Dar Caine threw down the werewolf, running to Scioto's side. "Will he survive?"

"I believe he will be fine, but he has lost much blood," Groith replied. "He cannot be moved."

"This is my fault."

Groith finished tying some cloth around the wound, restricting the loss of blood. "There's no time to wallow. You must reach the city and finish what you started."

"I cannot leave you and Scioto."

Groith smirked. "There is nothing you can do here."

Dar Caine knew he was right. "I'll be back for you."

Rising to his feet, the giant turned to the barge and boarded it, starting upriver. He felt guilty about Scioto's wound and for leaving him and Groith behind, but he had to reach the city.

On and on the barge sailed through the dark, until the city came into sight. Dar Caine rummaged about, finding rich linens, golden and sapphire rings, and a refined golden bracelet embedded with rubies and diamonds. He donned the linens and jewelry, disguising himself as a wealthy merchant. As the barge hit the dock, he noticed a jug of wine, and he picked it up, taking a swig.

"Who are you?" one of the dock-guards asked.

With a massive grin, Dar Caine jumped up on the dock, flaunting his rich appearance. "Can you not see? I am a wealthy merchant, looking to sell my goods! See my barge? It is filled to the brim with linens and jewels!"

The guard stepped next to him, examining him, and looking into the barge. Meanwhile, Dar Caine downed the last of the strong wine, and overwhelmed with confidence, he kicked the guard into the river.

At the sight of this, a second guard appeared. Dar Caine rolled his eyes, and with a swing, he crushed the empty jug against the second guard's head, and the guard fell unconscious.

The first guard grappled and climbed aboard the barge, clearly angry. Before he could say a word, Dar Caine jumped back aboard the barge, grabbed the guard, and repeatedly slammed him against the dock, until the guard slouched unconscious.

Dar Caine left the barge again and strolled to the temple. *Such a glorious temple*, he thought, looking at it. The outer walls seemed to be carved from ivory, and the burning incense inside filled the air with a peaceful aroma, though it bothered the giant's drunkened mind.

He made his way into the temple, and though he admired the outside, he awed at the temple's innards. Across from the great doorway, a gigantic statue of a golden serpent stood, and before it, there was a table with a bowl of blood, a bloodstained sword, and four pieces of electrum.

"This is too easy," he whispered to himself. With a smirk, he strutted toward the table, but as he neared the statue, the floor beneath him gave way to a pit.

Thud! The giant hit the bottom of the pit hard, and immediately, he wished he had not touched the bargeman's wine. After a moan, he chuckled to himself. *At least there are no spikes.*

The pit would have been deep to a jagg, but Dar Caine easily climbed out, and as he dusted himself off, he found company waiting for him. "Stop," a jaggaddi soldier ordered.

Dar Caine grunted. "Would your god be pleased if you spilt blood in this temple?"

"No jaggeddi may be slain, but you are a stranger to these lands," a high priest answered.

Dar Caine shrugged. "Dentar must be an exception?"

"He is a peace maker!"

"I have heard," Dar Caine replied, noticing a window above the great doorway. "As a giant, though, I have more surprises."

Quickly, he turned and grabbed the electrum, slipping it into his pack. The guards began to chase him. Then, Dar Caine scurried up the golden serpent, and many of the guards stood in shock, surprised that the giant would defy their god. Once atop the statue, though, Dar Caine pushed against the wall, tipping the serpent forward.

"Run!" the jaggeddi cried out, as the statue fell and crumbled on them.

While the serpent fell, Dar Caine leaped off, grabbing hold of a hanging chandelier. Rocking back and forth, the giant swung himself forward, taking hold of the next chandelier, and he continued doing so until he swung out the window.

"Fool!"

Fool? his mind echoed. He fell between a conscious and unconscious state of mind, but he could feel the jaggs taking hold of him.

"Let me go!" he shouted, beating them back.

"Calm down, Dar Caine," a familiar voice said.

"Jolon?"

"Yes, and your exit was quite impressive, my friend," Jolon said, laughing aloud.

Dar Caine rubbed his head; his senses were numb, but his memory was not gone. "Groith and Scioto?"

"We found them, and they are well."

Sitting up, Dar Caine looked around the city. The jaggarri were storming it, taking the jaggeddi by surprise. "How did you enter unseen? I never took out the guards."

Jolon laughed, again. "When we arrived, all of the guards were in the temple, so we quietly entered and then attacked."

"Chief Ohanzee?" Dar Caine asked.

"Ah," Jolon said, smiling, "I was going to pay him a visit. You may join if you wish."

Dar Caine rose to his feet, joining Jolon and several other jaggarri soldiers. They marched into Chief Ohanzee's home, where he had already been subdued.

"Oh, please! Mercy!" Chief Ohanzee cried.

"Why?" Dar Caine asked.

"Dentar commanded the jaggeddi to do his will, and I was only a pawn in his grand scheme!"

Jolon smirked. "That is what the giant tried to convey at the parley."

"I understand it now! I understand all things!"

"Be quiet," Dar Caine grumbled. Chief Ohanzee's pleas only worsened his headache. "I told you that I would free the jaggarri, but you would not listen."

"You win! You both win! I submit!"

Jolon sent a sharp kick to Chief Ohanzee's chest. "You are nothing but a dog's feast."

Chief Ohanzee's eyes widened. "N-no, please," he begged, "I will do anything to avoid death."

"Take off your clothes and go out to your people," Dar Caine ordered.

Chief Ohanzee began to weep. "Please, leave me my slice of dignity before my death."

"Strip him," Jolon said to his soldiers.

While the chief wailed, the jaggarri stripped him of his royal blue and purple silks, casting them all aside. Jolon and Dar

Caine each took hold of Chief Ohanzee, escorting him to the throne room's window.

"Tell your people to surrender," Jolon said to him.

"Help me! Help me!"

Jolon held Chief Ohanzee out the window, returning a cold glare. "Dentar is not here to save you, Ohanzee."

With those words, Jolon let go and Ohanzee fell to the streets below, bloody, bruised, and dead. Just as Jolon had said, the dogs soon found Ohanzee's body, feasting and devouring it. The second civil war was far from over, but the victory dealt a hard blow to the jaggeddi and Dentar.

CHAPTER XXIV

The Blue Dragon

Riding a black stallion, Telezzar approached the countryside of Greenwald, where leprechauns lived in the Hidden Forest. Of course, the Hidden Forest was not truly hidden at all. The old forest gained its name because of the many folks who lived in it, who enchanted their homes to keep them hidden from unsavory eyes.

Telezzar's slender stallion made her way down the winding, icy cobblestone walkways, past little cottages, and snow-covered gardens, where many leprechauns shot wary glances as they sat down for hot tea. He did not care, though. He took in deep breaths, savoring the scents of chilled blossoms and pipe smoke. He enjoyed the old and enchanted lore of the leprechauns, and even the short elves.

As Telezzar and the stallion reached the last little cottage, he slowed her to a stop. There, it sat. Lars's home, but it seemed no one was home, from the curtain drawn windows and soundless grounds.

"Lars, open the door," Telezzar said, knocking.

Placing his ear against the door, the wizard could hear the scampering of feet, and then a reply: "Telezzar, you cannot come in!"

Telezzar stared at the door, returning an odd look. "If you do not open this door, I shall."

"But—" Lars sighed. It was hopeless. *Snap, snap* went the locks, and the door cracked open. "Come in."

"That is better," Telezzar replied, entering.

"'That is better'! 'That is better'! Is that all you can say?"

"You have not been pleasant yourself, but thank you for letting me in."

"Oh, Telezzar, you've put me in trouble."

"Trouble?"

"I was a disgrace before, but now, it's even worse. Everyone thinks I killed William! But the worse part is the dark creatures, lurking about."

Telezzar tilted his head, surprised. "Dark creatures? What dark creatures?"

"Dire wolves," Lars replied, as he shakily poured himself a cup of hot tea, "and dozens of them. Its like they are after something."

Telezzar nodded his head, as if agreeing. "Well, you and I are about to have an adventure, so we will be far from your dire wolves."

"What if they follow us? Perhaps, I should stay."

"Nonsense," Telezzar replied, taking a cup of hot tea from Lars. "Everything has been set. We go to Thracia to see if they will join us in the coming war, and afterwards, we will hunt electrum with the bard, Bono Vox."

"The bard?"

Telezzar nodded his head, sipping his tea. "Dar Caine spoke highly of the bard. On my return from Gilon and the east, I met him in Thracia, and we arranged for him to join us, with a few companions."

Telezzar took another sip of his tea, cringing his nose. "This is quite strong, but good for the spirit."

"Yes—well, thank you," Lars replied, taking a sip himself. "Telezzar, it is good to see you again."

"I, too, always cherish seeing myself, even though I need a mirror."

The two laughed at the wizard's quip and finished their tea. Telezzar grabbed his staff from the mantle side, while Lars slipped on his lucky jacket and gathered his pack. He joined Telezzar by the mantle and stared fondly at a picture of William.

"Will I ever see him again, Telezzar?"

The wizard glanced at the picture, returning a fretful smile as his answer. "I think we should be on our way."

The two stepped out of the cottage, and mounted Telezzar's black stallion. With a whistle, she was off while Lars stared back, until the cottage disappeared.

For two days, nothing changed. Small willow trees, little streams, and cottages filled their view, as they bounded through the Hidden Forest. It was strange to Lars, though, since the journey should have been much longer, but there was a strange sensation—a magical sensation.

After those two days, the scenery changed, as the mighty evergreens and vast rivers of Res Publica came into sight. At the border, Telezzar slowed the stallion and set her free.

"How will we reach Thracia?" Lars asked, confused by the wizard's doings.

"Watch," Telezzar replied, and a thunderous laugh followed, as he began transforming into the Blue Dragon.

Lars's eyes widened in horror and disbelief. "Telezzar!" he shouted, staring in awe. "Your talons are like gold spears, and your hide glistens like an ocean of sapphires. You appear...you appear magnificent!"

"Magnificent?" the Blue Dragon questioned. "Do I not appear magnificent when I am a wizard?"

Lars's mouth fell agape, bumbling for an answer. "No! No, no, you do! But in this form, you seem majestic. Not that you are not majestic in your wizard form...I'd better stop talking."

Telezzar bellowed with laughter. "Come, Lars, you will ride on my back to Thracia."

Lars climbed up the dragon's great sapphire wing, positioning himself safely on Telezzar's back. With a roar, like a thousand shouting voices, the Blue Dragon jumped into the air, spread his wings, and flew off towards Thracia.

Lars stared at everything below, and everything seemed so small, with the trees like sticks and boulders like stones. The clouds, which seemed soft and large from the ground, seemed not so large, and they obscured the leprechaun's view, as the Blue Dragon flew into them and on higher.

Now a flight from Res Publica to Thracia should have taken some time, but Telezzar cast a spell, speeding the flight to Thracia. Below them, Res Publica gave way to Nethinims, Nethinims gave way to the Underground World of Ashturim, and Ashturim gave way to the Woodlands of Eliel, until finally they entered Thracia.

"Fort Hellen," the Blue Dragon said, "that is where we will be meeting Bono Vox."

With that, the dragon landed on the outskirts of Fort Hellen, where Lars dismounted. "Why do they have a fort?"

Telezzar grunted and groaned, as he transformed back into his wizard form. "It is always uncomfortable changing back," he said, gasping for air. He raised his head, combing back his black hair, and his blue eyes looked over the fort. "They believe the Copper Dragon is a threat."

Lars's eyes widened, surprised. "Is he?"

"Of course not," Telezzar replied, with a smirk. "Now come, we have dallied long enough."

The two entered the fort, through the massive iron gates. It was filled with soldiers and horsemen, wearing armor, chainmail, and clothes of forest green etched with a golden boar sigil. Even the horses were adorned in clothes and blankets of forest green with the golden boar.

"Everything is large again," Lars whispered, depressingly.

"What?"

"Nothing, Telezzar."

"All right, keep up."

Further into the fort, there were few merchants and tradesmen, dealing in weapons, food, and goods. There were several stables, an armory, a forge, and then it caught Lars's eye. The inn.

Telezzar led them straight into the inn and to a table, where Bono Vox waited with two unfriendly looking characters.

"Friends of yours?" Telezzar asked, taking a seat at the table.

"Best swordsmen in Thracia," Bono Vox replied, with a dazzling grin. "Gwydon and Riger Groundspeed, rangers."

Telezzar nodded his head at each of them, studying them. Both had long, hollow faces, wily and unkempt hair, and cloaks of black and forest green.

The wizard turned his attention back to Bono Vox. "What news of Thracia?"

"I couldn't receive an audience with the king, but I spoke to some contacts in the court. The generals are pushing for war, but—" Bono Vox stopped short, glancing about, and leaning towards the wizard. "Some of my contacts belive someone, or something, is counseling the king, secretly. Whatever it is, it has persuaded him against war."

Telezzar mused over the bard's words. "The seed has been planted, hopefully it blossoms. We can do nothing more now, so let us shift our attentions."

"The electrum?" Lars asked.

"Indeed, and I believe I know where all the electrum is located here, on Padavona."

"Where?" the other four seemed to whisper excitedly, in unison.

"Odie possessed three, and his brother, Arthur, had two. I believe that dwarf clerics gave these pieces to both gneiss, but we are still missing two. While I have heard rumor that one is in the Marshes of Cameroon, under the protection of the Bdellium Knights, I do know one rests with my old friend, Thaddeus, in the Forest of Shiloh."

"The Bdellium Knights have one?" Bono Vox asked.

"Yes, and if we intend to reforge all seven swords, we will need that piece."

"Who is Thaddeus, Telezzar?" Lars asked.

"Each plain is blessed with a Protector of the Land, with their purpose being to protect nature. Thaddeus is the one for Prixem," Telezzar replied, holding back hesitantly. "They are also skin changers, much like the giants of the north or doppelgangers of old Tartanzuma."

"Is it wise to trust a skin-changer?" Riger Groundspeed asked. "After all, they always seem to become corrupt in the end."

"Whatever you have heard, is nothing but foolish old wives-tales. Thaddeus is an old friend of mine, one who I trust with my life."

Gwydon and Riger Groundspeed exchanged glances and shrugs. "All right, Wizard, we are with you."

With those words, the rangers finished their lagers, while Bono Vox took Telezzar and Lars to one of the stables, where the bard had already purchased four horses. When the rangers were done, they exited the inn and mounted their horses, following Telezzar and Lars, while Bono Vox took up the rear.

CHAPTER XXV

Protector of the Land

The sky began to darken, as night creeped in, and the sun's last rays lingered in the western sky, like thin fingers. The lights of Fort Hellen's safety were dim, and almost unseen by the five companions. Ahead lay nothing, but to the right, the silhouttes of towering mountains—the Mountains of the Copper Dragon—could be seen.

"We should ride straight for Shiloh, rather than southward toward the mountains," Riger Groundspeed said to Telezzar, and Gwydon nodded his head in agreement.

"Nonsense, there is no reason to fear the dragon," Telezzar replied, looking to the mountains. He smiled and thought of his brother, Alwran, who was the Copper Dragon.

Lars had spoken of dark creatures in the Hidden Forest, and Bono Vox had spoken of evil counselors to the king. If spies of the enemy were afoot, they would not dare follow the companions so close to Alwran's mountains, in fear that Alwran might eat them. This plan eased Telezzar's mind, but he did not reveal this to his companions.

"I hear it preys on travelers," Gwydon said, backing Riger Groundspeed's concerns. "There are many tales that the dragon asks for payment, and if one cannot pay, it will eat them."

Telezzar laughed aloud. "He is a sly dragon that enjoys riddles and riches, but we do not need to fear."

"What about the tales of the dragon having six limbs? Are those false?" Riger Groundspeed asked.

"No, those are quite true," Telezzar replied. "As I said, he enjoys riddles and riches, with the occasional mischief, but we have nothing to fear."

Though Telezzar's assurance did not calm anyone, but himself, he was right. Alwran would not dare stop the group, not with Telezzar present, and leading them.

They pushed southward for two days, closer toward Alwran's mountains, and none of them slept well, save Telezzar. On the third day of their travels—and feeling it was safe—Telezzar had the group turn eastward, towards Shiloh. They kept this path for four days, until they came to the forest's edge.

The Forest of Shiloh seemed to have an infinite number of trees, but they were regarded as the fairest of Padavona. While folklore attempted to capture the beauty and nature of the trees, they always fell short. The trees of Shiloh had seen many life spans. They remembered the beginning of Prixem, the Fall of King Kota and the darkness that followed, High-King Draul, the rise of men and paladins, and the many great wars fought against the goblins. Indeed, there was much to remember.

"Amazing, aren't they?" Telezzar asked, marveling at the trees.

"If you find trees beautiful," Riger Groundspeed replied.

"Oh, I do," the wizard said, "this forest, remembers many things, and that is why dark creatures wish to tear it down. If what should be remembered is torn down, then how will we remember?"

The group moved on, silently. After a short while, they dismounted from their horses, as the forest became too dense, and they continued on foot.

As they traveled on, Bono Vox took out his lyre and played a melodious tune, while Riger Groundspeed and Gwydon trekked ahead and scouted. Lars dragged his weary body on, but Telezzar stayed by him, helping him along.

"We are not far from Thaddeus's hut," the wizard said.

Deeper and deeper, they traveled; and the deeper they went, the more they found the trees living closely together. Telezzar knew the right paths, though, and he took over guiding them to the hut.

Then, a great rumbling filled the air, and they all looked to each other in fear, save Telezzar. "Who marches so openly?" a deep voice asked.

"It is Telezzar," the wizard said, removing his hat and bowing.

"What is going on?" Riger Groundspeed asked.

Before the wizard could answer, a group of trees shuffled about and surrounded them, joyfully swarming the wizard. "Telezzar, our dear friend, how have you been?"

"I have been well. I have come to see Thaddeus."

The trees parted back, like a veil, at Thaddeus's name, and the companions were surprised to find his hut sitting on the other side of the trees.

From the hut, a stocky, giant man exited, brushing back his wily, chipmunk-brown hair. His leafy green eyes met the wizards, and he smiled with delight. "Telezzar, I have missed our long talks, my friend!"

"The oldest and wisest of us all, I have missed your tales," Telezzar replied, waving for his companions to follow.

"If your heart desires tales, then I shall tell them all through the night. Surely, you will stay and continue your travels tomorrow?"

"Of course," Telezzar replied. "Where are my manners, though? Please, let me introduce my traveling party."

Thaddeus gave a hearty laugh. "You are either utterly brave or exceedingly dim-witted to be traveling with this wizard!"

Telezzar laughed at Thaddeus's quip, bantering back, "What does that make you, for claiming me as a friend?"

The two laughed some more, but Thaddeus finally settled, and gestured for the companions to meet him. "Friends of Telezzar, you are most welcome here, in this forest and in my house. Come, tell me your names and ask for any wish, which your heart desires."

Bono Vox stepped forward, with a slight bow. "I am Bono Vox, a bard from Thracia. It has always been my wish to see the most powerful magical instrument."

"Ah, a lover of music," Thaddeus replied, musing for a moment. "I do possess such an instrument." He reached into his satchel, pulling out a beautifully fashioned harp of gold. "This was the harp of the former Elf Queen Eden."

Bono Vox stared in awe. "It is most eloquent."

"It is yours."

"Mine?" Bono Vox asked, voice quivering.

"Indeed," Thaddeus replied. "The harp's body is that of a golden horn from a chastel goat, and the strings are from the hairs of angels, which merfolk provided."

The bard's finger trembeled, as he reached out to take it. Even Telezzar was surprised. "How did you come by this?" the wizard asked.

"Her ladyship bequeathed it to me upon her death, for I was the one who provided the chastel goat's golden horn." Thaddeus smiled, reminiscing about Queen Eden, but it was only for a moment. "Come, which of you is next?"

"I am Lars, from Hidden Forest. I-I wish to see a jewel crafted from the stars."

Thaddeus reached into his cloak. "I possess a small collection of jewels crafted from the heavenly stars, and I bestow them unto you."

Lars stared in disbelief at the glittering starlight jewels. "I-I will always treasure these. Thank you."

Riger Groundspeed and Gwydon stepped forward, ready to receive their gifts. "I am Riger Groundspeed, and this is Gwydon. We both wish for immortality."

Thaddeus eyed the rangers, as if he had expected such a request. "Immortality is a myth, but I offer you both a vial of water from a secret stream, which gives the trees of this forest longevity."

The rangers greedily accepted the vials, marveling over them. "This water delays death?"

"Indeed," Thaddeus replied, "but you will not live forever, and the water can only delay aging death, not death by battle."

After passing out the gifts, Thaddeus ushered them into his hut, and they all sat around a great table, while he continued making vegetable soup. Lars and the rangers marveled at their gifts, while Bono Vox played a tune on his harp. Thaddeus poured them each a cup of meady ale, followed by rich bread and bowls of soup.

"This soup is quite good," Lars said, blowing gently on his and taking another bite.

"Thank you, it is not much, but I hope you all enjoy."

"Any news, Thaddeus?"

The giant man shook his head, resembling a lion with a wild mane. "All goes the same. Dire wolves enter the forest with goblins, they burn and tear down trees, and then go back to the marshes."

"It will only grow worse, I'm afraid," the wizard replied.

"Too true, my friend, though odd things are beginning to stir," Thaddeus replied, sitting back in his massive chair. "The goblins of the marshes are disappearing. Rumor is they are all being called to Ashdod."

"The dire wolves?"

"That's odd, too. Few go to Ashdod, most stay in the marshes, but many are going north, toward the elf woodlands."

Telezzar mused at these words. "Some have made their way to Hidden Forest."

"Dire wolves that far north?" Thaddeus asked, shaking his head. "That's not good, Telezzar. A war is coming, no doubt, but dire wolves have not been that far north since King Kota's fall."

"I know that is what troubles me."

"And me, I remember those darks days too well."

"What happened last time?" Lars asked.

Thaddeus gave a fretful look. "All fell into darkness and despair. With King Kota's fall, the elves were not the same. If it weren't for Draul and the giants, none of us would be sitting here."

"Was it that bad?"

Thaddeus grunted. "It was. None of the races, save the elves, dwarfs, and giants, were ready for the goblin onslaughts. You must remember the Shallow Bread eating had just happened; before that, the other races did not know of evil, war, or weapons. That is why the elves goverened them.

"Sadly, the dwarfs locked themselves away. The elves would not unite to fight the goblins, though they did fight. Draul rallied and united the malobathron clans, and he and his people saved us."

"It is not the same this time, Thaddeus," Telzzar said. "We are better prepared, with armies and fighters and even the Paladin Order."

"You may be right, but you're still outnumbered."

Telezzar gave a concerned look. "What else have you seen, Thaddeus?"

"Vampires and werewolves," Thaddeus replied, "they have been running rampant through the forest."

"Are they attacking?"

"No, they are going north, toward the elf woodlands," Thaddeus replied. "I don't know what is coming, Telezzar, but I hope you have a plan because I fear for the north and the elves."

All fell silent, as the conversation died. The bowls of soup, plates bread, and cups of ale sat empty. Telezzar thought of dismissing everyone, save himself and Thaddeus, but he chose not to.

"I do have a plan, and that is why we are here."

"I'm not joining your fight, if that's why you're here, Telezzar. My duty is to protect this forest."

"This forest would fall, if you ever left," Telezzar said, smiling and knowing it was true. "You have electrum, yes?"

Thaddeus smirked. "Your sister told me of this."

"Then, you know my intentions?"

"Of course," Thaddeus replied, "but I am torn. At first, I did not want to part with it, but after a long talk with her, she convinced me otherwise."

Thaddeus placed the electrum on the table and slid it over to the wizard. "I will trade you anything of equal value, my friend," Telezzar said.

"I need nothing."

"You give this freely?"

"There is nothing free about it, Telezzar. Electrum cannot save you."

CHAPTER XXVI

King of the Cavern

When morning came, Telezzar and the others were greeted by a lovely breakfast. Thaddeus had laid out a meal of honey biscuits with many jams and fresh milk. They ate and were merry, but no words were spoken about the night before and the electrum.

After breakfast, Telezzar and the companions gathered their packs, and Thaddeus gave them a bundle of food and fresh water.

"Where will you go, Telezzar?" Thaddeus asked, as he escorted the group to the edge of his land.

"The marshes, though I know they are not safe."

Thaddeus pulled at his scruffy beard, with a hesitant look. "You cannot enter by the main road, anymore. Birds and beasts have been whispering to me, the Bdellium Knights are hiding in the marshes."

"I mean to enter by a hidden path."

"What path?"

"There is a cavern that connects the Lake of Abdullum and the marshes. There is only one way in on each side of the cavern, and most of the chambers are flooded."

Thaddeus gave a worrisome grunt. "You speak of the King's Cavern. Be careful, I would not take that path, unless pressed."

"We already are."

"Will there be witches and warlocks in the marshlands?" Lars asked, interrupting the conversation.

"There's worse than that," Riger Groundspeed replied, snickering.

"It is no laughing matter," Thaddeus said, snippily. "There are vampires and werewolves in the marshlands, and to answer you, Lars, yes, there are witches and other foul creatures."

Lars gave a hard swallow. "Other creatures?"

"Yes," Thaddeus said, stopping and looking over the group one last time. "You must remain vigilant in the marshes, and I wish you each goodspeed and safety."

"You have been a most gracious host, as always, Thaddeus," Telezzar said, tipping his hat.

"I hope I may do it again," he replied, with an uncertain grin.

With that, Telezzar led the group on, away from the care and shelter of Thaddeus. Lars wished they had spent more time at the hut, but then again, the electrum was important.

The group trudged on, making their way to Abdullum, which was a two-day journey. When they arrived at Abdullum, the howls of dire wolves pierced the air. Though they were in Shiloh still, it was no longer safe.

For five days, they crept along Abdullum's banks, hiding, and making their way for the hidden path. Telezzar led them, but sometimes, the rangers would go off to hunt for small game.

Then as night came, a misty fog rolled in. The cool breeze gave them little comfort, it only put them on edge, and it became hard to travel, due to the slick mud.

"We are here," Telezzar said, slowly approaching the cavern's mouth.

The others stopped, gazing at the shallow, murky river that flowed from the cavern into the lake. Trees blocked the light of the stars and moon, casting shadows about the ground. The wizard waved his hand, gesturing for them to follow, and they did.

"Are you sure this is safe?" Riger Groundspeed asked.

"Most certainly," Telezzar answered.

Pebbles crunched beneath their feet, as they walked closer to the cavern's barren mouth. No light came from it, yet there seemed to be an eerie enticement about it. As it captivated their imaginations, a sharp howl filled the air, and they all glanced at one another. Then, silence.

"You were mad to bring us here," Riger Groundspeed whispered, with sword drawn.

"We can point fingers later, follow me."

Splash! Splash! Telezzar dashed into the cavern. A second sharp howl pierced the air, and quickly, the others followed him.

Did we lose him? Lars thought, as he followed Bono Vox. At least, he thought it was Bono Vox. Was he following anyone? He had entered with three—not including Telezzar who dashed off—but now, the leprechaun heard no splashing footsteps but his own.

The cavern was completely dark since the moonlight outside had faded from sight. Anxiety filled Lars. He opened his mouth to call for Telezzar, but before he could, a white light shone all around. It was the wizard's orb.

"Good, we are all present," Telezzar said, as Lars joined them.

Lars looked around, noticing gems and hidden treasures, which the orb's light revealed. "Telezzar, what is this place?"

The wizard grinned, and turned away, walking deeper into the cavern. "There is a myth, dear Lars. A myth that this cave was once overflowing with riches, until Men of Gilon claimed the cavern because of its beauty."

"What happened to them?"

"That is a fair question. Some say the men waged war against one another, and the cavern lost its beauty, becoming a bloody battlefield. Others claim the spirit of the cavern poisoned the water, thus creating the Marshes of Cameroon." The wizard paused, as he glanced about. "Nonetheless, the cavern's beauty is forever lost."

They weaved through the cavern, making their way to the end. Jagged rocks jutted upwards, cutting at their cloaks and boots, and at times, the ceiling was so low that they had to crawl. No matter the level of the ceiling, though, water continually dripped, echoing, and ringing and pelting the group.

"Something is not right," Telezzar said, stopping in his steps.

While the others looked at him, Gwydon looked ahead. "I see an exit!"

"No," Telezzar replied, but it was too late, Gwydon was trekking toward the light.

A shriek and a howl filled the air, as short, green figures tackled Gwydon, and started for the others.

"Goblins!" Riger Groundspeed shouted, drawing his sword.

The goblins were clad in ancient armor, carrying short swords and spears. They howled and they snorted, but they knew not to attack, for they were not foolish and knew Telezzar was a wizard.

"Surrender, you're outnumbered!" one of the goblins spat. The other goblins jeered, screeching, and making horrifying faces.

Telezzar studied the situation, but he knew a fight would be foolish. "Hand over your weapons."

The goblins laughed, as they collected the swords, spears, knives, and the wizard's staff. "You are now captives of the King of the Cavern," several of the goblins announced.

With that, the goblins pushed and prodded the group away from the exit. Despair settled in each of their hearts. The goblins led them down dark hallways, and none of them could see in the dark, save Lars since he was a leprechaun, but he was too afraid to keep track of the path. Riger Groundspeed and Gwydon attempted to track the way, by feeling their way, but the jagged walls cut their hands deeply. Telezzar listened to his surroundings, noticing the goblins were taking them deeper into the cavern's heart.

"Telezzar, who is the King of the Cavern?" Bono Vox asked.

"No one truly knows. The Men of Gilon fear and respect him, for he is neither an enemy, nor a friend, but he despises the Bdellium Knights."

"What will he do with us?"

"That remains to be seen."

The goblins pushed them into a large room, which they presumed to be the throne room. In the midst, there lay a pit ablazed with a mighty fire, and as the fire flickered, the walls glittered with precious, unmined gems.

Above them, elevated on a monstrous pile of skulls and bones of slain vampires and werewolves, the King of the Cavern sat on his throne. They could not see his face—he wore a mask of bones—but they could feel his cold glare, as his blood-red eyes stared at them.

"Oh, King of the Cavern, we bring trespassers!" one of the goblins proclaimed, while others chanted ritual prayers, waiting for him to spill their blood.

The King of the Cavern rose from his throne, reavealing his sandy, tanned skin. If he had been a man, it was long ago, for in blood, there were markings engraved on his chest that read: *Last of the Great Ones.*

"You fools," the King of the Cavern growled, "one of Balor's is among them. Would you have the Lord of the Void descend upon us?"

Telezzar was surprised by the turn of events, and he stepped forward. "He will spare you, if you let us leave."

The King of the Cavern eyed him carefully. "You are the one?"

"Yes, I am Balor's son. Telezzar the Blue, they call me."

"My apologies for this misunderstanding, Telezzar the Blue. I wish no wrath from your father."

Shrieks and howls filled the room. "No! Kill them! The gods wish for blood!" many goblins shouted in unison.

The King of the Cavern took out his dagger, cutting open the nearest goblin. "There is your gods' blood. Now, release these prisoners where they were found, and let no harm come to them."

Quickly and fearfully, the goblins obeyed the King of the Cavern, releasing the companions from their bonds, and taking them back to the cavern's exit. Once there, the goblins left them, going back to their dark tunnels.

"What was all that about?" Riger Groundspeed asked, confused by it all.

"These are ancient goblins, who worship pagan gods of old, and the King of the Cavern offers them shelter and safety to worship here. In return, they do his bidding and slay any aligned with the Bdellium Knights," Telezzar said.

"Yes, but why did they release us?"

"He knew I was a child of Balor, and he feared my father would punish him."

"What would he have done?" Lars asked, curiously.

The wizard shrugged. "Nothing, most likely."

"Nothing?" several of them asked, in unison.

"Our ways are not like yours. We are here to protect, not meddle," Telezzar said. "Now, let us shift our attention to the marshes."

"What is our plan?" Riger Groundspeed asked.

Telezzar mused silently, pondering what could have happened with the electrum. "The electrum is being used as bait, so we will spring the trap," Telezzar replied, "as for its whereabouts, the Bdellium Knights would be foolish to keep the electrum with them, so I believe that a trusted servant has it."

"Probably a witch or warlock," Bono Vox replied.

"No, I would give it to a vampire or werewolf," Riger Groundspeed said.

"No, no, the minds of vampires and werewolves are too crazed," Telezzar replied.

"A warlock or witch," Bono Vox pressed.

"A hag," Lars chimed in.

"A hag," Telezzar murmured to himself. "Yes, an ugly, powerful witch who has the ability to transform herself into a beautiful maiden. A perfect protector."

"Why a hag? I do not believe we are looking for one," Riger Groundspeed said.

"Why not?" Telezzar asked. "Does it bother you that the enemy might trust a woman with something important, whereas you would not?"

Riger Groundspeed's face turned red. "I still say you're wrong, Wizard."

"I say we should stop squabbling," Bono Vox cut in, as he cleaned the tinted lens to his glasses. "We should move on before something else finds us."

"Quite right," Telezzar said, leading them into the boggy marshes, "but first, we must find a place to rest, so I may restore my powers."

CHAPTER XXVII

The Hag

After trudging through the marshes, they found a hillside with a cave. Telezzar placed an invisibility spell on the entrance and cast a second spell to cover their scent.

Knowing they were safe, everyone found a spot to lie down and sleep. Telezzar could not rest, though. He sat at the cave's mouth, watching the mist roll over the marshy woodland below, like an eagle from a highly perched nest. He spotted several dire wolves roaming about and hunting for them.

All was silent, save the occasional owl's hoot or faint dire wolf howl. The sun was creeping in the east, but the sky was still a pale, cold blue of night.

Then, there came a ruffling from the bushes below, and Telezzar grabbed his staff. "Put your staff down, before you take an eye out," a fox said, coming out from underneath the bushes.

Telezzar grinned, happily. "And where have you been?"

"Gathering news for you."

"What do you have?"

"Not much, I'm afraid," Basil replied. "Leda arrived at Lithia long ago, while Nova returned with the electrum from Hell."

Telezzar waited a moment, but Basil did not continue. "And Troy?"

"He was captured, but your eyes and ears beyond Prixem claim he escaped and returned to Lithia. I cannot confirm this, though, since I have not been in Lithia."

"If they say he returned, then he has. Where have you been, if not Lithia?"

"I stayed with Gwendolyn for a time, and then I went to the Mountains of the White Dragon to visit Rathmel."

"Did you go south to the Black and Blue?" Telzzar asked.

"Yes, I did return home to the Blue, and I did some hunting around the Black."

"Any sign of Lorcan?"

Basil shook his head. "I found nothing, but I—" Before Basil could finish, howls filled the air, as the dire wolves were on the hunt again.

"You should go, it is not safe here," Telezzar replied, scouting the marshes below. "Go to Lithia and wait for my return."

"I will see you then, Telezzar." With that, Basil turned back to the bushes and disappeared.

"Who were you talking to?" Riger Groundspeed asked, waking to the howls.

"Do not concern yourself about it," Telezzar said, rising from his spot. "Wake the others; we have a hag to find."

Then, from behind a false wall, a playful voice laughed. "Hag you search for, but no hag you will find, for our little hag does like to hide."

Gwydon and Riger Groundspeed scrambled for their swords, while Telezzar pointed his staff to the wall. Bono Vox lay frozen still, and Lars scurried behind the wizard.

"Who is there?" Telezzar asked.

The false wall drew back, and an alien-like, gray-skinned creature emerged. "Do not fear me, though I know what I am, for I can help you find your little hag."

"Why should we trust you? Many of your kind are spies," the wizard replied, eyeing the doppelganger closely.

"Listen to me and what I have to say; for there is no game I'm trying to play."

"Quit speaking in rhyme, and make sense," the wizard said, lunging the tip of his staff closer to the doppelganger.

"I'm the evil one, though you wish to steal the electrum," the doppelganger snickered, lightheartedly.

"Our business is our own."

"True, true, but you know, Wizard, that your mind is not," the doppelganer replied, as its huge, sickly yellow eyes widened. "Follow me."

As the doppelganger turned away, everyone looked to Telezzar, unsure of what to do. "We will follow it. Beware your thoughts, though, doppelgangers can read minds."

They followed the doppelganger into the cave, and it took them to a door, which led to a tiny room. They were all surprised. The room held items, ranging from portraits of ancient kings and queens to rusted weapons of old to heaping piles of gold and silver.

"Welcome to my humble abode," the doppelganger said, happily. "I have not had guests since Whipstler the Silvershank."

"Who was he?" Lars asked.

"Who do you mean?"

"Whipstler the Silvershank," Lars answered, annoyed that he had to point out the obvious.

"Never heard of the fellow, but you should tell me about him sometime."

Lars's mouth opened to complain, but Telezzar placed his hand on the leprechaun's shoulder and shook his head.

"I am Snake," the doppelganger said, pouring cups of water for his guests.

"I am the Blue Dragon," Telezzar said, not wishing to reveal his name, since he did not trust the doppelganger.

"A dragon!" Snake exclaimed with pleasure. "I am pleased to have you as my guest, in such dreary hours."

"What can you tell us of the hag?"

"Ah, yes, the hag," Snake replied, passing out the cups. "Well, she does not live far from here, not far at all. There is a cave north of here, with a wooden bridge, and that is where her home is."

"The electrum?"

"Seen it myself! She keeps it in plain sight."

Telezzar leaned towards the doppelganger. "The Bdellium Knights?"

"Do not mention them. They are full of evil, coming and going as their master bids," Snake said, quivering at the thought.

Telezzar turned to his companions. "We have collected enough, let us go," he whispered. He turned back to Snake and continued: "Your assistance has been tremendous, but we must be on our way."

"Of course," Snake replied, opening the door for them. "Farewell and happy journeys! Dear Leprechaun, you will have to tell me of Whipstler at another time!"

As quick as they could, the companions backtracked to the cave's mouth. They collected their belongings and left, leaving the cave empty, as if it had never been occupied.

"That doppelganger was too cheery, Telezzar, something's not right," Riger Groundspeed said.

"I agree," Bono Vox said, adjusting his glasses nervously, "something bad is going to happen."

Telezzar glanced at each of them, plotting in his mind. "Bono Vox, take Lars and go back to Lithia. The rangers and I will pursue the doppelganger's lead."

"But—"

"Please, Bono Vox, do this. I do not trust the doppelganger either, but we have nothing else, and I fear what may be afoot."

The bard wanted to argue with the wizard, but he decided not to. In the end, Bono Vox and Lars left the group for Lithia; meanwhile, Telezzar and the rangers crept northward, toward the hag's location, which Snake had given them.

There were no howls from dire wolves, nor were any spotted. Then again, there was nothing about. The trees sat silent, no wind rustled through the branches, and the uneasiness only escalated.

The three reached the wooden bridge with ease, and indeed, it led to the mouth of a cave. After looking for spells or enchantments, Telezzar led the rangers across the bridge and into the cave.

"Hopefully, we can overtake her without much struggle and gain the electrum," Telezzar whispered.

"I doubt that," a figure replied, standing in the midst of the cave's room. Two other figures were present, and they laughed at the third's jest.

"Kirjath," Telezzar replied, somewhat taken aback.

"Hello, Wizard, we've been expecting you," Kirjath replied, tossing the hag's severed head at Telezzar's feet. "She reported your presence to Dentar, and when we arrived, she thought we were here to protect her. Sadly, she was mistaken."

Telezzar readied his staff, pointing it at the Bdellium Knights. "You cannot defeat me, Kirjath," he replied, "not even Citron can."

Kirjath smirked. "I am not going to fight you alone, as Citron tried. I have Malluch and Meremoth with me, and we will defeat you."

Angered at Kirjath's words, Riger Groundspeed and Gwydon charged the Bdellium Knights. Telezzar wished to join them, but his body felt stiff and frozen, not from fear, but rather a spell. Malluch and Meremoth raised their shields, blocking the first several blows from the rangers.

"You cannot defeat them!" Telezzar shouted.

The rangers did not listen, and soon, Malluch and Meremoth took the offensive, attacking. Hacking and slashing, the Bdellium Knights had little trouble cutting down Riger Groundspeed and Gwydon, slaughtering both.

Telezzar watched in horror. He felt helpless and empty, wishing to move, wishing he could have saved them. The Bdellium Knights only mocked his pain.

"I would enjoy giving you the same fate, but he has claimed you," Kirjath said. His fiery eyes gazed behind the wizard, to the sight of his master.

Strutting into the cave, the Demon Prince gave a dark, broad grin. "Bring me the electrum, Kirjath, for I have this fool bound by my powers."

Telezzar hung his head, as Kirjath started towards him, with the hag's electrum in hand. Immediately, the wizard cast his own spell, breaking the freeze spell; he cast a second, throwing Kirjath back into Malluch and Meremoth; and a third spell retrieving the electrum that Kirjath dropped.

Dentar gnashed his teeth. "Do not try my patience, Wizard," he said, summoning the Staff of the Scythians into his grasp, and pinning Telezzar against the far wall.

"See, Son of Balor, I have won, and now, my followers will hunt down and destroy your companions, and a new day will dawn on this land."

Telezzar clutched the electrum tightly. "You will never rule Prixem!"

Crazily laughing, Dentar's eyes beamed with eagerness and cruelty, and with a chilling tone, he finally replied, "But I already do."

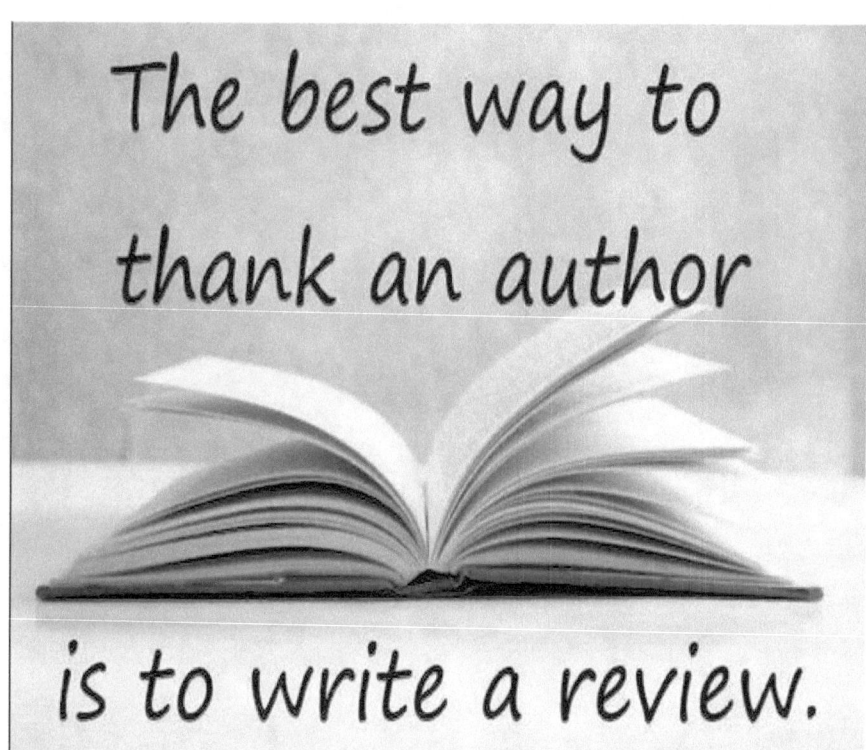

The best way to thank an author is to write a review.

<u>Appendixes</u>

- ❖ The Glossary
- ❖ The Plains
- ❖ The Calendar
- ❖ The Spans

Appendix I
The Glossary

Abaddon (ab·ə·dän ; Ab-uh-don) - King of Hell; head of the Nine Rulers

Abdullum (ab·d(y)ooəl·əm ; Ab-duel-um) - a lake on the continent of Padavona, on the Plain of Prixem

Abigor (ab·i·gôr ; Ab-ih-gore) - General of Hell; Baalzaphon's cousin; one of the Nine Rulers

Abner Wycuff (ab·nər wi·kuf ; Ab-ner Wi-cuff) – Chieftain of the Wycuff Clan

Abyssal Kidron (ə·bisəl kid·rän ; Abyssal Kid-ron) - a demon of Hell

Abyssal Kishon (ə·bisəl kiSH·ôn ; Abyssal Kish-on) - a demon of Hell

Abyssal Grihorn (ə·bisəl grē·hôrn ; Abyssal Gree-horn) - a demon of Hell

Achren Red-Dragon (āk·ren red-dra·gən ; Ache-ren Red-Dragon) - one of Troy's brothers

Alwran (ôl·rän ; All-ron) - eldest dragon/wizard; the Copper Dragon; Balor's son

Anneberg (annə·bərg ; Anna-berg) - a demon of Hell; one of the Nine Rulers

Aquilla (ə·kwil·ə ; Uh-quill-uh) - one of the Seven Great Plains, often referred to as the water plain

Arthur (är·thər ; Ar-thur) - a gneiss or rock creature; Odie's older brother

Arxy (ärx·zē ; Arx-zee) - an imp of Hell

Ashdod (aSH·däd ; Ash-dahd) - a land on the continent of Padavona, where most goblins and evil creatures live; conquered by Dentar

Asher (aSH·ər ; Ash-urr) - a elder of the yak folk

Ashturim (aSH·tər·rim ; Ash-tur-im) - (1) a former dwarf prince, son of King Ziklag (2) The Underground World of Ashturim is home to the dwarfs of Padavona

Azekiel (ā·zāk·ə·el ; A-zake-e-el) - King of Lithia; a renowned paladin; grandfather of Troy Red-Dragon

Baalzaphon (bā·ôl·zē·fän ; Bay-ahl-zee-fuhn) - Captain of the Guards of Hell; Abigor's cousin; one of the Nine Rulers

Balor (bà·lôr ; Baww-lore) - Lord of the Void; King of Formorian; creator of mankind and the Seven Great Plains; father of the first elves, Death, and the ten dragons/wizards

Basil (bāzel ; Bay-zill) - a fox; Telezzar's familiar

Bdellium Knights of Death (delēəm ; Bdell-yuhm) - seven servants of evil; created in the Void by Segomo

Beelzebub (bēl·zi·bəb ; Bell-zi-bub) - Prince of Hell; eldest of Abaddon's children; one of the Nine Rulers

Behemoth (bə·hē·məTH ; Buh-he-muth) - servants of devils and demons; some reside throughout the Seven Great Plains

Belial (bə·lī·el ; Be-lie-al) - Prince of Hell; youngest of Abaddon's children; Dentar's birth name

Belfast (bəl·fast ; Bel-fast) - a city in Gilon

Ben-Hadad (ben·hə·dad ; Ben-Huh-dad) - a city in Gilon

Birog (biróg ; Bir-og) - Balor's father; part of the Thebian Triad

Bono Vox (bänō väks ; Bon-o Vox) - a bard of Thracia

Boremon (bôr·män ; Bore-mon) - one of the Bdellium Knights of Death

Bucklin (bək·lin ; Buck-lin) - a city in the Hidden Forest, where most short elves live

Caelan (kāl·en ; Kay-len) - a minotaur prince; Caneal's twin

Caelix (kel·ik ; Kell-ick) - a minotaur outcast; King Claudius's brother

Cameroon (kam·roon ; Cam-rune) - marshes on the continent of Padavona

Caneal (kān·ē·el ; Kay-ee-el) - a minotaur prince; Caelan's twin

Carlton (kärl·tən ; Carl-ton) - a minotaur prince; eldest of King Claudius's sons

Citron (sit·rän ; Sit-ron) - the leader, and one of, the Bdellium Knights of Death

Claudius (klôd·ē·əs ; Claud-e-us) - King of the Minotaurs

Coalton McConnell (kôl·tən mə·kän·əl ; Coal-ton Mc-Conn-ell) - Chieftain of the McConnel Clan

Condorian (kän·dôr·ēən ; Con-dor-ian) - Dar Caine's sur-name, which he chose when becoming a chieftain

Cordorian (kôr·dôr·ēən ; Core-dor-ian) - a tribe of giants, usually evil

Couplet (kə·plət ; Cup-let) - a span of 50 days; there is 8 total couplets

Crokus (krō·kəs ; Crow-cuss) - a minotaur prince

Dagon (dā·gän ; Day-gone) - a forest on the continent of Padavona, where most giants live

Dalian (dāl·yən ; Dale-yuhn) - (1) a former king of Gilon (2) a castle where the Kings of Gilon live

Dalidon (däl·i·dän ; Dal-ih-don) - one of the four dwarf kings; King Rororoi's brother

Dar Caine Condorian (där kän kän·dôr·ēən; Dar Cane Con-dor-ian) - a malobathron giant; son of Chief Njord; grandson of King Draul

DeAth (dē·aTH ; Dee-ath) - the birthname of Death; father of the virgin valkyrie

Del Baeth (del bā·eTH) - Birog's brother, Elcmar's twin, and Balor's uncle; part of the Thebian Triad

Delirus (də·lir·əs ; Duh-lear-us) - one of the Seven Great Plains, often referred to as the crazed plain

Dentar (den·tär ; Den-tar) - a former Prince of Hell; Lord of Ashdod

Dion Caliguri (dē·ôn kal·ig·yoorə ; Dee-on Cal-ig-yoore) - King of Gilon

Doppelganger (däpəl·gaNGər ; Dopp-el-ganger) - a creature that can shape-shift into other beings or creatures

Drabog Dakin (drā·bog dā·kin ; Dray-bog Day-kin) – Chieftain of the Dakin Clan

Draul McAdoo (drôl mak·ə·doo ; Drawl Mac-ah-doo) - the first chieftain of the McAdoo clan; also known as the High King; Dar Caine's grandfather

Dunbar (dən·bär ; Done-bar) - the first King of Hell; the only being to be cast out of the Void; father of Abaddon and grandfather to Belial/Dentar

Ehud (ē·həd ; E-hud) - Dar Caine's youngest brother

Eldred (el·dred ; El-dread) - a race of evil elves

Elcmar (elk-mär ; Elk-mar) - Birog's brother, Del Baeth's twin, and Balor's uncle; part of the Thebian Triad

Elhanan (el·hanən ; El-hann-en) - a woodland on the continent of Padavona; home of traditional elves

Eliel (ē·lī·el ; E-lie-el) - a woodland on the continent of Padavona; home of elves who mate with the sons and daughters of men

Epsilon (ep·sil·än ; Ep-sill-on) - the second spring couplet, or the last 50 days of spring

Esther (es·tər ; Es-ter) - a quokka; Gwendolyn's familiar

Eta (ēta ; E-tah) - one of the eight couplets; the second autumn couplet, or last 50 days of autumn

Formorian (fôr·môr·ēən ; Four-more-ian) - a mountain in the Void; Balor's home

Gargouille (gär·gool·ā ; Gar-ghoul-a) - the gargoyle king

Geryon (gər·yôn ; Grr-yawn) - a dragon who guards the Gates of Hell

Geshur (gə·SHər ; Geh-sherr) - a brounie; Dentar's manipulated familiar

Gilon (gil·än ; Gill-on) - a land on the continent of Padavona, renowned for its warriors and architects; home to men

Gneiss (nīs ; Nice) - a rock creature

Greenwald (grēn·wôld ; Green-wald) - a city in the Hidden Forest, where most leprechaun live

Gremian (grē·mē·an ; Gree-me-an) - a gremlin servant of Dentar

Gilead (gil·ē·ad ; Gill-e-add) - Troy's oldest brother

Groith (groiTH ; Groy-th) - a goblin merchant

Gwendolyn (gwen·dō·lin ; Gwen-doe-lin) - the Green Dragon; Balor's daughter

Gwydon (gwī·dän ; Gwhy-don) - a ranger of Thracia

Hivitte (hiv·īt ; Hiv-ight) - a race of evil dwarfs

Ishtar (iSH·tär ; Ish-tar) - Prince of the yak folk

Jaggarri (jag·är·ē ; Jagg-arr-ee) - a race on the Plain of Tartanzuma; twin race of the jaggeddi

Jaggeddi (jag·ed·ē ; Jagg-edd-ee) - a race on the Plain of Tartanzuma; twin race of the jaggarri

Joarkoam (jär·kō·əm ; Jor-ko-um) - a fortress in the Forest of Dagon, where the McAdoo clan lives

Jolon (jō·län ; Joe-lawn) - a jaggarri elder

Kaulthar (kōl·THər ; Coal-thar) - King of the Spidermites

Kirjath (kir·jaTH ; Kir-jath) - one of the Bdellium Knights of Death

Knossos (näs·sôs ; Knaw-sus) - a northern city in Ashdod

Kota (kō·də ; Ko-tah) - a former elf king; all of Kota's lineage are sworn paladins

Lars (lärs ; Larz) - a leprechaun of Greenwald

Leda (lā·də ; Lay-duh) - a dwarf from the Underground World of Ashturim; kin to King Dalidon

Leviathan (lə·vīə·THən ; Leh-vy-eh-THan) - Grand Admiral of Hell; one of the Nine Rulers

Lilith (lil·iTH ; Lil-ith) - Princess of Hell; Abaddon's daughter; one of the Nine Rulers

Lithia (liTh·ē·ə ; Lith-e-uh) - a city in Nethinims

Lorcan (lôr·kan ; Lore-can) - the Black Dragon; Balor's son

Magnuson McGleish (mag·nəh·sən mə·gliSH ; Mag-nus-son Mc-Gleesh) - Chieftain of the McGleish Clan

Malluch (məl·uk ; Mal-uck) – one of the Bdellium Knights of Death

Malobathron (mal·ō·baTH·rän ; Mal-o-bath-ron) - a race of giants from the Void; on Prixem, their clan settled in the Forest of Dagon

Meldon (mel·dän ; Mel-don) - Treasurer of Hell; Murmur's brother; one of the Nine Rulers

Meremoth (merē·môTH ; Mary-moth) - one of the Bdellium Knights of Death

Mu (m(y) oo ; Mew) - one of the eight couplets; the first winter couplet, or first 50 days of winter

Mugwort (məg· wərt ; Mug-wart) - giants of Hell; some reside throughout the Seven Great Plains

Murmur (mər·mər ; Mur-mur) - a Count of Hell; Meldon's brother; one of the Nine Rulers

Naga (nägə ; Nah-guh) - a giant serpent; there are several Naga: Hidden Naga, Void Naga, and Divine Naga

Nethinims (neTH·ē·nims ; Neth-e-nims) - a woodland on the continent of Padavona, where Lithia and Starlight Forest are located

Njord McAdoo (nôrd mak·ə·doo ; N-ord Mac-ah-doo) - son of Draul McAdoo and father of Dar Caine Condorian

Nova (nōvə ; No-vuh) - an elf of Elhanan

Nu (n(y) oo ; New) - one of the eight couplets; the second winter couplet, or last 50 days of winter

Odie (Ōdē ; O-dee) - a gneiss or rock creature; younger brother of Arthur

Ogma (äg·mä ; Og-mah) - Balor's brother; Birog's son

Ohanzee (ō·hän·zē ; O-han-zee) - Chief of the Jaggeddi

Ovid (ō·vid ; O-vid) - the Minotaur's capital city

Padavona (pad·ə·vōnə ; Pad-uh-vonuh) - a continent on the Plain of Prixem

Pastilles (pa·stēls ; Pa-zells) - a bread made by the elves

Prixem (prix·em ; Prix-em) - one of the Seven Great Plains

Purslain (pər·slān ; Purr-slain) - an armadillo like creature, with cutting claw hands and a poisonous tongue

Pygarg (pī·gärg ; Pie-garg) - a friendly race of creatures from the Plain of Solarium

Quokka (kwäkə ; Quo-kuh) - a cat-sized kangaroo

Res Publica (rās poo·bli·kä ; Res Poo-blih-cah) - a land on the continent of Padavona; home to many races, including centaurs and minotaurs

Rho (rō ; row) - one of the eight couplets; the second summer couplet, or last 50 days of summer

Riger Groundspeed (rigər ; Rig-er) - Head of the Ranger's Guild in Thracia

Saladin (salədin ; Sal-uh-din) - a kingdom on the Plain of Thermidor

Segomo (səg·ōmō ; Seg-o-moe) - leader of the Scythians in the Void

Shelan (SHē·län ; She-lawn) - the dragon man, who appeared as a dragon but in the form of a man; Death's brother; Balor's son

Silloweb (sil·ō·web ; Sill-o-web) – an Eldred Prince

SinGoth (sin·gäTH ; Sin-goth) - a half elf, half goblin of Hell

Solarium (sōl·ôr·ēəm ; Soul-or-ium) - one of the Seven Great Plains, often referred to as the heavenly plain, or terebinth's plain

Staff of the Scythians (siTH·ē·əns ; Sith-e-ens) - Telezzar's staff, crafted by Segomo in the Void

Tamarisk (tam·ər·əsk ; Tam-air-isk) - a dryad from the Forest of Dagon

Tartanzuma (tär·tan·zoomə ; Tar-tan-zoomah) - one of the Seven Great Plains, often referred to as the jungle plain

Tau (tô ; tah) - one of the eight couplets; the first autumn couplet, or first 50 days of autumn

Telezzar (telə·zär ; Tele-zar) - the Blue Dragon; Balor's son; wielder of the Staff of the Scythians

Terebinth (terə·bēnTH ; Tear-uh-beenth) - seven adversaries of the Bdellium Knights of Death; former wielders of the electrum swords

Thermidor (THər·mi·dôr ; Ther-mi-door) - one of the Seven Great Plain, often referred to as the desert plain

Theta (THē·də ; Th-ee-tah) - one of the eight couplets; the first summer couplet, or first 50 days of summer

Thracia (THra·SHē·ə ; Thra-she-uh) - a land on the continent of Padavona, predominantly inhabited by men whose structure is much cruder than those of Gilon

Timuluk (tim·yoo·lək ; Tim-u-luck) - a pygarg and elevator conductor of Hell

Torrok (tôr·äk ; Tour-ahk) - a dwarf imprisoned by King Kaulthar

Troy Red-Dragon (troi red-dra·gən ; Troy Red-Dragon) - an elf of Lithia; grandson of King Azekiel

Turuk (tər·ək ; turr-uck) - a race of giants found on Thermidor, sometimes referred to as sun-giants

Upsilon (əp·sil·än ; Up-sill-on) - one of the eight couplets; the first spring couplet, or the first 50 days of spring

Urijah Durand (yoor·i·əh də·rand ; Ur-i-uh Dur-and) - Chieftain of the Durand Clan

Uther (oo·THər ; Oo-ther) - a dwarf ranger and Leda's father

Virgin Valkyrie (vər·jən val·kirē ; Virgin Val-cry) - the thirteen daughters of Death; ride unicorns amongst battles and claim the dead souls for their father's house

Wildermenn (wil·dər·men ; wil-der-men) - wild tribes of men that roam the fields near the Mountains of the Green Dragon

Ziglo (zig·lō ; Zig-low) - a hivitte king

Ziklag (zik·lag ; Zik-lag) - (1) a former dwarf king, quite renowned; father of Ashturim and King Oreslayer, and great-great-great grandfather of King Dalidon and King Rororoi (2) the original name of the great caverns on Padavona, the Caves of Ziklag, before Ashturim renamed them, the Underground World of Ashturim

Zinzinc (ziN-ziNGk ; Zin-zinc) - one of the Seven Great Plains, often referred to as the snow plain

Appendix II

The Plains

The Void

The Seven Great Plains:

    Solarium

    Zinzinc

    Tartanzuma

    Prixem

    Aquilla

    Thermidor

    Delirus

Hell

Appendix III
Calendar

50 days – 1 couplet

400 days – 8 couplets

400 days – 8 couplets – 1ballad/1year

Spring Couplets: Upsilon and Epsilon

Summer Couplets: Theta and Rho

Autumn Couplets: Tau and Eta

Winter Couplets: Mu and Nu

Appendix IV

The Spans

The Void

- Birog's wife bears two sons, Ogma and Balor
- Balor takes Shoshoni and Nakota as his wives (Shoshoni's children, being abundant, become known as the elves; Nakota gives birth to Shelan, the Dragon-Man, and DeAth)
- Creation of races leads to Balor becoming Lord of the Void
- 1st Holy War
    - Shattering of the electrum swords
    - Dunbar cast into Hell
- Creation of the Seven Plains and more races

1st Span (Creation of Time)

- Days of Elves (reign of King Kota and Queen Eden)
- Shallow Bread (the fall of all races)

2nd Span (Death of Dunbar)

- Days of Giants, Dwarfs, and the House of Balor
  - DeAth becomes Death
  - Nakota gives birth to the ten wizards
  - Draul the Malobathron Giant becomes High King of Prixem
  - Death's thirteen daughters, the Virgin Valkyrie, are born
  - The ten wizards are sent to the Plain of Prixem
- Days of Centaurs, Minotaurs, and other races
  - King Abaddon establishes the Council of Nine
  - Salvatore crafts the chess set
  - Betrayal of Belial
  - Rise of the elf paladins

3rd Span (The Coming of Dentar)

- Dentar claims Ashdod
- Telezzar's doings
- Hunt for electrum

About the Author

Originally from Columbus, Ohio, Dakota McElhinny also spent time growing up in Morganton, North Carolina. Between the two, he gained the 'bustling city life' and 'rural country life' experience. After receiving his Associate of Arts degree from Western Piedmont Community College, he obtained his Bachelor of Science from North Greenville University.

In addition, Dakota holds a certification in Old Norse Mythology from the University of Colorado, and a certification in Magic in the Middle Ages from the University of Barcelona. Currently, he lives in South Carolina, where he serves on the board of the South Carolina Writers Association.

-For more about Dakota, visit dakotamcelhinny-author.com

-For all questions and inquiries, Dakota can be reached at dakotawrites100@gmail.com

Indie Published Titles:

The Realm Series:

The Realm (2016)

The Realm: Rise of the Demon Prince (2017)

The Realm: The Chess Master's Ring (2020)

Poetry Compilations:

Time Frozen Mirrors (2018)

Black October (2019)

Dreams of Glass (2020)

The Cutting Room Floor (2021)

The King of Wordplay (2022)

Half A Truth, Half A Lie (2022)

Envoi (2023)

Short Story Collection:

The Art of Time (2020)

Magical Realism:

Crumpet Court Chronicles (2021)